By Which We Are Judged

Les Finlayson

This is a work of fiction. Names, characters, businesses, places, events and incidents are either the products of the author's imagination or used in a fictitious manner. Any resemblance to actual persons, living or dead, or actual events is purely coincidental.

Les Finlayson reserves the right to be identified as the author of this work.

Artwork image used under licence.

Acknowledgements

Time is a precious commodity, so I am incredibly grateful to those people who have freely and willingly given theirs to help my journey in writing my first novel. My son, Alex, and my good friend and Table Tennis partner, Paul Clarke, need recognition for reading the first draft and offering suggestions and corrections.

My dear sister, Jackie Kelly, helped her little brother by working on the first edit and correcting an embarrassing number of mistakes, as well as re-evaluating the second draft and helping with the artwork. The delightful Angie James and her demon red pen also deserves acknowledgement for reading and highlighting errors in the second draft. The third wonderful woman I need to thank is the most important; my wonderful wife Debbie. Not only does she mean the world to me, without her support, this book would not exist.

Professionals have also had a hand in my journey to self-publication. The Literary Consultancy provided an insightful assessment for the first manuscript, and the editing skills of Nicola Simcock on the final version were quite exceptional. I have no hesitation in recommending their services.

My final words are reserved for my friend and neighbour, Jonathan Alper, who helped me negotiate the finer points in the use of anaesthetics and narcotics. Of all the people who I spoke to in the process of writing this book, Jonathan understood the challenges of writing more than anyone else and I treasured his endless encouragement. His illness claimed a very special man far too early in his life, and I can do little else other than dedicate this book to his memory.

A modern, civilised society does not give its people freedom; that privilege is provided by the people themselves.

The State provides its people with the complicated mechanism for administering justice, but it is the people who make the final decisions about culpability and guilt. Full devolution of the judiciary to the people has not happened for a simple reason.

The State says you are innocent until proven guilty.

The people say you are guilty until proven innocent.

MARCH

Had she opened her eyes? It felt like it, but darkness surrounded her, with light as absent as her ability to process her location. New, alien senses slowly woke her, one by one gently unfolding like flowers in early spring, each one unveiling a new clue to decipher.

A heavy, damp odour filled the air; it reminded her of Rocket when he used to bound energetically into the house after chasing imaginary cats in the pouring rain, before shaking himself dry in the kitchen. It made her and her sister squeal in anticipation of getting sprayed with water infused with the scent of a happy and excitable Irish wolfhound. But it couldn't be Rocket, he died years ago.

Synapses in her brain re-activated as neurons re-established their connectivity, but something still impeded their normal function and her thoughts were heavy and clogged. Her mouth was arid, and her chapped lips tingled as they moved. The first noise to rise out of her stinging throat was nothing more than a gentle whimper.

Her clothes were different to the ones she had been wearing before. Gone were the mimosa yellow soft fit jeans she bought with her mother's birthday money, and vague memories of wearing a light tan leather jacket swirled around in her head – but it wasn't on her now. Covering her instead, was a simple garment that felt like a plain tent dress with the sterile smell of TCP, but it came with the sharp prickle that accompanies hospital gowns which have been boil washed a thousand times before.

Her memories remained resolutely nebulous and she fought to wrestle a confused dream world away from reality. Had she been in an accident? She was lying on a bed, facing up into a blackness that had yet to reveal what it was hiding, but it didn't feel like a hospital.

No gentle bleeping sounds coming from patient monitoring systems, no hint of medical professionals quietly scurrying around as they cared for their patients. The silence was as total as the darkness.

A tingling sensation snaked up her right calf into her thigh muscles and she tried to shift her weight to the left to allow more blood to flow through the restricted veins. A distinctive sound crashed through the dark and in an instant all the remaining wiring in her brain reconnected with a startling efficiency that could only be facilitated by a massive dose of adrenaline.

The unmistakeable clatter of chains.

Blind terror caused her chest to rise and fall rapidly as she gasped for oxygen to give her a fighting chance to cope with the shock. More clanking sounds greeted her attempted arm movement, and as the sensation in her limbs returned, she felt tight rings of cold steel around her wrists and ankles.

Hidden amongst the sound of chains was another, gentler, metallic creak. She kept her arms and legs still, before pushing her backside downwards. The response was the sound of woven steel wire grating against itself. The last time she had heard that noise was when her aunt had come to stay, and she had been forced to sleep on a metal framed camp bed. She hated it; it was the same one her father used to sleep on when he had had a row with her mother, and it always smelt of his misery.

Tears welled in her eyes and she instinctively called out for help. The dryness in her throat imposed a cap on the volume and her first attempt barely rose above a hoarse rasp. Her second try was louder as her vocal chords organised themselves to cope with a lack of fluids, and it triggered a noise above her head. The creak of aged floorboards gave way to the gentle thud of footsteps, twelve of them in slow succession, each one louder than the last.

A shaft of muted yellow light broke into the dark, bringing with it a new raft of revelations to process. Her eyes darted around a windowless room with ageing white paint interspersed with patchworks of ashen grey mould. Hoary, flaked paint clung to lifeless plaster on the ceiling and old wooden joists were visible where the render had crumbled through age. A single light flex dangled motionless from the ceiling, the bayonet fitting missing a bulb. The illumination that penetrated the room came from the other side of an uneven doorway. Behind it, a flight of tired oak stairs stretched upwards towards the source of the light.

Before she could fully process the sight unfurling before her, her eyes were drawn to the person who entered the cellar and now stood barely two metres in front of her prone body.

'You're awake I see.'

The figure was silhouetted against the dim light so she could not make out any facial features, but the tone of voice and outline of a lean musculature left her in no doubt he was male.

'Are you thirsty?' His calm voice held a hint of genuine concern.

She nodded, unable to formulate an intelligible sentence.

'Here.' He reached down to the floor and brought up a bottle of spring water. The top made a gentle cracking sound as the seal opened and with one hand lifting and supporting her head, he offered the water up to her lips.

'Thank you,' she mumbled. Her strict upbringing meant that good manners remained instinctive, even when they weren't deserved.

He sat down on the bed, his right buttock resting on the metal frame and his hip gently touching hers. The light now illuminated the left side of his face, accentuating a rugged cheek bone covered with stubble.

It was enough to recognise him. She let out an involuntary gasp.

'You! You bastard!'

'Now now, that's no way to speak to your new owner.'

'Owner?'

'Yes, you're mine now. I own you.'

Apoplexy took control, and her adrenal glands went into overdrive. Her heart rate doubled, blood flooded into her aching muscles and the pain that had gripped her limbs temporarily vanished. She screamed every ounce of air out of her lungs and swung her arms up towards him, readying herself to claw each square inch of skin away from his face.

Her hands barely made it half way to their destination when the iron manacles that bound her to the bed did their intended job. Her arms slammed to a halt, bringing the attack to an end barely half a second after it started.

'You can scream all you like, no one will hear you.' He traced his index finger up the inside of her leg towards her thigh.

'Although I wouldn't recommend it. You're going to need all your strength for our games.'

She twisted her torso away from him, breaking the contact with his finger and lurched upwards in an endeavour to break away from the bed. The chains were unforgiving and told her with agonising clarity that she wasn't going anywhere, and she slumped back on the bed.

'Why are you doing this?' she sobbed. 'You know who I am and you know people will be looking for me.'

He leaned in towards her and for the first time she could smell the ketones on his breath.

'You're correct, people are looking for you.' His tone was matter-of-fact. 'But I can tell you they are not looking anywhere near here. It will be ages before you are found, plenty of time for us to have some fun.'

Her anger subsided fractionally as her predicament came into harrowing focus. She wanted to ask what he meant by fun but didn't want to give him the satisfaction, resorting instead to as much defiance as she could muster.

'You can go fuck yourself.'

He stood up and walked around the bed until he was standing behind her head. Grabbing her auburn hair, he fiercely yanked it backwards, pinning her head tightly against the thin mattress. He bent over her so their noses were two centimetres apart and all she could see were two rows of teeth in need of dental hygiene.

'The first lesson, bitch, is the use of manners.'

She couldn't reply even if she wanted to. A searing pain clawed at her skull and it took all her strength not to cry out in agony.

'There's a debt to settle and I fully intend to enjoy myself while I make you pay it.' He twisted her hair again and grinned when her face contorted with pain. 'Trust me, it won't be quick and it won't be comfortable.'

He let go of her head and without saying another word walked out of the cellar. As the door closed behind him, her world plunged back into total darkness.

One

Courtroom number one at Bristol Crown Court creaked with age as it struggled to keep pace with the 21st century. The wainscot that served to insulate the room from the external sandstone had become chipped and lifeless, and what natural light was able to break through the two lancet windows was woefully inadequate. Consequently, the court relied on pendant lights for its illumination, which had last been upgraded in the 1980s. A dusty smell radiated out of the worn green and grey frieze carpet, which blended with the vintage leather aroma coming from the bound copies of *Comyns' Digest* that flanked one wall. The ambience of antiquity that permeated the room was heightened by the presence of the presiding judge. Dame Joan Hind was three months away from her enforced and highly unwelcome retirement. Arthritis had recently teamed up with Parkinson's disease and the combined effect aged her appearance by a decade more than her seventy-four years. Despite these ravages, she remained one of the most astute and respected judges on the circuit.

From a dark inconspicuous corner of the public gallery, Inspector Lucas Cornelius watched the trial of Marcus David Weavell unfold with a growing sense of unease. At the start of the trial the prosecuting counsel, Davina McAlister, declared herself happy with the Crown's case. Heroin had been found in a flat belonging to the defendant and a witness was going to testify that he had stowed the drugs on Weavell's behalf. Marcus Weavell had not been arrested at the time of the raid, however, he had been seen exiting the first floor flat by a bathroom window barely wide enough for his slender frame. The witness had identified Weavell in a line-up, and she was waiting in the wings to give her evidence. The charge was possession with intent to supply, and McAlister confidently predicted a custodial sentence in excess of ten years. Judging by the ragged expression creeping on to McAlister's face, it was a prediction she wanted to rescind.

The defence barrister was Tobias McMillan, a product of a 1970s Eton education, whose razor-sharp intellect was still imbued with the social prejudices which blighted that decade. He retained a full mop of unkempt blonde hair which contrasted starkly with his dark blue eyes and grey pinstriped Canali suit. McMillan's client, Weavell, was better known to Bristol's underworld as Weasel, a moniker not solely attributed to the similarity of pronunciation. He also had a long thin body with short legs which hadn't developed at the same rate as his torso. A thin pinched face with swept back pepper brown hair completed the mustelid look. The loud red floral shirt he was renowned for wearing was absent, dressing instead in a pale blue shirt, paisley tie and plain herringbone tweed jacket. From the other side of the courtroom, Cornelius thought Weasel looked quite respectable, although he recognised the outfit from his last court appearance.

The trial started well enough. The first witness was a woman in her early sixties, her snowy white hair pinned up into a bun and a fashion sense that centred on comfort rather than aesthetics. She nervously took the stand and under genial cajoling from McAlister, confirmed seeing the accused climbing out of a window at the time the flat was being raided by the police. She spoke quietly and elegantly about seeing him squeeze his slender frame through a hopper window, shimmying across a narrow ledge, before dropping on to the pavement and running off. He'd landed three metres in front of her which is why, she declared, she was confident it was him. Cornelius frowned when Tobias McMillan declined the opportunity to cross examine. His normal tactics involved putting everyone else on trial except his client, and Cornelius found it unnerving to see him pass up an opportunity to demolish a prosecution witness.

The next witnesses to take the stand were Cornelius's colleagues who had worked with him in building the case against Weasel. Cornelius was forced to sit in agonised silence as, one by one, his colleagues' working practices were attacked by McMillan's sardonic questioning. The crime scene manager had climbed down from the witness stand with tears in her eyes after the barrister's oral bombardment about minor inaccuracies in the staff entry and exit log at the time Weasel's flat had been raided. And forensic evidence that showed traces of heroin on Weasel's clothing was torn apart when McMillan raised the spectre of cross contamination by a technician who had not correctly stored samples taken at the scene.

With the case against Weasel crumbling by the minute, it was Cornelius's turn under the cosh. As the inspector in charge of the case he expected McMillan's questions to be harsh and imperious, and dryness clawed at his throat as he took the affirmation. McMillan's first question came from an unexpected angle.

'Inspector Cornelius, why did you specifically ask for this case to be assigned to you?'

'I didn't,' Cornelius lied.

McMillan paused for three heartbeats longer than he needed to. His head tilted forward slightly as he stared at Cornelius over the top of his tortoiseshell brown Bvlgari glasses – his way of telling the jury that he didn't believe him.

'Have you had previous dealings with my client?'

'I've arrested him in the past if that is what you are referring to.' Cornelius was determined to score a few points of his own with the jury, and a warm sense of defiance washed over him. It didn't last long.

'Was that before or after you assaulted my client, inspector?'

Davina McAlister raised an objection to the question, which Justice Hind immediately sustained. She gave McMillan a withering stare leaving him in no doubt that a serious rebuke was one misdemeanour away. He didn't mind, he had sowed the seeds of doubt regarding Cornelius's integrity and was about to work his way towards harvesting them. After a polite nod to the judge, he rephrased his question.

'Can you please tell the court the circumstances that led to you hitting my client in the face with a saucepan, causing him to lose one of his molars?'

Before Cornelius had a chance to answer, Davina McAlister raised another objection on the grounds of relevance. McMillan swiftly countered that it was an entirely pertinent line of questioning that had significant implications which could affect the outcome of the case. This time Justice Hind sided with the defence but warned McMillan to tread carefully in his line of questioning. She turned to Cornelius, nodding at him to proceed with an answer.

'We had a warrant to search some premises owned by Mr Weavell. Whilst executing the search, the accused lunged at me, armed with what I believed to be a knife in his right hand. I instinctively defended myself by grabbing a kitchen utensil and swinging it at Mr Weavell, regrettably loosening one of his teeth in the process.'

'Yet, no knife was ever found, was it inspector?'

'No, it wasn't,' he confirmed. So far, this was going to the script Cornelius expected. He turned his torso slightly towards the jury, as he wanted them to be crystal clear about his rebuttal.

'However, the incident was investigated by the Independent Police Complaints Commission. They concluded that a weapon had been used but had been removed in the immediate aftermath of the attack by another person or persons unknown. The probability being, that this was done whilst I administered first aid to Mr Weavell.'

'My client was never prosecuted though, was he?'

'No, he wasn't. No drugs were found on the premises and without the knife there were no grounds for an assault charge either.'

'That's always bothered you, hasn't it, inspector?'

Cornelius tightened his grip on the brass rail surrounding the witness stand. McMillan's cross examination tactics were not unique to him, they were used in courtrooms around the globe. Destroy the credibility of the witness and you ruin the reliability of their testimony. Cornelius hated this approach, and now he was on the receiving end of it. Blood crept up his neck from his collar line, and he took a gentle deep breath to control his rising anger.

'My only regret is that the knife was never found, however, I specifically asked for no further action be taken against Mr Weavell after his attack.'

A brief watery smile crept on to McMillan's face as he paused for three heartbeats again, using the silence to garner the full attention of the jury.

'Would you please tell the court the precise nature of the goods that were lost ten months ago from the evidence room of Gloucester Road Police Station?'

Cornelius closed his eyes as he realised how the next five minutes of questioning were going to play out. Tobias McMillan had sucker punched him, and he wasn't going to get up. His only remaining hope of a sustained objection from Davina McAlister was waved away, and Cornelius had to answer a question he would rather not have been posed in a court of law.

'A consignment of seized drugs was taken away from the evidence room before it could be processed and destroyed.'

'Taken away? You mean stolen don't you, inspector?'

'It's an internal matter within the constabulary and it's being investigated by the Professional Standards Team.' He was bursting to ask a question of his own, like where did McMillan get that fucking information from but, instead, had to wait for the next difficult question.

'It's far from an internal matter inspector. What drugs in particular were stolen?'

'Heroin. Two kilogrammes of it.' Cornelius braced himself for McMillan's theatrical summary.

'Heroin.' McMillan loudly reiterated as he faced the jury again. 'The same drug that was found in my client's flat which he denies ever seeing before.' He turned back to Cornelius and took one step closer to the witness stand. 'I put it to you Inspector Cornelius, that you know exactly where the missing heroin went. You removed it from the evidence room and were responsible for planting it in my client's flat in revenge for failing to secure a successful prosecution the last time you tried to persecute him!'

Davina McAlister sprang to her feet, but Judge Hind cut in with her own intervention.

'You do not need to answer the allegation if you do not want to inspector.'

Cornelius did want to answer, but first he first needed to relax the muscles in his jaw that had wound themselves up into a constricted knot. He tried for as much condescension as his temperament would allow.

'That's complete rubbish and you know it.'

Tobias McMillan knew it was rubbish, but he didn't care. It was the jury who mattered, and now, they were unsure what to believe.

***

As the court reconvened after lunch recess, Cornelius seethed. Tobias McMillan had ripped his credibility apart and he had to suffer the ignominy of seeing Weasel gloating from the dock. Cornelius put all vengeful thoughts out of his mind; another question was taking priority. How the hell had McMillan found out about the missing drugs from Gloucester Road station?

The arrival in the witness stand of one of the key witnesses for the prosecution brought Cornelius's attention back to the trial. Manny Thompson owned a grimy garage on a run-down industrial estate, and in addition to offering vehicle repair services, he also provided storage facilities for a wide range of clientele. Legitimate goods were stored in lockups behind his garage, however, the site he used for the storage of illegal goods had eluded Avon and Somerset Constabulary for years. The declaration to the court that Thompson had been storing solar lights for Weasel was something Cornelius agreed with Thompson before the trial. In reality, it had been a consignment of smuggled tobacco, which Cornelius had been prepared to overlook. The heroin had been hidden in the middle of it and Cornelius knew damn well that Thompson knew nothing about it. Against all regulations he had coached Thompson on the likely questions he would be subjected to in court, and now it was about to be put to the test.

Manny Thompson looked thoroughly uncomfortable as he took the witness stand. Even from his viewpoint in the public gallery, Cornelius could see the oily grime of a thousand cars indelibly etched into the tips of his fingers. His charcoal grey suit looked like it had been bought in a charity shop, and his white shirt was one collar size too small. Judging by the horizontal and vertical creases it still sported, it hadn't been ironed since being taken out of the original wrapping.

Davina McAlister opened with an entirely predictable line of questioning. What did he think he was storing for Mr Weavell? How did he react when told by the police that heroin had been concealed inside the consignment? When did Mr Weavell admit to him that it was his heroin? Why didn't he go directly to the police when he first knew he had been duped? Manny Thompson mumbled his way through his answers with the sluggishness of a Galapagos tortoise but managed to keep to the line of responses previously agreed with Cornelius.

With little deviation in Thompson's testimony, Cornelius felt a degree of confidence that a conviction would be secured after all. Thompson had been precise and ultimately damning when he declared under oath that the defendant had admitted to him that he had deceived him into storing heroin.

With McAlister's questioning completed, Tobias McMillan gently rose from his seat, his red leather-bound notebook remaining closed on the light beech table in front of him. He fixed Thompson with a hard stare before speaking.

'Mr Thompson, do you know a man called Ronald Daniel Palmer?'

The woman in dark tweeds sitting next to Cornelius in the public gallery glowered disapprovingly at him, and he realised that instead of thinking, *oh fuck*, he'd said it out loud. He quickly returned his stare to Thompson, who looked like a rabbit blinded by the headlights of a forty tonne juggernaut.

'Answer the question please, Mr Thompson. You may know him better as Danny Palmer.'

'Yes.' He said eventually. 'I know him.'

'What is your relationship with Mr Palmer?'

Thompson's eyes darted around the courtroom as he looked for Cornelius. This question hadn't been rehearsed and he didn't know how to respond. He knew he had little choice but to tell the truth but first tried to dilute it.

'I did some business with him a few years ago.'

'Please tell the court what you mean by "some business".'

Thompson tried relying on partial truths to bail him out. 'I stored some equipment for him.'

'You did more than that, didn't you Mr Thompson? You were employed by Mr Palmer to provide vehicle maintenance for his taxi business for two years, is that correct?'

'Yes.' Thompson lowered his head.

'Are you aware of the vendetta Mr Palmer has had with my client since being sent to prison for drugs offences two years ago?'

'Yes, and I know Mr Palmer blames Weas ... Mr Weavell for planting drugs on him, but that has nothing to do with this!'

If Thompson had looked up at the public gallery he would have seen Cornelius burying his head in his hands, not wanting to listen to the remainder of the exchange between the two men.

'Mr Thompson, did Danny Palmer instruct you to give false evidence against my client?'

Thompson's jaw hung open but no words came out.

McMillan increased his ferocity. 'Yes or no, Mr Thompson?'

'No!' Thompson yelped.

'No?' Another three heartbeats as he prepared his *coup de grace*. 'So why did you visit him in prison last week?'

Cornelius didn't wait to hear Thompson's response; he stormed out of the gallery, fantasising about the slow and painful death of Tobias McMillan.

***

The Portland stone gallery which swept the length of Bristol Crown Court was a bustling thoroughfare of barristers, legal clerks and reporters, all with an air of purpose, as they briskly glided over the pillowed flagstones and went about the business of administering justice. Any blank or confused faces belonged to one-time visitors, unsure of how they should conduct themselves in the imposing gothic surroundings. Witnesses and family members, all wanting different outcomes from the trials being played out in adjacent courtrooms.

Cornelius was oblivious to the routine maelstrom of activity unfolding around him. His demons demanded sedation by alcohol, but they had to make do with weak coffee from a vending machine that refused to honour its pledge of giving change.

'Ah, there you are.' Davina McAlister's tone was brisk and clipped. 'You do realise that Avon and Somerset Constabulary have pissed all over the Crown's case?'

Cornelius struggled to formulate a response. He couldn't work out whether her acerbic comment was rooted in the knowledge that it was Cornelius himself who had cocked up. He opted for deflection rather than acknowledgement of McAlister's accurate assessment.

'Why are you out here? Has the trial closed already?'

'No, Judge Hind has called a recess to consider legal argument. My learned colleague has requested two new witnesses be allowed to give evidence. Apparently, they have only just come forward and will be testifying that the defendant was with them at the time of the raid.'

'Two witnesses?' Cornelius's voice carried down the length of the corridor, earning him a hard glare from a passing clerk. By way of appeasement he brought his voice down to a hoarse whisper which was still audible from five metres away. 'That can't be right? We know damn well Weasel was in the flat and ...'

McAlister put her carefully manicured hand up to stop Cornelius from speaking any further.

'It doesn't matter inspector. I'm afraid Tobias has played a proverbial blinder, greatly aided by someone with impressive inside knowledge. The case is as flimsy as hell, and if the judge allows these witnesses to be heard, I'm afraid you can kiss goodbye to a prosecution.'

Seeing the court clerk gesturing her from the entrance to the courtroom, McAlister turned on her Christian Louboutin heels.

'Judgement time,' she muttered. 'Wish me luck inspector; I think we are going to need it.'

Two

Bristol sulked under a steel grey February sky that stretched an unforgiving gloom over the rooftops. A fine blanket of icy drizzle was gearing itself up to transform into a torrent, just in time to soak the morning commuters. Seven thirty in the morning, and achingly slow traffic inched its way along Cheltenham Road. A cavernous hole had appeared overnight on the northbound carriageway, courtesy of the water board, and the temporary lights that controlled the flow of vehicles around it changed twice but nothing moved. On any other day, Cornelius would fume about the congestion that ate chunks out of his day. Today, he barely gave it another thought. All his brain power was dissecting the previous day's events at the trial of Marcus Weavell, and his mood was as grim as the sky above him.

It took all his self-control to remain silent in the public gallery as he listened with incredulity to the two female witnesses that McMillan had produced in the dying hours of the trial. They both declared Weasel had spent the evening of the raid with them in a pokey pub, called The Wagon and Horses, on the edge of Hengrove. Cornelius knew the establishment well, the landlord being no friend of the police largely because of his prosecutions for handling stolen goods. Disproving the liaison between Weasel and the well-dressed ladies took place would be almost impossible. There were no CCTV cameras on The Wagon's premises and none in the surrounding streets. At least half the regular clientele had spent time being detained at Her Majesty's pleasure, so helping the police was not part of their social make up. Anybody from The Wagon brave enough to assist the Crown with a case of perjury was likely to end up having the direction of their kneecaps altered.

Cornelius didn't agree with Davina McAlister that Tobias McMillan had played a blinder. In his opinion, McMillan was a slimy shit who dealt his legal cards from the bottom of the pack. He'd somehow managed to acquire some inside information and had twisted it to undermine the Crown's case, spectacularly. McMillan didn't care that he had helped a drug-pushing pimp return to the streets of the city; all he wanted was to win his case. The denial of justice was nothing more than inconsequential collateral damage.

Despite all the ire that Cornelius vented at the defence barrister, he knew a sizeable chunk of the blame lay squarely at his feet. Manny Thompson had history with a gangster who held a colossal grudge against Weasel. If that wasn't bad enough, he'd also visited him in prison in the weeks leading up to the trial. Cornelius had missed it all, and he would have to spend his morning explaining to Superintendent Liatt how he had cocked up so spectacularly. His other choice was to return to the courtroom, listen to Judge Hind's summing up and wait for Weasel's inevitable acquittal. The fact he chose a roasting from the superintendent over the sight of Weasel's smug self-congratulatory grin was an unwelcome reminder of how much Cornelius hating losing.

***

Gloucester Road Police Station went up during the post-war rebuild of the late 1940s when construction speed won hands-down over aesthetics. It had all the appearance of being designed by unimaginative primary school children playing with Lego and looked like three large, grubby reddish-brown boxes randomly left by the side of the A38. Half a century's worth of city grime had been absorbed into the plain brickwork, which had not been cleaned since the day it was built. However, it retained a degree of popularity with the police as it had a good-sized car park at the rear, which more than made up for the ageing internal facilities.

Easing his tiny car into a space only a handful of vehicles could access, Cornelius climbed out into the driving rain and headed for the station's side entrance in the vain hope he could get to his desk without having to run the gauntlet of gossipers who would want to quiz him about the trial. He was still shaking the rain from his coat when he was spotted by Sergeant Malcolm Williams who was trying to carry four mugs of coffee and two packets of plain crisps without the aid of a tray. The sergeant's face lit up when he saw the bedraggled inspector standing in front of him.

'She's looking for yooou!' he sang with his deep tenor voice. 'I think her actual words were,' he paused to arrange his vocal chords so he could mimic her voice. '"Will the next person who catches sight of Inspector Cornelius please send him directly to my office, without stopping at the vending machine first."' The words directly and without were delivered with an increase in volume. Williams's eyes glinted as he praised himself for his vocal artistry, Cornelius's shoulders merely dropped.

Cornelius had ended the previous working day by phoning through an update on the trial's developments before seeking solace in The Flask. He'd carefully avoided giving the superintendent too many details, particularly the ones which highlighted his incompetence. He had opted to speak to the Super this morning, thinking that managing the bad news would be easier face to face. But it sounded like she was abreast of developments and was already on the warpath.

Climbing the stairs to the office which housed the CID, he passed a nervous looking Detective Constable Andy Statton. He inadvertently made eye contact with Cornelius and felt obliged to pass on the message he had heard boomed out across the CID office.

'The Super wants to see you, sir.' His expression indicated that he and everyone else in the station knew what was heading his way. Cornelius acknowledged his effort with a brief nod of his head and carried on up the stairs. Once inside the CID office, another DC,

Rita Sharma, got as far as opening her mouth before Cornelius barked,

'I know!'

Instead of heading to the superintendent's office, he headed for the vending machines which dispensed the caffeine and sugar supplies that he relied on to function. To Cornelius's dismay, John Brawley was already there, audibly cursing the machine for taking his money without recompensing him with the appropriate goods. He turned away in disgust from his inanimate tormentor, but his scowl was replaced by an ill-disguised grin as he saw Cornelius approaching him.

'Ah, Inspector Cornelius ...' but before he could deliver his gloating message Cornelius told him to piss off. 'Charming,' uttered Brawley, as Karen Liatt's considerable bulk came into view. Her eyes focused on Cornelius as he retrieved a Mars bar from the machine.

'Lucas, did Inspector Brawley not pass on my message about seeing me immediately?'

'Never said a word, ma'am,' and before an open-mouthed Brawley could form a reply, Cornelius disappeared into the superintendent's office.

Karen Liatt had been drafted into Gloucester Road two years previously, following an inspection from the Criminal Justice Inspectorate. Her brief was to improve the effectiveness of the station whose practices were as old as the creaking infrastructure. With a tenure originally set at six months, she'd set about changing all manner of procedures most of which had been met with ill-disguised resentment from staff who were waiting for her time at the station to come to an end. It soon became obvious that her transfer had more to do with getting her out from underneath the feet of the Portishead hierarchy than anything else, and consequently, she had never left Gloucester Road.

Cornelius reluctantly followed the formidable superintendent into an orderly office, her tidy workspace a stark contrast to the disorganised heap that constituted Cornelius's desk. Bare light blue walls surrounded a slate grey tanker desk, which never had more than two sheets of paper on it at any one time. She had positioned it adjacent to the external window so she could keep an eye on the station's comings and goings, two floors below. The semi-glazed wall directly in front of her provided a view stretching right across the CID office. Visitors were made to sit with their back to the glass in the full knowledge they were being watched by the CID staff who, today, would be wondering what fate was befalling Cornelius.

'Sit,' she ordered. Cornelius dutifully did so, deliberately sipping loudly on his coffee.

Superintendent Liatt fixed her gaze on Cornelius. An ominous crimson colour rose in her cheeks, the pen in her hands close to snapping. After what felt like an eternity, she eventually spoke.

'In your own time, Lucas ...'

Cornelius knew he had to come clean about his own shortcomings but decided to expose the failings of others first.

'We have someone in the station leaking information, ma'am.'

He glanced at Liatt's expression to see if this revelation had deflected any of her anger away from him. She remained impassioned and the intensity of colour in her cheeks suggested her wrath was not subsiding.

'Tobias McMillan knew we had a packet of Afghan's finest stolen from our evidence room, he also knew about my history with Weasel and that I asked to take on his case. He twisted the lot, making it look like a conspiracy to convict his hard done by, and obviously innocent, client.'

'Maybe I should employ McMillan as an inspector rather than you.' Her mouth formed into a contorted pout at her own rhetorical question – a sign she was mulling over unpleasant options.

'Ma'am?'

'How did he know about Thompson's working history with Danny Palmer, when you, an inspector, didn't have a fucking clue?' The superintendent's pen snapped, sending splinters of shattered plastic flying across her office.

Cornelius winced. When Karen Liatt swore, nothing good ever came out of it. He was one badly worded answer away from transfer or demotion, so he opted for a small amount of contrition.

'Yes, I know I missed the link, but the list of Manny's known associates is seriously long, and yes, Palmer is on it but only because Manny is the go-to person for any self-respecting thief who needs to store their ill-gotten gains away from our prying eyes. We knew nothing about him looking after Palmer's taxi fleet, and anyway, how the hell was someone like Manny allowed a visiting permit to see Palmer in Prison?'

'I'm raising that with the prison governor later this morning, but it doesn't excuse you not knowing.'

'Okay,' Cornelius held his hands up as a sign of surrender. 'Our intelligence wasn't good enough, but someone in here fed

McMillan information. I'd bet six months' salary he coached the last two witnesses into providing false alibis. I'll look into it, but he chose the location for their alibis carefully, and I reckon he'll have moved them on by now, so even finding them will be difficult enough.'

Silence descended as Liatt stared out of the grey steel framed window; she seemed transfixed by the rain doing its best to force its way through the ageing seals. Cornelius was on the verge of interrupting her train of thought before deciding he was probably better off sitting quietly and waiting for her to finish deliberating.

'Who knew you asked to take on Weasel's case?'

Cornelius puffed his cheeks out, mentally checking off possible candidates.

'Apart from DCI Laverty, I really don't know. It's possible our conversation was overheard.'

Liatt nodded imperceptibly. 'I'll refer that to professional standards, however, if you uncover any further information, you refer back to me, clear?'

'Of course, ma'am.' Cornelius felt grateful at being temporarily off the hook.

'Find Thompson and dump any charge you can muster on him. I want him to pay for his part in screwing up the case.'

'With pleasure.' Cornelius stood up and made it as far as opening her office door when Liatt called after him.

'Oh, and Lucas,' she paused until he looked directly at her. 'Make a mistake like that again and I'll transfer you out of CID.'

Cornelius just stared at her. She had deliberately waited until he'd opened the door so the staff outside could hear. Punishment by humiliation, dished out with a single sentence. As he walked out though the CID office, everyone had their heads down, trying to make it look like they weren't listening. Everyone except John Brawley, who looked directly at him and grinned broadly.

Three

Cornelius spent a listless morning seated at his cluttered desk, attempting to look busy. He tried to focus his mind on anything other than the Weavell trial but failed. At noon precisely, he was put out of his misery. The call came from a court clerk who Cornelius had once helped get off a speeding charge. Not guilty – a unanimous decision. What a surprise. The jury had deliberated for less than two hours, a new record for one of his cases. It would take him months to shake off the humiliation.

It was barely lunchtime and, so far, the day had been an unmitigated disaster. The thought of a lunchtime pint was lodged in his head, and he wondered which one of his cases would conveniently take him past The Flask. Before he could formulate an exit strategy, his phone rang.

'Inspector Cornelius? Malcolm Williams here, sir. I have a lady asking for you, she wants to report a missing person.'

Cornelius quickly scanned the room for some other poor sod to dump this call on. Nobody suitable appeared in his eye-line, but he remembered seeing John Brawley heading off in the general direction of the exit. It was less than five minutes ago, chances were, he was still in the building. Perfect.

'Brawley's down there with you, isn't he? Why don't you ask him? Even that incompetent idiot could manage a missing person case.'

'As it happens, sir, Inspector Brawley did offer. However, the lady is insistent she speaks to you, and you alone.'

Cornelius sighed. 'Okay, I'll be there in five minutes.' It dawned on him that Williams called him sir twice during the call. 'Malcolm, are you on speaker phone?'

'Yup,' replied Williams, promptly disconnecting the call before the puce-looking Brawley standing alongside him had a chance to retort.

Grimacing, Cornelius replaced the phone. Today was not his day for getting anything right.

***

Hoping Brawley had now gone and he wasn't going to be asked for an apology he had no intention of giving, Cornelius weaved his way through the station's narrow, poorly lit corridors. They still stank of the magnolia paint which had been slapped on the walls to try and rejuvenate the place. Cornelius gave it a month before the first scuff marks appeared, another year and it would be back to its normal battered look.

Interview room two was a windowless, battleship-grey box with barely enough room for four people to sit around the small white table in the middle. Cornelius lowered himself into one of the seats and looked at his visitor, as she scrunched up a bag from Jane's Bakery. He guessed the woman opposite him was in her mid-seventies. Her grey hair, tied in a bun, was partially hidden under a cream felt bucket hat. With a neat green and brown Harris Tweed jacket and skirt, a string of pearls and piercing blue eyes, she reminded Cornelius of Miss Marple. He dismissed that idea the moment she opened her mouth.

'You be Lucas Cornelius?' she said, removing doughnut crumbs from the corner of her mouth with her sleeve.

'I be, I mean I am,' said Cornelius, offering his warrant card by way of reassurance.

'Me neighbour's gone missin'.' She leaned back in the metal framed chair, waiting for a response.

Cornelius's reply didn't help. 'I see.' It was as much as he could muster, mostly because he was wondering why she had asked for him specifically.

'Not like 'er at all. Good girl she is, always looks out for me.' Specks of icing sugar not cleared by the previous sleeve wipe, flew from her mouth towards Cornelius.

Why do I always get them? he thought as he tried to work out the best way to deal with his visitor without increasing his workload. At this point he realised he didn't know the doughnut eater's name, but she volunteered the information before he could ask.

'Name's Bettie. Elizabeth Bettie, Mrs. I ain't seen 'er for nigh on two weeks and I tell 'ee it ain't right. There's summat wrong.'

Barely thirty seconds in and Cornelius had had enough. 'Well Mrs Bettie, for a case like this I think that Sergeant Williams, on the front desk, can take all the details.' He stood up, put his pen back in his pocket and tucked his unused pad under his arm. He gestured for Mrs Bettie to leave the room.

She didn't budge.

'Neil said I should insist on seeing you.'

'Neil?'

' 'E said that you were the only one 'ood take me serious.'

Cornelius felt a slight pang of guilt. Elizabeth Bettie seemed oblivious that he was standing, ready to leave. She carried on.

'Last time I came to see you lot I wus 'avin' trouble with the little shites three doors down. Four times I came 'ere and no bugger ever called to see me. Went on for bloody ages it did.' Tears welled in her eyes. 'Neil said you were the one decent policeman in 'ere and you'd 'elp.'

'Sorry, who is Neil?'

For the first time Mrs Bettie looked him in the eye, her expression indicating she had misjudged him after all and that, perhaps, he was completely thick.

' 'E works 'ere with you!' Despite her increasing agitation, Cornelius still sported a blank expression. 'Now 'ow did 'e describe you?' She paused, searching her memory banks, eyes widening as she remembered. ' 'E said you're a bit cranky, but when you say you'll do summat you always do – and that you're a ten ... ten ... ten something or other little bugger.'

'Tenacious?' offered Cornelius.

'Yeah, that's it – tenacious! Whatever that means.' She grinned, giving herself credit for recalling the descriptive terminology, pieces of doughnut still visible between her yellow teeth.

You obviously don't know what cranky means either, thought Cornelius but elected not to enlighten Mrs Bettie. 'I don't recall anyone called Neil working here,' he said in the absence of anything more meaningful and made a mental note to ask Malcolm

Williams who this Neil might be. He stared at the woman who clearly, and wrongly, held him in high esteem. She sat back in the chair, folded her arms and stared at him, not even blinking. Deciding his visitor had no intention of going anywhere until she had what she came for, Cornelius took a deep breath.

'Okay Mrs Bettie,' he said. 'Let's start at the beginning.'

He sat back down at the table, opened his pad and embarked on his journey into a whole world of trouble.

MARCH

As a young child, she hated the onset of nightfall. Once the safety of daylight eased away it was replaced not by night but by a deep black void waiting to be filled by the active imagination of a five year old. When the shadows in her bedroom lengthened and darkened, her thoughts persuaded her that a man in an ugly black top hat, with straggly greasy hair and a long pointy nose was watching her from the furthest corner of the bedroom. The nightmare had begun one wet Sunday afternoon when she watched *Chitty Chitty Bang Bang* over her sister's shoulder. Effortlessly convincing herself that one day, the child catcher would come for her.

From her darkened bedroom, she'd scream for her mother, who responded with an empathy that came from knowing her daughter had inherited a fertile imagination. Her mother would give the gentle reassurance of a tender cuddle, the type that can only come from a protective parent. It would settle her for a while, but barely ten minutes later, he was back, silently waiting in the dark corner for her to go to sleep, and she'd scream again.

Eventually, her mother became exhausted by the broken nights, and for her own sanity as much as her daughter's, she bought a Peter Rabbit night light. The gentle glow banished all the shadows away and peaceful sleep made a welcome return. Although the days of watching *Chitty Chitty Bang Bang* were decades behind her, the legacy had been mild nyctophobia. By her late teens, she convinced herself that her fears had been successfully hidden from those around her, so was furious when her elder sister gave her an Iron Maiden CD for Christmas one year. As soon as she read the cover, she'd thrown it to the floor and stormed out of the room. Sibling love temporarily shattered over a CD entitled *Fear of the dark*.

One of the reasons she opted for urban life as an adult was for the ambient neon lights that reached out across the city at night. A dense population meant a permanent absence of complete darkness, and without the dark the child catcher could never return to haunt her dreams.

Now, darkness had returned, but it wasn't the child catcher from her nightmares that tormented her. It was someone much, much worse.

Four

Not for the first time that day, Cornelius rejected his body's call for alcohol's numbing properties, deciding it would better to head for home and try to spend some time with Daniel. His relationship with his son had been on a rollercoaster since his wife, Jane, had exited their lives, and he was hoping to try and repair some of the damage that still existed following a massive argument from a month previously.

He left Gloucester Road station and fought his way westwards through the dense traffic. The driving rain gave way to sleet and he jeered the radio presenter for playing ELO's *Mr Blue Sky*. Cornelius's four-bedroomed house sat on the edge of Durdham Down, built in the mid-eighties on the site of an old manor house which had fallen into a state of disrepair. The land had been carved up and seven dwellings created within the curtilage. He'd not wanted to move there, but Jane fell in love with the generous gardens at the front and back. She saw the potential to develop her hobby as a horticulturist, whereas he saw a shed-load of work in simple routine maintenance. What eventually sold the house to him was the location at the end of a no-through road with only a narrow footpath on the eastern border and a sturdy six foot wooden fence surrounding the full perimeter, making it secure and private.

Opening the solid six-foot gates, Cornelius hoped Shagalong Charlotte wasn't there with Daniel. He'd developed an irrational dislike of his son's girlfriend the first time they had met. She'd handed him a birthday card, signed Lottie with an overly large loop dotting the letter 'i', and she called him Luke, one of his pet hates. She seemed permanently glued to Facebook and was a ferocious gossip who gleefully shared any information she found remotely scurrilous, its accuracy being entirely inconsequential. Add the unsubstantiated rumours about her previous sexual proclivities he unwillingly listened to at Daniel's 18th birthday bash and the nickname was born. He promised himself he wouldn't share the epithet – a feat achieved so far, whilst sober at least.

A thunderous beat greeted him as he opened the front door. With the music that loud, Cornelius surmised Daniel couldn't be on the PlayStation as well, which gave him a jot of hope. Persuading him to lower the volume of his music was challenging enough, but extracting him from the games console would be nigh on impossible, and he wanted to spend some time with Daniel without it descending into an almighty row.

Knocking on Daniel's door was probably the most pointless thing he had done all day. With the decibel level on his speakers set to dangerous, the sound of a fist on wood was hopelessly lost. Cornelius partially opened the door, and only then did it occur to him Daniel might have been trying to drown out the sound of him and Shagalong having sex. To his relief his son was on his own: to his dismay Daniel was multitasking by listening to music and playing a game which seemed to involve the wholesale slaughter of a strange alien species.

'Sup?' Daniel mumbled, his eyes not moving away from the screen.

Cornelius resisted the overwhelming urge to tell him to turn the fucking music down and at least grant him the courtesy of eye contact.

'You hungry? I'm feeling the need for a pizza delivery tonight ...'

Nothing.

'Daniel?'

'What?' Obvious irritation rising in Daniels voice.

'Do ... you ... want ... pizza?'

The briefest of head shakes indicated Daniel had no intention of breaking away from the digital massacre unfolding before him to do anything as trivial as eat. Cornelius sighed. The dialogue he wanted with his son was not going to happen.

'Is this a two player game?'

A head nod.

'Budge up then ...'

***

After fifteen minutes of assisting Daniel in alien genocide, Cornelius's mind started to wander, and he quietly mulled over the problem of finding Elizabeth Bettie's neighbour. He had her address and approximate age along with a physical description but no name. It had taken twenty minutes to establish that Elizabeth Bettie knew nothing other than the fact that the kind woman who lived in her block of flats was missing. Cornelius tried to tell Elizabeth this kind of disappearance was much more common than she probably appreciated but that tomorrow he would call by the flats and ask a few questions.

Social media seemed to be a good place to begin the search, but the worlds of Facebook and Instagram were anathema to him. His son however, was rarely without his smart phone or laptop. Asking Daniel for help seemed to be a good starting point.

Still playing the game, his question was innocuous enough; what were the likely social media sites that women in their thirties might use. Daniel said nothing; there was no change in his facial expression and nothing to indicate the emotional tsunami about to envelope them both. Thinking Daniel hadn't heard the question, Cornelius asked it again. This time he had a response, Daniel's voice as cold as ice.

'I'm not going to help you find another tart.'

Daniel was still staring at the screen, but the veins in his forehead had started to bulge. Cornelius realised his mistake and quickly tried to back track.

'That's not what I mean, I have to ...' but Daniel had come to his own conclusion and no amount of reasoning was going to change it.

'Isn't one enough for you?' he screamed, 'Why are you doing this? What is your problem?'

The questions were fired like bullets from a Browning. Cornelius had tried to answer them before but always to deaf ears. Daniel's tirade concluded with the most painful proclamation he could think of.

'She will come back!'

Deciding he could do nothing else to help the situation, Cornelius quietly put the game controller down and left Daniel to his rage. Just before reaching the door, he looked back at his son, whose head was shaking with fury as he stared at the monitor.

'That's not why I asked Daniel. And sooner or later you and I will need to talk this through properly.'

His statement had been quiet and gentle, and not expecting a response, he shut the door on a problem that was escalating between him and his son – one which he had no idea how to tackle.

MARCH

Waking up to find herself chained to a bed in a dark cellar wasn't a scenario that she had ever contemplated – not even in the murkiest recesses of her imagination. She closed her eyes and concentrated on bringing her breathing under control. After fifteen minutes of deep, regular breaths her head started to clear and rational thinking clawed its way back, but all she had were uncertainties. She didn't know her location, her reason for being there or how she came to be chained to a bed. Her mouth was still dry, she was cold, could barely move, and her bladder needed emptying.

She desperately attempted to recall the events that led to her living nightmare, trying to work out how she had allowed herself to become so susceptible without realising it. Before she could arrange the pieces of that particular puzzle in her mind, she heard the unmistakeable creak of floorboards. The regular tip-tap sound of leather soles on wooden stairs followed, and dingy yellow light once again streamed into the cellar.

His lean silhouette filled the doorframe, where he stood, silent and motionless. He was savouring her vulnerability and she hated it, but she needed some respite from her confinement.

'Can you loosen these chains, please?'

'Why? Are you planning on going somewhere, Alisha?'

She paused, as her mind danced. Perhaps he had the wrong person and it was all a mistake. She'd promise not to go to the police, if he would just leave her somewhere – anywhere – as long as she could walk back to freedom. A long hike, barefoot in the pouring rain was suddenly an enticing proposition.

'You've got it wrong,' she cried. 'Have a look in my handbag, it will tell you who I really am. I'm not Alisha, I'm …'

She didn't finish her sentence. He took two rapid strides and swung his right arm across her face. The back of his hand connected with her cheekbone with a savage ferocity, sending her skull spinning sideways.

'Your name is the one I give you!' He grabbed her chin and twisted her head back towards him. 'I told you, I own you now, and I am calling you Alisha.'

She nodded briefly, knowing she was in no position to fight back. He let go of her chin but stayed standing over her, his eyes carefully taking in every inch of her restrained body.

'I need to pee,' she whispered. Even in these wildly abnormal circumstances, the mention of bodily functions to a stranger still warranted the discretion of a lowered voice.

He moved to the base of the fold-up bed and reached down. When he straightened up, she could see him holding a bright orange bucket which he carried to the side. He walked behind her and remembering what he did last time he stood there, she braced herself for the stinging pain of having her hair pulled harshly again. Instead, the sound of clanking iron chains filled the room, and a few moments later, he moved away from the bed and leaned against the mildew covered wall.

'Go on then.'

She shuffled again and realised she could now move her limbs beyond the restriction that the chains had first imposed. Swinging her legs over the side, the chains rattled and complained but granted the movement.

She stared down at her makeshift toilet and up at her captor, who had returned to the door frame.

'Can I have some privacy please?'

'You don't get to make any requests. I'll do want I want with you and that includes watching you piss.'

His dismissive tone was condescending but not as unpleasant as the sight of his right hand rummaging in his baggy front pocket.

She knew this degradation was the start of it; from here on, it would only get worse. She had two options – escape or die.

Five

The leaden grey backdrop that had shrouded Bristol for the previous week had been replaced by overnight snow and a freezing northern wind. Dull grey slate rooftops had been transformed into an unseasonal wonderland and untreated pavements glistened with ice. The army of daily commuters buried under layers of warm clothing teetered uncomfortably, struggling to keep their balance as they gently edged their way to work. An elegantly dressed woman in her mid-fifties went sprawling as the ice claimed her balance. As she began to fall, she involuntarily grabbed the arm of an unsuspecting student standing next to her. Her respite was brief as they both crashed to the ground in an undignified heap.

From the safe warmth of Cornelius's car, Daniel burst out laughing at the spectacle and promptly claimed he wished he had caught it on his phone, so he could share it on YouTube. Cornelius put aside any concerns for the lack of sympathy displayed by his son, grateful for anything to help break the icy atmosphere that had developed between them since the previous night.

Earlier that morning, Daniel was still giving his father the silent treatment. Their last argument had resulted in a silence that went on for days, and Daniel had refused to acknowledge, let alone accept, Cornelius's offer of a lift into college. But the morning's freezing temperature had beaten teenage belligerence, and with a barely perceptible nod of the head, Daniel had finally accepted his father's offer.

For the remainder of the journey, Cornelius sought to capitalise on the thaw in Daniel's mood, trying to make small talk with him but carefully avoiding anything that could take them back to the fighting ground of twelve hours earlier. It had been a marginally successful strategy, as Daniel even mumbled, bye, as he exited the car – something Cornelius happily interpreted as progress.

Cornelius had not factored the unexpected detour via Daniel's college into his journey time. Only when he pulled into the station car park, did he realise he was five minutes late for the morning briefing. Ignoring the genial nods given by two officers heading home after their night shift, he bounded up the stairs two at time, somehow thinking this would help atone for his lateness.

The Gloucester Road CID office was a second floor room, half the size it needed to be. Too many desks had been levered in to accommodate all the staff and despite Karen's Liatt's efforts to introduce a paperless environment, five floor-to-ceiling filing cabinets lined one wall; they had been in place since the mid-1970s. Apart from Liatt, no one wanted to see the back of them and her insistence they should be removed had been met with universal disquiet. A perpetual smell of damp plaster constantly filled the air, although no one ever managed to find the source.

Bursting into the office, he was relieved to see the briefing had yet to start, although DCI Laverty still fixed him with a hard glare.

'Lucas, gracious of you to join us.'

Cornelius said nothing but scanning the room gratefully noted Superintendent Liatt wasn't there to stick her spiteful oar in. It took another five minutes before everybody had their morning requirements of coffee and doughnuts safely in their hands. Laverty was wise enough to know that if he started before they were suitably armed with sugar and caffeine, he would not hold their attention beyond five minutes.

At six feet, four inches tall, with a lean frame and dome shaped head, Detective Chief Inspector Ross Laverty was easy to spot from a distance. His usual attire of dark suits and heavy rimmed photochromic glasses had earned him the nickname of Meninblack although no one said it to his face. His skilled and analytical insight into the workings of criminal minds had brought many men and women to justice who might have otherwise walked away unpunished for their misdemeanours. However, when it came to speaking to more than three people at once, Laverty tended to drone. This morning he was in particularly fine fettle as he mumbled his way through the extensive CID caseload. Cornelius couldn't help but wonder how someone as astute as Laverty seemed to be oblivious to the fact he bored the arse off his team.

Within twenty minutes the briefing had ended, and the assembled officers dispersed to start their respective tasks for the day. Cornelius tried to exit the room before anyone could dump extra work on him – he had his own agenda today. He darted for the door, but Laverty was too quick for him.

'Lucas, a word please,' he said, pointing to the seclusion of Karen Liatt's empty office.

Ushering Cornelius in, he began without any preamble or social niceties.

'The Super filled me in on the trial.' He stared at his inspector to invite comment. Cornelius simply rammed his hands in his pockets.

'Not good, Lucas. I know Karen has already bawled you out over it, so I'm not going to add my two penn'orth.' Cornelius doubted it but said nothing. 'However, I do want Thompson nailed for going back on his word. What deal did you strike with him?'

Cornelius felt his neck hairs prickling. He paused a fraction too long whilst wondering how much information to divulge, and Laverty pounced on his hesitation.

'You're a good inspector Lucas, but no one is going to get the likes of Thompson to give evidence at trial unless they have some kind of hold over him. McMillan was wrong to suggest Palmer had influenced him, so that leaves you as the likely culprit. How am I doing so far?'

Cornelius said nothing but felt very uncomfortable; Laverty was going to have his two penn'orth after all. His expression gave away his guilt.

'Thought so. Why didn't you tell me?'

Cornelius puffed his cheeks out; he had to come clean. Laverty offered an olive branch to help him.

'I'm not blameless. I had to extract Liatt's boot from my arse for not knowing about his link to Palmer. Just because you didn't tell me about your deal – which you bloody should have by the way – doesn't make it right. Now, did you let him off a serious crime in order to persuade him to testify?'

Laverty's stare indicated he had no intention of uttering another word until he heard what Cornelius had to say for himself.

'I didn't know about Palmer. There's never been anything to suggest Thompson had worked for him in the past.'

'You don't have to be Sherlock to work that out, but's that's not what I asked – what was the deal?'

Cornelius sighed. He'd never have made it as a practising Catholic but here he was, having to confess all.

'Given his history of looking after other people's goods, I thought he was worth checking out for the wholesale whisky job, the batch taken from the warehouse on Bath Road.'

Laverty nodded, he remembered it well. 'We put that lot away though ...'

'But at the time we hadn't recovered the goods, and if ever there was a person who would happily look after a consignment of whisky it was Manny.' He paused long enough to see Laverty agreeing with his logic.

'So, I paid him a visit, I didn't find any whisky there but he had twenty, top of the range, wide screen televisions in his lockup. He was trying to stack them as I walked in. Unsurprisingly, he wasn't prepared to tell me where they came from, but he looked shit scared about what would happen if he lost them.'

'Storing them for one of Palmer's mob?'

'My thoughts exactly. I had grilled him before about his alleged role in looking after the drugs for Weasel and ...'

Laverty groaned and Cornelius realised he didn't need to finish his confession – Laverty did it for him.

'So, you offered to look the other way regarding the televisions in exchange for him changing his mind about testifying against Weasel. For crying out loud Lucas ...'

'It's not as if I asked him to lie – we know damn well Weasel asked him to hoard the goods.' Laverty didn't look mollified. 'Look, he was a damn sight more scared about upsetting Palmer over twenty poxy televisions than the prospect of putting Weasel away. I just used it to my advantage.'

'What, so you could get to Weasel?' Laverty threw his arms in the air in exasperation.

'Thompson is a criminal, there's no denying that, but in the scheme of things he's low level, he's never involved in violence and apart from helping out Weasel, he never does drugs either. As far as villains go he is the lesser of two evils, and that's what I made my call on.' Cornelius tried to look more defiant than he felt.

'More likely, you saw a chance to get one over on Weasel.' Cornelius opened his mouth to object, but Laverty had his hand up. 'Christ, what a cock up. Right, get your sorry arse over to his lockup. Superintendent Liatt wants Thompson taken down and I agree with her.'

'I'm on my way.' Cornelius made for the exit before Laverty could say anything else, but he didn't move quickly enough.

'Lucas, take Andy Statton with you, I don't want you tackling this on your own and screwing up again.'

Cornelius opened his mouth ready to protest but Laverty's fixed stare indicated it was non-negotiable. He also knew Laverty was right, so far, he had screwed up big time. What he didn't know was that his life was about to become a whole lot worse.

***

'Grab your coat, Andy.'

Detective Constable Andrew Statton looked up from his monitor, his lips still attached to a large mug of coffee with *Keep calm and call Batman* written on the side. His expression told Cornelius all he needed to know about whether he had been told in advance about his task for the day.

'Uh, sir?'

Cornelius stared at the immaculately dressed DC, wondering how much time he spent in front of the bathroom mirror every morning.

'You're coming with me.' He'd almost said, we have a score to settle but didn't want those words heard within the office. Someone in the station was leaking information, and at this stage he couldn't rule anyone out, especially a young detective constable who obviously spent considerable sums of money on his appearance.

Statton shrugged, shut down his computer and slinging his Italian double-breasted coat over his arm, dutifully followed Cornelius out of the office. He didn't say a word until they were out in the car park and had walked past the fleet of pool cars.

'Are we walking, sir?' He failed to hide his disappointment at having to walk anywhere on a freezing cold day.

'No, we're taking my car.'

Statton stopped in his tracks. 'Really? Shouldn't we use one of the ...'

Cornelius turned around and caught sight of the young DC's expression. 'Surely you're not embarrassed to be seen in my car are you Andy?'

The pause in reply was enough and Cornelius grinned. 'I'm so sorry if my Smart car doesn't match your urbane style, but I can park virtually anywhere in it, and that is a real asset in this city, so stop whingeing and climb in.'

Statton thought better of saying he hadn't actually whinged but hoped he wouldn't be seen by anybody he knew.

***

The thought of having Statton babysitting him all day put Cornelius in a mood, and although it was probably the last thing the detective constable wanted as well, Cornelius made a churlish point by not saying a word on the journey out. By the time they reached their destination, Cornelius's mood had softened slightly and he decided to brief Statton before interviewing their suspect.

'I'd never tell him,' Cornelius began, 'but I almost like Thompson.'

Statton fixed him with a quizzical stare.

'He's part of dying breed of criminal, one who has his own moral code about what he will and will not get involved in. His stock-in-trade is storing stolen goods and he's good at it. Businesses and people with more money than sense are fair game as far as he is concerned, but he won't touch anything if he thinks it's been lifted from your average Joe. He will not get involved with drugs and he doesn't use violence. Manny's also incredibly polite, even when he is lying through his teeth.'

Statton looked puzzled. 'But didn't he store Weasel's drugs?'

'Yes, but he claims Weasel lied to him. He thought he was storing some smuggled tobacco, and I believe him. That's one of the reasons he agreed to give evidence.' Cornelius had no intention of divulging his off-the-record negotiations with a junior officer.

Exiting the car, Statton cursed the icy wind as it stung his face. Cornelius told him to stop being such a wimp, despite feeling exactly the same. They entered the yard and trudged past a couple of abandoned lockups and scrap merchant's that sat alongside Manny Thompson's garage.

Hort Bridge Trading Estate was a collection of red brick Victorian buildings, originally constructed as a Woollen Mill, which had survived the Bristol blitz largely unscathed. There had not been much in the way of repairs and maintenance since it became home to small business units in the late 1970s. Wrought iron fencing had been added to the perimeter, but the gates to the site were rarely closed. The yard, which linked the collection of battered buildings, had fared even worse when it came to general upkeep; it was now a sea of crumbled tarmac and diesel spills. Cornelius walked steady and straight across the yard; Statton picked his route carefully to protect his new wingtip brogues from the mud packed potholes.

The old wooden sign fixed above the garage's double doors said, *E. Thompson - Garage and Storage* – or at least it did originally. It had not been renovated since first erected and the elements and the years had combined to wear it down to a barely readable mix of faded and flaked paint. The telephone number had a 0272 prefix, but locals knew it as *Manny's* and judging by the number of vehicles parked outside, it wasn't short of customers.

The large dark grey plank and batten doors which gave access to the workshop were shut, so Cornelius and Statton entered via a side door with the word *Office* only just readable through the grime and oil stains. The room's status as an office was highly questionable. It was just a dumping ground for old boxes of papers with an over flowing and battered 1960's filing cabinet in the corner. There was a desk covered in files, papers and discarded wrappers, and something positively disgusting covered the floor.

With no one in the office to greet them, they made their way through the inner door, which was as grimy and discoloured as the first. It opened out into the main workshop and Cornelius and Statton were immediately hit by a wall of fumes – a mixture of diesel and cigarette smoke. Statton hesitated, pausing to take in one last lungful of air. Cornelius strode straight in and stumbled over a pair of legs protruding from underneath a twenty year old black BMW that looked like it was held together with duct tape. The legs did not belong to Manny Thompson; his were longer and stockier. Nevertheless, Cornelius did not intend to start with an apology.

'Police!' he barked with as much authority as his fume filled lungs could muster. 'Can I have a word please, sir?' The legs didn't move, and there was no audible response. 'A word please, sir,' he repeated, injecting a tone of irritation. Still no response from the legs, although a gentle movement suggested their owner was, at least, alive. 'Either we chat here or we can do it down the station but not until I've filed for a warrant to search this dump from top to bottom – your choice.'

'I'm sorry, I didn't realise you were talking to me officer, what's all this about a warrant?'

Cornelius was about to advise the owner of the legs that he was an inspector and not an officer, when he saw they belonged to dark-haired, brown-eyed and quite beautiful woman.

'Oh, er sorry, I ...' a flustered Cornelius tried to regain his composure in the face of a bemused woman and a detective constable trying to suppress a grin.

'A woman working in a garage? Who'd of thought it, eh?' said the owner of the legs, winking at Statton.

'And you are, madam?' invited Statton with his most genial smile.

'Megan.'

Cornelius looked her up and down. 'Megan Thompson?'

Megan said nothing but grinned broadly.

'The last time I saw you was ...'

'Nine years ago, when you searched my dad's house. Detective Sergeant Cornelius isn't it?'

'Inspector,' he replied, fumbling for his warrant card.

'No need for that, inspector. My – haven't you grown up.' Megan held Cornelius's stare but from the corner of her eye she could see Statton stifling a laugh. 'Now, what can I do for you?'

The sight of Manny's daughter as a grown woman and now working for her father unsettled Cornelius. He always liked the impact his rank had when questioning suspects and the fact that she was playing with, and getting the better of, him in front of his colleague riled him. He needed to regain control.

'I'm looking for your dad, where is he?'

'I'm afraid you just missed him – and no, he didn't say where he was going.'

Cornelius said nothing, waiting for Megan to disclose more information. Statton simply wondered if she was single.

Megan broke into a grin again. 'I'm sorry. I had forgotten your default position is not to believe people. Here ...' She threw a bunch of keys at Statton, harder than she needed to, stinging his hand as he caught them. 'Feel free to check the lockups out the back.'

Cornelius nodded at his colleague who, reluctantly, trudged out to search for Thompson. He knew it was pointless, but he had to go through the motions.

Whilst Statton was searching through the lockups, Cornelius idly looked around the workshop, committing as many of the number plates to memory as he could; he would check on the owners back at the station. Turning down the offer of a coffee from Megan, he decided to quiz her again about Manny's whereabouts in the hope she might contradict herself.

'Was it nine years since I last saw you? You must have been about 15 or 16?'

Megan picked up a tool that would have looked more at home in a mediaeval torture chamber, but instead of crawling back underneath the BMW she turned and faced Cornelius.

'Mr Cornelius, for the record I am 23 years old. I have never been in trouble with the law, nor do I have any intention of being. I know my father has previously operated on the fringes of legal activity, but he has never tried to involve me in any of it. Now, it doesn't matter in how many ways you ask the question you are about to ask me, I have no idea where Dad is right now. I'll happily give you his mobile number, but he is a complete Luddite and rarely bothers to turn it on let alone answer it, even when the caller is his beloved daughter. I have no idea why you want to speak to him and I don't want to know. Now, if you'll excuse me, I will have a very unhappy customer on my hands if I don't have this Beamer on the road by the end of the day.'

Without waiting for a response, she slid back underneath the car and the sound of gentle percussive maintenance started to emanate from the engine.

She's her father's daughter alright, thought Cornelius. Megan's dismissal left him doing nothing more than staring around the disorganised garage, waiting for Statton to return. It took a further five minutes before he reappeared, shaking his head.

'Did you check the lockup at the far end of the yard? Your lot tend to miss that one,' yelled Megan from beneath the vehicle.

Cornelius gave his colleague an enquiring stare; Statton's embarrassed look suggested he hadn't, and once again he disappeared off into the freezing yard. He returned shaking his head.

'Thank you for your time Miss Thompson,' Cornelius called out as he turned to leave. 'Please tell your father I would like to speak to him – he can either ring me or I'll call again soon.'

Megan's response was muffled, but he thought she said she would be delighted to pass his message on.

It didn't occur to Cornelius or Statton to check the boot of the BMW Megan was working on. If they had, they would have saved the life of Emmanuel Thompson.

JANUARY

Her mind had drifted off, back to happier days when she played with her younger sister Marie in the rolling green fields which surrounded their home. In the field where Farmer Bill grew his maize, they'd run around in-between the tall stalks until they were sure they were lost, then try and find their way out. They would laugh, uncontrollably, when they found their way to the edge of the field, only to realise they were as far away from their house as it was possible to be. Then, they would play in a small brook that ran adjacent to the field, trying to build a dam to stop its gentle trickle, but the water always found a way through the various stones and branches they'd put its path. There must have been grey cloudy days but the recollections of those had faded over the years. Her childhood memories were of warm summer holidays spent in the West Sussex sunshine, her mother's cheese scones, and her little sister's blue and white floral dress which she insisted on wearing everywhere she went.

The thunderous roar of a grimy flatbed truck loaded with scaffolding snapped her back to reality. Its radial tyres sprayed a freezing mix of grit, diesel and rainwater over her bare legs and she shivered uncomfortably underneath the faded red awning of the betting shop. She liked touting here; the manager of the shop never asked her to move on and occasionally he would bring out a cup of tea and two digestive biscuits wrapped in foil. She was always grateful but suspected he did it because he wanted a freebie. One day, she might have to oblige, but not today. Today she needed money. A tingling sensation had started, the first signs of restlessness creeping through her body. Another few hours and her joints would ache as they seized up, like heavy door hinges in need of lubricating. She could just about cope with that but not the abdominal pains – those were too much. She must get a hit before then. Servicing a punter when she had those was almost impossible; it crippled her stomach and she could barely stand. Two more hours, then she'd move on to Cannon Street. Trade was brisker there, but it came at a price. The city's psychos and perverts went to Cannon Street to get their kicks. You had to be desperate to work there, and you could easily pick up a punter who would give you a black eye as part of the payment. Cannon Street meant painful work, but not as painful having to go without a hit.

She hated being broke, so tried to keep some money stashed away for emergencies. Knowing she could get a hit when needed was the only assurance she wanted – but the last of her cash was gone. Her trade had dropped by half recently and it had hit her hard. Some of her regular punters had stopped showing up at their usual times. Perhaps they had found out about her new boyfriend. Everyone was scared of him, but he knew what she did and would never try and stop her.

She had a theory that there were two types of punter. The regular ones knew the ropes and were savvy with the rates. It made them easier to deal with as they knew the rules, but they were much more difficult to rip-off. The others were the first-timers; the ones who thought condoms were optional or hadn't given any thoughts as to where they could go for their liaison. The compensation came when negotiating the rates. Newbies were usually so nervous they'd accept the first price, as long as it wasn't too high. After that, they could be tapped up for all kinds of extras. On a good day, she could make twice as much from a naïve new customer, as she could from one of the regulars.

Even from the other side of the road, she could see the man staring at her was a first-timer. He watched her but tried not to look at the same time, uncertain of what to do next. He was middle-aged, clean-shaven and reasonably dressed in light blue denim jeans and a John Rocha slate grey overcoat – a good sign he had money to spend. She watched, smiling, as he tried to look like he was doing anything else other than thinking about picking up a prostitute. He appeared to be shy and was probably gullible, just the way she liked them. She waved at him, beckoning him to cross the road. He acknowledged her with the briefest of waves and a hint of a smile. The muscles in her body relaxed slightly, knowing that within the hour, heroin would once again be coursing through her veins.

Six

By the time Cornelius and Statton drove away from Manny Thompson's garage, thin shafts of sunlight were breaking through the previously impenetrable cloud, gently thawing the lines of snow that remained glued to the sides of the roads and pavements.

Cornelius couldn't help comparing Megan, the girl he had encountered nine years earlier, with the beautiful woman that had so deftly put him in his place, today. He wondered how such a transition had happened before concluding it was nothing more than a sign of his own age. Statton was trying to think of any conceivable way he could ask her out without getting a bollocking from professional standards.

Lost in their own thoughts, the two men sat in silence as they fought their way back through the travel chaos. It was not until Cornelius saw the road sign for St Werburghs that he remembered Mrs Bettie and her missing neighbour. He didn't really want Statton in tow while he asked questions about a case he hadn't yet logged, but as the address was on the route back to the station, he thought it worth a quick look.

Maitland Gardens was a misnomer for four blocks of flats surrounding a courtyard of grey paving slabs that used to be a garden. The plants that once grew there had been neglected over the years and in the 1980s the trees were uprooted and the flower beds were paved over. Air pollution had eroded the slabs along with the brickwork of the buildings, resulting in a depressing looking complex. Residents were offered a vote on whether to keep the address as Maitland Gardens or change it to something more apt like Maitland Court. Those who voted opted to keep the name, because they couldn't be bothered with all the form-filling that a change of address would result in. Apathy won, and Maitland Gardens lived on, without a blade of grass to its name.

Exiting the car, Statton sniffed the air and screwed his face up.

'Oh, bloody hell, that's worse than the contents of my nephew's nappy.'

Cornelius set off briskly in search of Mrs Bettie's flat, Statton falling in beside him with a handkerchief held over his nose.

'Put it away!' barked Cornelius.

'But it stinks here, what is it?'

'Have you never smelt a blocked drain before? You wait until you are called to a building where a body's been liquefying for two months during the summer heat.'

Statton thought better of calling him a patronising git and turned his attention to the reason for their visit. 'Remind me, why are we here?'

Cornelius was going to ignore the question but decided limited information was better than none.

'I've had a report about a missing person. I'm pretty sure it's straightforward and the person in question has just moved on, but I'm checking it out before we have to do a shed-load of paperwork.'

'I'm not surprised. I'd want to leave this dump as well. Who is it that is missing?'

'One of the residents, apparently.'

He couldn't remember the missing person's name, which is why he was looking for Elizabeth Bettie's flat. They entered the dingy hallway and took the stairs. By the time Cornelius reached the top floor he was mildly out of breath; Statton looked as if he could climb another 20 flights without breaking into a sweat.

They walked along the narrow, covered balcony that straddled the length of the flats until they came to the last one, with faded floral curtains framing the inside of the windows. Cornelius rang the bell, but no sound came from inside so he rapped on the door frame. Through the frosted glass he could see a woman waddling towards the door.

'Alright, I 'eard 'ee the first time. 'Bout bloody time you came as well, that bloody smell 'as been getting on everyone's nerves and I ...' Elizabeth Bettie flung her door open and her face went from thunderous to a broad smile when she saw Cornelius. 'Oh, it's you. Neil was right, you are a ten ... ten ... thingyorother little bugger.'

Cornelius didn't bother to correct her this time. 'Hello Mrs Bettie, we're following up your report about your missing neighbour, Miss, uh ...' The pause was brief, Cornelius banked on Mrs Bettie not allowing for awkward silences and she didn't disappoint.

'Pippa, dunno 'er surname. I told 'ee that last time. 'Er flat's two doors down, number 32. What 'av 'ee found out then?'

'Nothing I can divulge yet. I assume you have heard nothing else since we last spoke?'

She fixed him with same withering stare that she had done in the interview room. 'I'd 'av told 'ee if I did. Not goin' to waste police time, am I?' Can you do anythin' about that smell?'

'I'll get Detective Constable Statton here to raise it with the relevant authorities. Do you have a key for Pippa's flat?'

'Nah, she's a private one that girl, 'eart of gold though. Always getting me bits of shoppin' an 'elpin' me with me cleanin'. Really missin' 'er I am. 'Ere, where are me manners? Do you two want tea?'

Both men shook their heads in unison.

'Thank you, but we'll be on our way. If you hear anything from Pippa, please let us know.'

Elizabeth Bettie mumbled something about stating the bloody obvious, as she shut the door on them.

Before Statton had a chance to ask why he had been delegated a task that was outside Avon and Somerset Constabulary's remit, Cornelius took a few short strides to the outside of Pippa's flat and tried to peer in through the windows. Heavy net curtains obscured the view inside the flat and a look though the letterbox didn't reveal anything, as all her mail dropped into an internal post-box.

For the first time, Cornelius felt a sense of unease about Pippa. Her flat was designed to keep people out; the door had a double mortise lock, with what looked like vertical dead bolts. Heavy duty key locks and restrictor cables guarded the windows. Maitland Gardens wasn't the best of areas, but even so, the security was higher than normal for a flat of this type. No signs of life were visible inside, but from what little he could make out, it did not look like the place had been abandoned.

'Sounds to me like all that batty woman wants is to have her unpaid skivvy back,' chipped in Statton. 'I'd move away from a neighbour like her.'

'That's not our call to make Andy, and when we are dealing with the public it helps if we get their names right. Her name is Mrs Bettie not Batty.'

'I know what I meant, sir.'

Cornelius walked away and tried not to smile as he returned to the car. He had one hand on the door handle when he heard a familiar noise from a balcony on one of the flats above him. Whatever ailments Elizabeth Bettie may have suffered from in her autumn years, a weak pair of lungs was not one of them.

'Inspector! Wait!'

Cornelius and Statton looked up to see Elizabeth waving; she had something in her hand and a smile on her face. 'Wait there ...' She pointed to where they were standing.

It took three minutes for Elizabeth to descend the stairs and walk over to Cornelius and Statton.

'I 'ad a thought,' she said as she approached them, breathing deeply and heavily, the mild exercise taking its toll. 'Well, I go to bingo on Thursdays. Last Christmas we 'ad a bit of a do, all of us 'oo share a table. The Thursday group, that's what we call ourselves, an' well, someone took a photo of us, see ...'

Elizabeth held out a photograph, it was of four women, each in their seventies, standing in the foyer of the bingo hall and grinning at the camera. Elizabeth was instantly recognisable; she was wearing the same Miss Marple outfit as when she visited the police station.

'This is Maud's. Real camera she 'as, not like them camera phones you young people 'ave.'

She poked Statton in the arm, as if he was entirely to blame for the demise of analogue photography, then turned her attention back to the picture.

'Me, Joan, Kathy and Maud,' she said pointing.

'I thought you said Maud took it?' said Statton.

'Well, it's Maud's camera. Neil took the photo.'

Cornelius wondered why she was sharing a Christmas party photo with him.

'And Neil is the man who suggested you talk to me?'

Elizabeth Bettie nodded, the smile on her face suggesting she was pleased with herself. Cornelius didn't want to disappoint her, but his patience was running out.

'Sorry Mrs Bettie, but what exactly am I looking at here?'

'Oh, sorry. Look ... just there.'

She pointed at a fifth person on the far left-hand side of the photo, standing in a dark corner about two metres behind the group of bingo players. The power of the camera flash had diminished by the time it bounced off her face, but it was enough to reflect some of her angular features. Cornelius took the photograph out of Elizabeth's hand, squinted at the woman in the background and he felt his neck hairs rising.

'That's Pippa. She walked with me to bingo that night; I told 'er she 'ad to come in an' say 'ello to me friends.'

Cornelius didn't hear the rest of Elizabeth's story about their Christmas celebrations; he was focused on the grainy image of the woman standing uncomfortably to one side.

He knew Pippa but not by that name.

Seven

Cornelius had achieved the square root of bugger-all that day, so when they returned to the station later in the afternoon, he was pleased to see neither Laverty nor Liatt were on hand to grill him about his lack of progress – progress he was prepared to talk about, anyway. Recognising Elizabeth Bettie's neighbour had unsettled him, but he planned to keep that nugget of information to himself for the moment.

Cornelius had first met Pippa in the middle of November at a ghastly house party he had been dragged to by one of his squash partners. It was in a large three storied house in a secluded cul-de-sac in Clifton, and the evening had descended into a condescending game of one-upmanship as each guest regaled the others about their Tuscan villas and the value of their property portfolios. Cornelius spent the evening helping himself to generous measures of a single malt whisky someone unwisely left unattended on the polished granite kitchen worktop. He knew it was time to leave when he was on the verge of telling the remaining guests what a bunch of self-centred vacuous wankers they were. Without realising it, he had been muttering it under his breath, and the petite brunette woman standing to his left leaned over to him and whispered that he'd missed out pompous.

She introduced herself as Phil and responding to Cornelius's raised eyebrow, added that it was short for Philippa. Carefully eyeing Cornelius from top to bottom, she declared to him she thought she was the only interloper that night, and why didn't they slope off and find a decent pub where the locals fought with fists rather than words.

It was the start of a short and chaste relationship.

During the eight weeks that followed their initial encounter, Pippa retained an enigmatic persona. She never divulged her surname, saying it was so embarrassing she was desperately looking for a husband so she could change it. When she caught sight of the look on Cornelius's face she laughed so hard tears ran down her cheeks. She'd always arrange to meet him in a pub or restaurant and would never let Cornelius anywhere near her place – her rationale being that she was one of four living in a house share and there was no chance of any privacy.

For Cornelius's part, he was still reeling from Jane's disappearance earlier in the year. Part of him felt uncomfortable for spending time with another woman, but Pippa's sparky attitude drew him in. She never pressured him into any type of commitment and seemed perfectly content to hear from him once a week. He never tried to get emotionally close to Pippa and it seemed to be an arrangement she was happy with.

One disastrous Saturday night in January, Cornelius and Pippa had enjoyed a meal in a cosy Thai restaurant off Whiteladies Road. Without even thinking through the consequences of his words, he suggested they finish off the night with coffee at his house. He meant it too; it wasn't a euphemism for sex. Whether Pippa knew that or not was to become a moot point. Daniel was at home.

Their journey back to Cornelius's house was relaxed, neither party having any expectation of a conjugal encounter. Arm in arm they walked into Cornelius's kitchen, still laughing about the impressive comb-over their waiter had had and how it had flapped in the breeze whenever the restaurant door opened.

Daniel was sitting at the large walnut table that was the centrepiece of the kitchen. His eyes remained glued to the laptop open in front of him, and he failed to respond to the greeting his father offered him. Pippa quickly recognised a hostile teenager defending his territory, one who believed his father should not be spending time with any woman other than his mother. She quietly suggested this may not be the best time for introductions. Cornelius was having none of it, insisting Daniel say hello to their guest with increasing agitation rising in his voice. Daniel said nothing, simply rising from the table and snapping his laptop shut. Cornelius barked a warning 'Daniel' delivered with a menacing undertone, his irritation rising. Daniel eventually replied that he had no intention of speaking to his father's new tart – and the fireworks started. With a temper to match his father's, Daniel headed for the door and Cornelius grabbed his arm to try to stop him from leaving the room. Daniel responded by lashing out with a fist that missed its intended target of his father's chin but glanced the side of his head. He wasn't a natural fighter, so Cornelius felt little physical pain, but the act triggered the emotional volcano that had been building in Daniel since Jane disappeared, and it erupted in style. Smashed Royal Worcester china and a volley of hurtful and abusive language left Cornelius reeling. Bewildered at his son's meltdown he was unable to respond. It was only when he turned around to apologise to Pippa, he realised she had quietly left the house.

He never saw her in person again. He'd rung the following day to say sorry. She said she understood perfectly and gently implied that most of the fault lay with Cornelius – that he needed to spend some quality time with his son. She was right of course, but he was far too proud to admit it.

In the wake of the battle, Cornelius and Pippa spoke by phone a few times but didn't arrange to meet again. Cornelius felt embarrassed by having a family fight in front of a woman he was fond of, so he feigned a busy caseload as an excuse to put off a discussion to clear the air between them. Ten days after the event, and feeling suitably contrite, he left a message on her phone asking if she wanted to revisit the waiter with the comb-over. She never returned the call or replied to his text messages, and he assumed he had frightened her off for good. Now, he knew differently. She was missing, and he wanted to know why.

He nestled himself into his battered chair with a cup of something declaring itself to be coffee from the vending machine and logged on to his computer. His heart sank when he saw 67 unread emails demanding his attention in his inbox. A quick scan of the subjects indicated the bulk of them were about the mundane protocols of police life. Policy reviews, changes in stop and search protocols and reports of meetings regarding new software implementation projects, all demanding inordinate amounts of his time. Malcolm Williams had sent out a blanket email asking to be sponsored for a charity bike ride across Costa Rica and one was from the new DC, trying to organise a social event at the bowling alley in Nelson Street. Clearly, she hadn't yet discovered they were mostly a bunch of unsociable gits who preferred to drink together only when they had a successful prosecution. He admired her efforts though and mulled over accepting the offer until he saw Brawley had replied, saying that he was looking forward to *whipping their arses*. Cornelius resisted the temptation to reply to the message saying that was fine but what about the bowling? Instead, he decided to spend some time digging into the life of the missing resident of 32 Maitland Gardens.

Elizabeth Bettie had not been able to give any of the kinds of details which can help piece together the life of a missing person. No known employer, no friends or family seen visiting Pippa's flat. When he mentioned Facebook and Twitter, Elizabeth said she didn't know what television programmes her neighbour watched. The rest of the interview continued along these lines, showing that Elizabeth Bettie's grasp of reality was slim at best. When asked if she knew whether Pippa was on drugs, Elizabeth prattled on about her taking something for a skin condition and proceeded to tell him about a rash she had spotted on Pippa's foot. All Cornelius learned from interviewing Mrs Bettie was that once she started talking, she was difficult to stop.

A quick call to the Missing Persons Bureau confirmed they had no reports of a missing Pippa or anybody with variants of that name. They promised to follow it up with the various charities they worked with in case they had a matching case which hadn't made it into their database yet.

With rising levels of frustration, Cornelius switched his attention to Pippa's flat. She had lied to him when she said that she lived in a house share; Pippa appeared to be the only occupant. He discovered that a company called AWF Holdings Ltd owned 32 Maitland Gardens, with an office based in Milton Keynes. No telephone number was listed, just a generic email address. Cornelius checked out the location of the office using Google Maps and saw immediately that whatever AWF Holdings was, it did not have a substantial head office. It was located in a narrow, one-way street close to the city centre, and judging by the size of the building and the number of business name plates he could see attached to the side of the door, AWF Holdings was probably no more than a single office based operation. He fired off an email, asking to be contacted immediately, as he needed urgent information on their Maitland Gardens tenant and was rewarded with an instant reply, telling him his email had been received and someone would make contact within two working days.

Cornelius carried on digging and found out that the forty-eight flats that made up Maitland Gardens had their maintenance managed collectively by the imaginatively titled MG Trust. At least he had a contact number this time, and Cornelius found himself speaking to a Bristol based solicitor who sounded as if he still wrote with a quill and ink. He made it abundantly clear he only dealt with the legal aspects of the maintenance and suggested Cornelius speak to the Chair of the Management Committee, a Trevor

Montgomery. Cornelius audibly groaned when he gave his address as 28 Maitland Gardens.

Cussing himself for not doing these checks first and thinking about the time he could have saved, Cornelius was pleasantly surprised when Trevor Montgomery answered his phone on the second ring. His feeling of cheer was short lived, as he quickly realised the Chair of the Management Committee could give Elizabeth Bettie a run for her money in the talking stakes. Montgomery chuntered on about his role on the committee whilst Cornelius imagined what a resident meeting would sound like with Mr loves-the-sound-of–his-own-voice in one corner and Mrs not-got-a-clue-about-reality in the other.

Ten minutes later, Cornelius was none the wiser. Montgomery confirmed he didn't know Pippa's surname nor did he have any contact details for her. Judging by his efforts to find out though, Cornelius suspected Montgomery had taken a shine to Pippa.

He checked the council tax charge; it was issued against Pippa Hobbs, so at least he now knew her surname, and it wasn't as horrendous as she had implied. Not that it helped him much; he couldn't find her profile on any social media sites. No prior convictions, no bad debts and her name wasn't known to Adult Social Care or the Mental Health Team. All other checks proved fruitless; this was a woman who had a low profile, and the enigma surrounding Pippa Hobbs only deepened. Reluctantly, Cornelius concluded he should refer this case to the Missing Persons Bureau, although he had every intention of running his own, off-the-record, investigation.

Cornelius spun around to see who else was in the office. His eyes focused on the digital clock perched on Andy Statton's desk, 5.45 p.m. on a Friday, hardly anybody about and the only sound was a vacuum cleaner humming gently in a nearby office. Whistling what sounded like a Lady Gaga song, Malcolm Williams appeared in the doorway with a tray in his hand, ready to load up on drinks and snacks to take to his colleagues about to start the Friday evening shift.

'Ah, Malcolm, just the person ...'

Williams's face lit up. 'Ah, you're going to sponsor me, are you? Excellent, it's for a wonderful cause and ...'

Cornelius put his hand up to stop the sergeant's sales pitch. 'I wondered if you knew whether we have someone called Neil based here at the station.'

Williams sighed. 'And there was me thinking you were the detective inspector. Let's think ... uh ... I don't think we do.' He promptly headed for the door before he could be asked anything else but stopped half way and turned around. 'Come to think of it, the cleaner is called Neil.'

'The cleaner? Which one?'

'We've only got one male cleaner you dimwit, I mean, sir. He was standing right behind you ten minutes ago.'

Cornelius had known the sergeant for many years and waved him off with a two finger salute.

As Cornelius stretched in his chair, his joints and ligaments all complained in unison, and he decided it was time to go. One question remained; an evening with Daniel, his belligerent attitude, loud music and Shagalong twittering on or one quiet pint in The Flask – followed by five noisy ones.

There was only ever going to be one winner in that debate.

JANUARY

He always found it difficult to find the right woman, particularly with his needs. Normally, he didn't care what they looked like, as long as they did what they were told. Sometimes they said no, but they only said it once. Sex was his right, and when he wanted it, he was going to have it. What he wasn't going to do was pay for it; that was for weak-willed men who didn't have the balls to take what they wanted.

He had something special in mind. If he could find a desperate enough hooker, he could wave a wad of cash under her nose and she'd go along with his plan. He'd only have to be nice to her for a while, yes – he could do nice if he had to.

Two months. Two fucking months it had taken so far. He'd walked every shitty backstreet, searching for the right one. At the beginning, he trawled his way through the filthy whorehouses, but they didn't have the right girl and so he walked away. The bleached haired madams with their collagen trout pouts and silicon tits were always gobby when he left without taking a girl – that he could cope with. But hunting in bordellos one unproductive Saturday afternoon, he found his exit route blocked by an enormous shaven-headed bouncer in a black tee shirt and arms covered in tattoos. Meathead demanded he take a girl or pay for the privilege of looking. With no intentions of doing either, he'd darted for the door. Meathead had grabbed him, put him in a headlock, taken him into the side alley and kicked the shit out of him.

He made sure Meathead got his comeuppance eventually and smiled as the memories came flooding back of the police busting him. It had taken eight of the bastards to take him down. Eight! Even then, they had to taser him. Watching that little episode unfold was not only satisfying, it gave him some fresh ideas.

It was cold, grey and pissing with rain. A couple of months was all he needed and his work would be done. He could fuck off to wherever he wanted, maybe spend a year sitting on a beach somewhere nice. Vietnam, yes, that was a good idea. He'd heard stories from people who'd been there, it would be perfect.

Then he saw her. She was on the opposite side of the road, standing under the betting shop awning. Her skirt was so short it was up around her arse and even from this distance he could see she wasn't wearing a bra. The only thing missing was a for sale sign hanging around her neck. She looked like she was waiting for some unsuspecting punter to come out of the betting shop loaded with winnings, like a silent unobtrusive predator lying in wait to ambush its prey. He watched her discreetly for a while to make sure she was exactly what he wanted.

Sensing his presence, she glanced across the road and caught his eye. She smiled and beckoned him to come over.

At last. All he had to do now was be nice to her, yes, he could do that.

Eight

Deep within his bed, Cornelius became vaguely aware of a buzzing sound coming from the pile of clothes he had left on the floor the previous night. His pounding head granted him no mercy, and as he drifted back to consciousness he wondered, for the umpteenth time, why he wasn't capable of leaving it at just the one. Fumbling for his watch, he recalled the house had been empty when he stumbled through the door sometime after midnight. Not for the first time, the landlord had removed his car keys from his jacket and bundled him into a taxi. One day, Cornelius would thank him properly, but then he remembered how much money he had put over the bar in the last few months – no wonder he received excellent customer service.

His mind was still clogged by the ravages of alcohol when he located his phone, expecting it to be Daniel, asking for a lift back from some remote party location. There were two missed calls, both from Laverty. Before Cornelius could check his voicemail, Laverty rang again.

'Lucas, where the hell have you been?'

'It's my day off, sir. I had a late night and I'm having a lie in.' He wanted to add, 'so fuck you,' but, wisely, didn't.

'That is where you are wrong, inspector – report to Portishead at 11 a.m. sharp.'

'What, why?' He mumbled through his hangover.

'No questions, Lucas. 11 a.m. and don't be one minute late.' Without waiting for a reply, he hung up.

Cornelius groaned. Whatever Laverty wanted, he guessed it would not end well.

***

Cornelius hoped his overworked liver had processed enough of last night's beer to make him safe to drive. Being summoned to the kremlin at short notice on a Saturday was never a good sign. Suspecting Weasel's trial to be the reason behind the call, he decided to set off earlier and call by Manny Thompson's garage. With luck Thompson would have returned and he could at least wring some meaningful information out of him, which could be used to defend himself.

He stepped out into a cold grey morning; the sky was a solid bank of gloom, offering no respite from his dark mood. Thirty minutes of brisk walking later, he arrived at a narrow side street to find his car still waiting for him, unmarked with four wheels still attached. Leaving a serving police officer's car out overnight on a public road in the middle of a city wasn't the wisest of ideas. All it needed was for one person who knew he was a copper to spot him getting out of it and, with the aid of social media, half the criminals in Bristol would know where to find some sport.

With mercifully light Saturday morning traffic, his detour to Thompson's garage took only twenty minutes. Parking as close as possible, he picked his way through the diesel filled puddles until he reached the battered garage. He rattled the doors but they were steadfastly locked; no signs of life could be seen inside or outside the dilapidated building and there were no lights on behind the grime covered windows. In mild desperation, he tried the numbers he had for Thompson. The first one caused the garage phone to ring and the mobile number went straight to voicemail. Cornelius cursed and cut the call; he was going to have to face his inquisitors without any new information.

***

The Avon and Somerset Police Headquarters was situated in a sprawling forty-seven acre site on the edge of Portishead. As well as housing Senior Management, it was home to the main Criminal Investigation Department as well as Armed Response, Counter Terrorism, Air Operations and the Major Investigation Team. If you were an ambitious, career focused officer, Portishead was the place to be. Today however, Cornelius couldn't think of any place worse, and his sense of trepidation ratcheted up a notch as he arrived at the south gate.

Once he had cleared security, Cornelius was directed to the main reception and was invited to sit and wait with nothing but crime prevention propaganda to distract him. At 11 a.m. precisely, a petite blonde woman in a blue Armani business suit arrived in reception and confidently introduced herself as Katherine. Her bright and friendly demeanour suggested to Cornelius that she didn't realise her job was to escort him into a pit of vipers.

Katherine shepherded Cornelius through a series of modern, well-appointed offices that were flooded with natural light, and he couldn't help but make comparisons between these palatial surroundings and the battered rabbit warren of Gloucester Road. Not that he yearned to work in a sterile environment like this but getting any kind of repair work done at Gloucester Road was a major battle, and HQ seemed to get anything it needed.

They arrived at a large open plan office with light blue and green walls, furnished with plain white desks and computer monitors; it was the kind of paperless environment that Karen Liatt was battling to achieve at Gloucester Road. Katherine guided him to the far corner where a private office had been created with glass walls, making it look like an overly large fish tank. The middle section was obscured by an adhesive film designed to give the effect of frosted glass. Cornelius could just about make out the dome of Laverty's head and at least two other people inside, the altered opacity shielding their identities.

The door opened, and Cornelius was confronted by what looked like a very unpleasant interview panel; he was in more trouble than he'd thought. A tired looking Laverty sat on the far right. Superintendent Karen Liatt was next to Laverty and didn't even look up from the papers spread out on the desk. Next to her, was a Staffordshire bull terrier also known as Deputy Chief Constable Rick McCartney, and making up the inquisition was a woman that Cornelius guessed to be in her mid-fifties, elegantly dressed with short cropped silver hair and eyes of steel. All four had a cup of coffee in front of them, but Cornelius wasn't offered anything. Instead, McCartney ordered him to sit down in the chair with no arm-rests, facing the panel. The DCC launched straight in with no introductions.

'You've not been asked to bring a representative with you this morning as this is not a disciplinary hearing, inspector.' Cornelius relaxed slightly and McCartney sensed it.

'Yet,' he added, not taking his eyes off Cornelius, 'yesterday at 15:27 you sent an email to AWF Holdings enquiring about the tenant of 32 Maitland Gardens.'

McCartney's eyes remained fixed on Cornelius. Of all the possible scenarios Cornelius had played out in his mind, this one had never occurred to him. The silence in the room seemed to last for an eternity.

'Well?' the DCC barked.

'Sorry, sir, I didn't know if that was a question or a statement.' Cornelius saw Laverty dropping his head slightly, shaking it from side to side with quiet disapproval.

'Don't get cocky inspector, right now you are up shit creek without a paddle. Did you send that email?'

Time for contrition. 'Yes, sir.'

'Why?'

'I received a report that the occupant had gone missing and yesterday, whilst attending an unrelated incident with Detective Constable Statton, I happened to be in close proximity to the address in question, so I decided to have a quick look at the property. Whilst there I saw …'

'Who reported it?'

'A neighbour, Elizabeth Bettie, she …'

'When?'

'Thursday.' The grilling Cornelius had previously received from Tobias McMillan seemed like a picnic compared to McCartney's non-compromising style.

'Did you know about this DCI Laverty?' McCartney's eyes were still transfixed on Cornelius.

'Not until yesterday evening, sir.'

Karen Liatt snorted slightly. 'There's a surprise,' she said quietly.

DCC McCartney turned his head ninety degrees to his left to glare at Liatt who had the grace to blush slightly. He turned back to face Cornelius, his voice cold and level.

'Why were you, an inspector from CID, investigating without even issuing a case reference number?'

In the cold light of the fish tank office in Portishead HQ, Cornelius started to suspect something had happened to Pippa. If he was right, he might be formally investigating after all. A carefully worded response was needed.

'Her neighbour came to the station and asked for me by name; she wouldn't speak to anyone else. It would appear she had previously had bad experiences with other officers at the station and had been told I was reliable ...' Karen Liatt scribbled furiously and Cornelius knew another grilling about that waited for him further down the line – if he made it that far. 'I didn't process it formally, because of logistics. On the face of it, it looked like a simple case of someone moving on without telling her neighbour. Hardly a police matter and issuing a case reference would mean generating unnecessary paperwork at a time when we are all feeling the strain of our caseloads and ...'

McCartney sensed an impending rant and stopped him short. 'I get it inspector. You didn't follow protocol; it's as simple as that.'

'Yes, sir, sorry, sir, but I intend to alert the Missing Persons Bureau on Monday morning as I now have concerns about the missing person.'

'So, the fact that you have been called to Portishead on a Saturday morning for the Spanish Inquisition has alerted you to something more sinister? We'll make a DCI out of you yet, inspector.'

Cornelius berated himself for not thinking his comment through but decided to keep quiet. Silence hung in the air for two minutes whilst McCartney and the nameless person with laser eyes quietly consulted with each other. His salvation came from an unlikely quarter.

Karen Liatt still had not made any eye contact with Cornelius, when she turned to the Staffie.

'Sir, whilst DI Cornelius has not followed protocol ...' For the first time she looked directly at him, 'and that is something we will be addressing ...' Her eyes flitted back to McCartney. 'His version of events is backed up by our enquiries and I have no reason whatsoever to question his loyalty. He is an excellent officer and would be an asset in leading this case.'

Cornelius's jaw almost hit the floor. Not even twenty-four hours had passed since sending the email, but in that time his movements and activities had been checked. If he'd told any kind of story a disciplinary charge would now be raining down on him. Laverty had gone a mild shade of pink which told him all he need to know about who had done the digging; no wonder he looked tired.

McCartney said nothing but looked at the mystery woman to his right, quizzically raising his eyebrows. The lady with the steel eyes spoke with a soft Irish lilt.

'Inspector Cornelius, my name is Jacqueline Kelly. Thank you for taking the time to see me this morning.'

Like I had a say in the matter, thought Cornelius. She'd paused and for a brief second and he worried he had said it out loud. It was a huge relief when she carried on.

'As you have probably fathomed by now, Pippa Hobbs is a cover name; she is on the witness protection programme. Pippa was a key prosecution witness in a Manchester trial three years ago and her testimony helped put away four high profile villains with links to drugs, gambling and prostitution. They had a long history of violence and intimidation, and she showed great personal fortitude in giving evidence.'

'That explains a few things,' said Cornelius, but she ignored him and continued.

'She last made contact with her case officer four weeks ago and was scheduled to make contact again next week. Her disappearance is of considerable concern to us and it is important we find out what has happened to her as soon as possible.'

McCartney resumed control. 'This is a high priority investigation, inspector, but we need to keep this information under wraps. It will be a disaster if a witness under our protection has gone missing.'

Cornelius wondered whether the DCC's concerns were about Pippa or the Force's reputation. He wanted to run this investigation but needed more information.

'I think her cover was good, sir, I couldn't find any evidence that she had used anything other than her assumed name. I think she was cautious about the company she kept and the amount of information she divulged about herself. All I have is a brief description from a woman you wouldn't put anywhere near a witness stand and a man who likes using ten words in place of one.'

He turned directly to Jacqueline Kelly, she'd not given her rank but he suspected her pay grade was at least twice his. 'Any additional information you can give me, ma'am would be helpful.'

Her laser eyes were still locked on him and he felt she could see right into his soul.

'You don't need to call me ma'am,' she quietly said before turning to McCartney. 'If you have no further questions for the inspector, may I suggest that he and I start without any additional delay?'

Taking the hint that they were no longer wanted, McCartney, Liatt and Laverty gathered up their papers and shuffled out of the interview room.

Cornelius felt a sense of relief at their departure, his grilling had ended but the revelation that Pippa was a protected witness intrigued him even further. Without saying anything more, Jacqueline Kelly passed over an unmarked manila folder. Cornelius looked inside and scanned a document with all Pippa's details, including her picture. A passport style photo showed a stern looking woman with blonde hair hanging in a ponytail. When Cornelius and Pippa met back in November, she was sporting a chestnut brown bob. The difference in style gave enough grounds for plausible deniability – if he had to declare he knew her later in the investigation. For the moment at least, he intended to keep quiet; this was a case he didn't want to be taken off.

Pippa, who he now knew to be Freya Louise McAndrews, was an only child with no surviving parents. She had once been in a relationship with Leroy Jenkins who, on the surface, was a successful businessman owning a portfolio of properties and businesses with a net worth of approximately three million pounds. Behind the façade he ran a drugs import ring, owned at least three brothels and carried the nickname of Pliers. If anyone ever dared to ask him how he acquired the name, he always said it was because he looked like the Jamaican reggae singer. The reality was that pliers were his weapon of choice, and he wasn't fussy on which bodily appendage he used them. Freya and Jenkins had been together for two years, and according to the file, originally, she had been unaware of his violent alter ego. She reported meeting a good-looking man with charm, style and money. However, he couldn't supress his psychopathic tendencies indefinitely.

In time, Jenkins became bored with his girlfriend; he didn't really want her anymore, but he had no intention of releasing her either. The first beating came when she tried to walk out of his house in Salford Quays after an argument and declared she was not coming back. By the time she regained consciousness, she had been locked in a spare bedroom with a bucket, a large bottle of water and three packets of plain crisps for company. Two days passed before he let her out.

She quickly learned to acquiesce to his demands, but quietly and carefully she plotted against him. She bought a recording device which looked similar to the remote control they used to open their garage, so it looked entirely at home on her key fob. It cost less than ten pounds online, but it held a miniature camera and was able to record sound. Jenkins regularly scanned his house for bugs, but Freya's device didn't broadcast a signal; it recorded all the information on to a miniature SD card stored within the fob itself. Freya used to place her keys on the top of her handbag and leave them on the worktop in their extensive, marbled floor kitchen where Jenkins liked to discuss his drugs and prostitution business arrangements. And so began the downfall of Jenkins.

In one chilling statement, Freya said she knew that if the device was ever discovered, she would be killed. She reckoned the only way she would ever be able to leave Jenkins was in a coffin – it was just a matter of when, so she didn't have much to lose.

After a further six months and five beatings, Freya McAndrews walked into a Greater Manchester police station armed with an extensive selection of SD cards. Within twenty-four hours, Jenkins and six other men were arrested and he never saw life as a free man again. Freya McAndrews also died that day. She was taken into witness protection and was reborn as Pippa Hobbs.

Pippa went to start a new life in Brighton, but intelligence emerged that from his cell, Jenkins had ordered two of his henchman, who had avoided jail, to track Pippa down and kill her. The information about the contract on her life didn't make it to the protection team in time and shortly after, a witness protection officer was found buried in a shallow grave, in woodland close to her home. The post-mortem showed that all her fingers and toes had been crushed whilst she was still alive. An absence of cuts indicated that a blunt force tool had been responsible for her injuries, and given that pressure had been applied equally to her all her digits, it seemed likely that a pair of pliers had been used. Jenkins's henchmen were interviewed and charged, but a lack of DNA evidence linking them to the murder, meant the case was dropped before it went to trial.

As a precaution Pippa was moved from Brighton and kept moving every six months for the next two years. It was only when Jenkins was killed in a fight in Strangeways that the moving stopped, and by that time she was living in Maitland Gardens.

Cornelius looked out from the Portishead fish tank into an office which seemed to be running at one-third capacity. He surmised that this was probably normal for a Saturday lunchtime at Portishead HQ. Jacqueline Kelly stayed with him, not wanting to leave him unattended with the sensitive case notes about Pippa Hobbs. She quietly worked on something else whilst he read through the file. Only when Cornelius leaned back in his chair to stretch his legs did her laser vision lock on to him.

'Your thoughts, Lucas?'

So, it was Lucas now the hierarchy had left and she was trying to build a rapport with him. The heart melting tone of her soft Irish voice drawing Cornelius in much faster than someone with a coarse Bristolian accent. He puffed out his cheeks as a rumbling stomach briefly distracted his thought process.

'I'll need to see her flat.'

'Not possible – yet. I can't rule out the fact she may have been spooked and gone into hiding. It could be that she has noticed somebody watching her flat. If that is the case I need to know who it is and if you go marching in with your size tens you're likely to scare them off.'

Cornelius conceded the point, but before he could say anything else, she cut him off.

'And anyway, I've already had it checked out overnight under the cover of darkness. We couldn't do a thorough search, obviously, but we found nothing untoward. Her clothes are still in the wardrobe and the flat is tidy but lived in. If she has gone into hiding, she left quickly.'

'Wouldn't she have told you what she was doing?'

'Did you not read the case file? After what happened in Brighton we lost her trust, and if she thinks her position has been compromised, it's us she will hold accountable. She took the death of the protection officer to heart and held herself responsible. I had to intervene to stop her from driving herself up to Strangeways to try and see Jenkins.'

'That sounds about right,' said Cornelius, smiling warmly.

Her eyes narrowed. 'Why do you say that, inspector?'

He looked up at her unsmiling face and realised his mistake. He needed to backtrack.

'Her profile indicates she's not exactly a shrinking violet; someone that brave is not likely to sit back and do nothing.' He quietly praised himself for his reply, hoping he had repaired the damage.

Jacqueline kept staring at him but said nothing. Cornelius held her gaze for as long as he dared without trying to look defensive. Distraction came in the form of Cornelius's rumbling stomach which drew a wry smile from his inquisitor.

'You need lunch, Lucas.' She was using his first name again – he was off the hook.

Eager to escape the fish tank and avoid another grilling about his opinion of Pippa, Cornelius leapt to his feet.

'Good idea, there must be some food around here somewhere. Want me to bring you anything?'

'I'll come with you,' said Jacqueline, unnecessarily putting her jacket on. It may have been quieter than normal in the office, but it didn't stop the heating system from over compensating for the February chill. She walked briskly alongside Cornelius as they set off in search of sustenance.

'So, why does Superintendent Liatt have such a downer on you?'

Cornelius's defences shot up. 'Didn't you hear her describe me as an excellent officer?'

'I did. Stop avoiding the question.'

'I thought the inquisition was over.'

She stopped walking and once again fixed Cornelius with one of her disconcerting stares.

'You two don't get on, that much is obvious – even to your average muppet. That leaves me wondering why she thinks you should lead on this case.'

Cornelius wondered the same question, but he wanted to be at the heart of this investigation, so kept his thoughts to himself.

'Oh, I think she loves me really,' he lied. 'Although, we disagree about procedural issues from time to time.'

'You mean she is pernickety and a stickler for detail, whereas you are busy with your case load and your clear up rate would fall by half if you did everything by the book.'

Jacqueline Kelly had only spent a few hours in their company but had worked them both out already. She smiled at Cornelius.

'I hope she's not setting you up for a fall ...'

Nine

Weak daylight peeked through Cornelius's bedroom curtains. It was his first Sunday off in two weeks, and he lay in bed wondering how to spend his day. An extensive range of domestic chores were bidding for his attention. Despite that, he knew the most likely victor in the battle for his time would be his Edgar Wallace book and a lunchtime pint in The Flask. The warm contentment generated by the thought of a whole day to himself promptly disappeared as he remembered that Elaine had invited herself over for the afternoon. Maybe some morning cleaning was in order after all, and he made a mental note to hide his supply of beer and wine from his alcoholic sister. He eased himself out of bed, to make himself a strong coffee before starting the long overdue housework.

Usually, he would have to extract his son from his slumber pit – not a task for the faint hearted, but here he was at 9.30 a.m., awake, dressed, sitting at the kitchen table and seemingly chatty.

'Hi,' he chirped whilst uncharacteristically making eye contact. Daniel never used any kind of paternal greeting with his father, nor did he ever ask him any questions about his work or other aspects of his life. Cornelius never knew whether this was a symptom of adolescence or whether he genuinely did not care.

'Good morning.' Cornelius decided against making any sly comments about his son being awake so early. Daniel buried his nose back into his laptop. 'College work?' Cornelius asked.

'Yup. Got a big assignment to hand in by tomorrow, thought I'd better crack on with it.'

Cornelius tried not to look too surprised, nor did he voice his suspicion that this was probably a piece of work Daniel should have started about two months ago. He had been exactly the same during his college days in Taunton but was never going to admit that to his son.

Cornelius plonked himself at the table with a steaming mug of coffee in hand, readying himself for the housework. He was bracing himself for Daniel's likely reaction when he told him that Elaine was visiting in the afternoon, when his son surprised him again.

'Do you think we will see Mum again?'

The question was a bolt out of the blue from a young man who had lived in a state of denial ever since his mother had vanished from the family home a year previously. Daniel had gone to great lengths to avoid talking about a subject that had ripped his soul apart. He had refused counselling or any other kind of help that his father or college tutor had thought of. Whenever the subject of Jane was raised, he either clammed up or lashed out.

Cornelius took a deep breath, aware of the question's gravity. If he screwed up a response he could send Daniel back into the deep abyss of depression. He looked up at his son and saw that he had shut his laptop in anticipation of a conversation and showed no outward signs of tension or agitation. Finally, he appeared to be ready to at least try and understand what happened. With all the truth he could muster, Cornelius barely whispered his reply.

'I genuinely don't know. What I have never understood, is why she walked out on you as well. Walking out on me? I could understand that. We were going through a difficult patch – although I didn't think it was that bad – but she loved the bones of you and to not even contact you ...'

Cornelius was unaware of his breaking voice; he needed to talk to Daniel more than he realised.

'Why did she go to Greece?'

'It wasn't Greece, it was Turkey.' Cornelius didn't want to sound contradictory, so quickly carried on. 'She flew to Adnan Menderes airport where she was met by someone who we were never able to trace. They took a taxi into Izmir and after that I don't know what happened to her.' Emotion stuck unforgivingly in his throat. 'I tried hard to find her, Daniel. You'd think that being a police officer I could find something out – but I wasn't allowed to conduct the investigation myself ... I ...' For so long he had wanted to have this conversation, and now he had the opportunity, words were failing him.

'I know you tried,' Daniel's eyes moistened. 'Why didn't you uncover anything when you went out to find her?' This was the first time he had delivered this question calmly, rather than scream it as an accusation and not wait for a response. He'd stopped looking at his father now, focusing instead on not crying.

'I didn't go to Turkey in an official capacity. Once she was picked up on CCTV footage at Bristol airport travelling alone, we knew she hadn't been abducted by criminals and the investigation was downgraded on the assumption that she'd just had enough and travelled of her own free will. It wasn't deemed necessary to send an officer out after her – bloody budget cuts – so the investigation was conducted with the Turkish police long distance, from the comfort of our own offices.'

'Not by you though?'

'No, we're not allowed to investigate anything which we have a personal interest in. Not that it stopped me. That's why I went to Turkey. The problem was that I needed the co-operation of the local police to find out anything meaningful.'

'But I thought you lot looked after each other?'

'Not always. I had been there barely a day when someone rang the Turkish police to tell them I wasn't investigating in an official capacity. They immediately withdrew their help and told me I needed to fill in a missing person's report and they would let me know when they found something out. It was as good as saying they had no intention of doing anything more than a few cursory checks.' Tears streamed from Cornelius's eyes. 'Do you know how many people go missing in Turkey each year? She was at the bottom of a long list, and I couldn't do anything about it.'

This was all news to Daniel, whose full attention remained fully focused on his father.

'No one has admitted making that call of course. Although I have my suspicions, I can't prove anything. Without access to the resources of the Turkish police there was little I could do. I hired a private investigator over there, but he rang me two weeks later with nothing to report. She had simply vanished.'

'But ... you're a police officer, why didn't you have more help?'

'When she first went missing all the alarm bells went off. It's not just a matter of the police looking after their own; the missing relative of a senior police officer is a serious matter. The fear was that someone had abducted her for revenge or to force me to do something I wouldn't normally do. A lot of resources were put into trying to track her down. All the CCTV in the area was checked, but that showed nothing conclusive. We leaned on all our informants but gleaned nothing.'

He paused, wondering whether to give Daniel all the details. He was dealing with this torrent of new information well, so he deserved some honesty.

'Her mobile phone was checked for calls and messages. All the numbers she contacted within the previous month checked out with the exception of one. It was a pay-as-you-go mobile number and she made six calls and sent four text messages to it. We were never able to trace it, but it raised an uncomfortable question.' Cornelius paused, unsure how to continue. Daniel did it for him.

'Was she having an affair?'

'I didn't think so – I still don't. But, if I was looking at it in an impartial way, it's a question I would ask as well. It's why they asked me to look for her passport. When I couldn't find it, they immediately checked it against the national database we hold. That was how I learnt she had left the country. CCTV showed her at Bristol airport. She was unaccompanied all the way on to the plane and according to the flight attendants she was calm and relaxed for the whole journey. As soon as the top brass knew she wasn't being held against her will, they lost interest.'

'She might have been seeing someone though.'

'Yes, it is a possibility, but the sole reason I don't believe that, is you. She may have not wanted to be with me, but there is no way on this earth she would have left you.'

Cornelius's voice finally cracked and he started sobbing. Daniel leaned forward and did something he hadn't done since he was thirteen years old.

He hugged his father.

Ten

Wanting to be at the station early, Cornelius left his house at 6.45 a.m. He'd woken Daniel before he'd left, knowing it was probably the most pointless task of the day. Judging by the abusive mumble that emanated from underneath the duvet, Cornelius knew that Daniel would be asleep again by the time he shut the front door. His son's grand plan of completing his college assignment in time for the 11 a.m. deadline would fly out of the window and his morning journey would be taken up by concocting plausible excuses as to why he was not able to hand his work in on time.

The previous day's conversation had been a cathartic experience – more for Cornelius than Daniel – and it had helped to bridge the gulf which had been expanding between them. They both promised to talk more about Jane, although Daniel shied away from Cornelius's suggestion of visiting the college counsellor. Not wishing to damage the truce that had been created, Cornelius hadn't pushed it. Daniel didn't even dive for cover when Elaine called at the house to see her brother. He managed thirty minutes with his father and aunt before offering his college assignment as an excuse for leaving them. The noise that subsequently came from his bedroom suggested he was studying with the aid of a PlayStation. Elaine didn't comment on her nephew's exit; she was too busy dropping hints about being thirsty. Pretending he didn't know what she was implying, Cornelius made her a coffee. Barely one hour after arrival, Elaine suggested that they walk into the city centre, ostensibly to do some shopping together. She'd managed twenty minutes of strolling around Broadmead Shopping Centre before telling Cornelius she needed to sit down. Elaine chose a street side café with exposed wooden flooring, fake vintage signs on the walls advertising Pear's soap and crucially, a licence. It was when she started on her third large glass of merlot that Cornelius decided to leave her to it. Before he left, and without any subtlety, she reminded him her fortieth birthday was only two weeks away, so he opted to go in search of a present.

Cornelius drank too much but he was a mere amateur compared to his younger sister. His own addiction meant he wasn't willing to lecture her, but when he was with her he pretended not to have any kind of alcohol problem. He said he was there for her if she needed him. Elaine limited herself to smiling sweetly at her big brother; she already knew he was on the verge of being a functioning alcoholic.

Pulling up at Gloucester Road station Cornelius forgot about the weekend and his plan to find Pippa Hobbs became uppermost in his mind. Laverty's mind-numbing briefing started at eight o'clock, which meant he could make a good start on tracking down any known associates beforehand. Not wanting to get too bogged down in grunt work he'd co-opted Andy Statton to help him and despite his initial protestations, he met Cornelius back at the station on Saturday afternoon. Using the information he'd been passed by Jacqueline Kelly, the two men had drawn up a list of contacts which needed to be followed up.

Cornelius had barely lowered his backside into the chair when Detective Constable Rita Sharma walked past his desk, and the smell of her coffee wafted up his nasal passages. He was never going to focus on the task in hand until his own caffeine levels were significantly increased, and he went to get a coffee.

His mind was so focused on finding Pippa that he hadn't noticed Brawley standing by the vending machine, thumping the coin slot and calling the machine a thieving bastard. Both men looked visibly disappointed to see each other, but instead of opting for stony silence, Cornelius saw an opportunity to put the boot in.

'Technology getting the better of you again, Jonny Boy?' Brawley scowled at the, deliberate, use of a name he hated.

'Get out of the bed the wrong side did we Lukey?' said Brawley. 'What is your problem anyway?'

'Problem? You mean I only get to have one as far as you are concerned?'

'Listen to me you little fuckwit,' snarled Brawley. 'If ever I ...'

'Good morning, Gentlemen,' breezed Laverty. Whether it was pure coincidence or deliberate intervention, Cornelius couldn't tell, but Laverty was smiling at them both, one hand in his pocket ferreting for change – at least Cornelius hoped so.

Brawley's aggression immediately deflated and he wandered off in search of a hot drink from another source. Laverty leaned over and thumped the machine high on the left side; it immediately sprang to life, subserviently offering up a choice of drinks.

'Loose connection,' offered Laverty. 'Briefing starts in ten minutes Lucas – don't be late.'

***

The briefing room was the largest single room in Gloucester Road station but had disproportionately small windows and was reliant on fluorescent strip lighting for illumination. With windows that were either difficult or impossible to open fresh air was often in short supply, and on quiet days the CID team preferred to stay at their desks in their own office whilst Laverty ran through the day's agenda. The briefing room had recently been redecorated, but for a reason Cornelius could not fathom, some idiot, who presumably never intended to set foot in the room, chose a shade of light grey for the walls. Andy Statton chirped that the dull walls matched the DCI's vocal delivery, before turning several shades of crimson when he realised he had been overheard.

Today, Laverty was living up to his reputation as an uninspiring orator. He droned his way through the usual collection of burglaries, muggings and assaults that had occurred since their last briefing, but it was not until he raised the discovery of a human finger that the assembled staff snapped to attention.

'This,' he proudly announced, 'was found yesterday evening on the edge of Broadmead.'

A photograph of a single severed finger flashed up on the screen at the front of the briefing room.

'No one has tried to claim it from lost property yet.' Laverty paused, expecting a laugh which never arrived. He cleared his throat and carried on. 'It was found yesterday afternoon wrapped up in muslin and had been left on the side of a bench just off the shopping precinct. Early analysis suggests it is the ring finger from the left hand of a female, probably in the thirty to forty age range.'

'Is that significant, sir?'

Laverty glared at Statton 'I think we'll only find that out when we find the owner, don't you, Andy?'

Cornelius was intrigued; he'd been in Broadmead that afternoon and hadn't noticed any commotion.

'What time was it found?'

'About 17:00, by a woman walking her dog. It was having a good sniff at the package and curiosity got the better of the owner.

She opened up the muslin and the severed finger fell out. She promptly threw up all over it. Shame really, nothing like a large pile of vomit to help with the DNA analysis.' This earned a modest ripple of laughter. 'CCTV is limited in the area where it was found, but we are checking in case we see anyone walking away from the scene minus a finger.'

Laverty was giving the assembled team a warning that the press had been alerted when Cornelius's phone rang. Laverty threw him a glare for interrupting his monologue. Grateful for an excuse to extract himself from the briefing, Cornelius answered it.

'DI Cornelius, you are one fortunate bastard, today is your lucky day.'

'And good morning to you Sergeant Williams,' he whispered, not wanting to distract Laverty any further, 'to what do I owe the honour of your call?'

'You have a female visitor; she insists on speaking to you and only you.'

Cornelius could rarely tell if Malcolm Williams was being serious or not. But if there was a female visitor wanting to see him it was going to be Elizabeth Bettie, thus Williams's description of Cornelius as lucky was his sarcastic humour in full flow. Cornelius weighed up his options which were listening to Laverty's dronings or Elizabeth Bettie's ramblings. Neither option held any appeal, but if Mrs Bettie was made to wait, she might just give up and go home. He'd need to talk to her soon but wanted more background information under his belt first.

'Ask her to wait, I'll be there as soon as I can,' he lied.

Williams snorted. 'As you wish, I wouldn't keep her waiting that's for sure.'

'Fine, I'll be there in ten.'

Twenty minutes later he descended the stairs of the station, trying to think of excuses for an early exit from his impending conversation with the batty woman. He made a mental note to bollock Andy Statton for planting the nickname in his head.

Malcolm Williams passed him in the corridor and fixed a wicked grin on Cornelius.

'About time. She's in interview room three, and I've just given her a second cup of coffee seeing as you seem to be happy to ignore her. You can thank me later by sponsoring me.'

'You did what?' Cornelius lowered his voice. 'I don't need you to give that woman any encouragement to come here; it's bad enough she asks for me anyway.'

Williams shook his head and wandered off. 'I worry about you lot in CID sometimes.'

Cornelius paused at the door of IR3 and took a deep breath before walking in, a breath he rapidly exhaled when he saw who was waiting for him.

Megan Thompson barely looked up at Cornelius when he entered. Her long dark auburn hair hung loose instead of being tied up functionally, and the baggy oil-smeared overalls had been replaced with designer jeans and a Burberry lambskin biker jacket that Cornelius guessed cost his whole month's take home pay. If this was a game of *What's my line?* the panel would have been far more likely to opt for model than mechanic.

'Megan,' Cornelius sat down opposite her, unsure how to proceed. 'I didn't expect to see you here this morning.' Thinking that was an early candidate for most obvious statement of the week, he let his raised eyebrows ask the question about why she was there.

Megan opened her mouth, but it was a few moments before she could speak.

'It's Dad – he's missing.'

No longer distracted by her beauty, Cornelius sat bolt upright.

'What do you mean he's missing? When was the last time you saw him?'

'Friday.'

The day I came calling thought Cornelius.

'He ... he felt bad about the trial.' Her words were barely audible but she had Cornelius's full attention. 'Dad knew he'd let you down and was furious Weasel tricked him into hiding his drugs. It's one of the reasons he agreed to give evidence.'

Cornelius didn't bother to tell Megan the real reason was because he had Manny in his pocket and he thought he would be done for possession of stolen goods instead. He was reluctant to steer the conversation away from the trial, but Megan had closed up and didn't offer anything else.

'When was the last time you saw him on Friday, Megan?'

'He received a text from someone at about 5.30 that seemed to worry him. Later in the evening he told me he had to go and meet someone, and I haven't seen him since.'

'Why wait until now to come and see me?'

'It's not unusual for Dad to be missing for a few days at a time. I'm ... not always nice to the women in his life so he tends not to bring them home. Why he can't pick a decent one I don't know.'

Cornelius quietly noted that as far as children were concerned, he had more in common with Manny Thompson than he thought.

'Anyway, if he's shagging someone he will often disappear, but it's rarely more than a day or two and he's always at home on a Sunday to play around with his Spitfire. When he didn't come back yesterday, I rang him but didn't hear back. He might not always get to the phone, but he always returns my call. That's why I'm worried.'

'Have you contacted anyone else before coming here? He may be with friends or acquaintances.'

Megan Thompson felt uncomfortable at having to involve an organisation that had been a thorn in her father's side for years. She stared at the floor, hardly blinking.

'I tried a few people he knows.'

'Such as?'

She stared at him. 'Seriously?' The fiery Thompson attitude sparked up again. 'I'm not about to give you names, am I? Dad would rather die in a ditch than see me hand over his contacts.'

Manny Thompson's contact list was a who's who of Bristol's criminals, so Cornelius had thought it worth a punt. But something else bothered him. 'Did you pass on my message?'

'Ah ... uh ... yes, it's just that ...'

Megan tried to find an answer which wouldn't come, and Cornelius knew he'd hit a nerve.

'What is it you are not telling me, Megan?'

Silence hung in the air; all that could be heard was the sound of creaking noises coming from the ancient radiator and the distant sounds of someone being restrained against their will. Eventually, Megan cracked.

'He panicked when he saw you coming and jumped into the boot of the Beamer I was working on. It was quite funny to watch you look everywhere but there.' A wry smile crept on to her face.

Cornelius tried not to let his anger show – how bloody daft could he be? He composed himself and carried on. 'Why did he hide?'

'Dad knew you would be angry with him, but he wasn't ready to speak to you. I think he had a few business matters to clear up first.'

'I don't suppose you happen to know what these matters were, do you?'

Megan shook her head. Cornelius would have been a damn sight more surprised if she'd told him. Manny Thompson would have known it was only a matter of time before the police came calling with a search warrant, so it made sense that he needed a day or so to offload any stolen gear he was hanging on to.

'Why did you ask for me, specifically?'

'Dad always said that if I ever needed to speak to anyone in the police, I should come and see you. He's not overly fond of your lot; he reckons half of you are on the take. But he thinks you are alright – as far as coppers go anyway.'

Cornelius tried not to smile at the back-handed compliment, but he could see Megan was holding something else back. Her next question threw him off guard.

'You don't know where he is, do you?'

'Why would I? I didn't know he was missing until ten minutes ago.'

She bit her bottom lip, wondering what to tell him next. 'It's … It's just that when he left, he told me he was off to meet a copper.'

She looked uncomfortable again.

'Did he say who, Megan?'

She gently nodded her head. 'He said he was meeting you.'

***

Cornelius climbed the stairs back to the CID room. The briefing had finished and most of the team had taken the opportunity to spend the rest of the morning out of the office. Only Andy Statton and Rita Sharma were at their desks, deeply engrossed in their PC monitors. Grateful for the peace of the quiet office, Cornelius slumped into his chair to digest the morning's developments. He reckoned Manny told his daughter the first thing that came into his mind when he told her had to go out. Megan seemed sceptical at this version of events but equally seemed to believe Cornelius's assertion that he had not arranged to meet her father. As it wasn't unusual for her dad to disappear for two days at a time, she agreed to wait a further twenty-four hours before officially reporting him missing.

Despite his reassurances to Megan, Cornelius felt uneasy about Thompson's disappearance. In the past week, he had been a prosecution witness in a trial and had his testimony ripped apart by a barrister who knew more about his past than Avon and Somerset Constabulary did. He had hidden from Cornelius in the morning but agreed to meet him in the evening. Now he was missing.

And it wouldn't be just the police who were pissed off with him. Thompson had broken the criminal code by giving evidence for the prosecution. Weasel might have got off, but he would have a score to settle. But Weasel was a smart operator and would not have acted immediately against his new enemy. He was far more likely to wait, then stitch up Thompson at a later date, as he had done with Palmer.

Palmer – he was the second option. Danny Palmer was still a major player in Bristol and his incarceration was nothing more than a minor inconvenience when it came to running his criminal empire. Would he want to punish Thompson for cocking up his witness testimony? The Palmer versus Weasel battle had yet to play out, but Cornelius couldn't see Thompson being abducted as part of that scenario. He sat back in his chair, closed his eyes and rubbed the sides of his temples in the vain hope it would stimulate his brain and give him the answers. Opening his eyes, he saw Andy Statton sitting at his desk staring at him with a half-cocked smile.

'Want some good news?' Statton had the expression of a child who had done the washing up without being asked.

'As long as you don't want a medal for it – yes.'

'Medal, no. Bacon butty, yes. Those contacts you asked me to work through?'

'Contacts?'

'For Pippa Hobbs ...'

'What about them?' said Cornelius.

'Mostly dead ends, seems your Miss Hobbs led a sheltered life.'

Cornelius wanted to tell Statton he couldn't have been more wrong if he tried, but he needed to keep information on a strict need-to-know only basis.

'I thought you had good news?' He stared into his empty coffee cup.

'She had an employer, a ...'

'Kelway's Office Supplies, I know, they went bust at the beginning of January – we established that on Saturday in case you had forgotten.'

Statton's mouth formed into a pout and it looked like a sulk was brewing. He paused before speaking again.

'We did,' his voice was clipped and measured as he stared at his notepad. 'But I think she may have had another job, working for a food importer just off Fishponds Road.'

Tossing his empty his cup to one side, Cornelius took five rapid strides to Statton's desk and without saying a word, whipped the notepad out of his hand.

'Slowik Foods?' He glared at Statton. 'This wasn't in the file; how did you find this out?'

Statton puffed his chest out, 'Good old-fashioned police work'. A smug grin crept across his face, but it wasn't there long.

'Don't get cocky, you have discovered information that Superintendent Liatt doesn't know about. She will be suspicious if you can't give a bloody good explanation as to how you have come by it.'

With his bubble burst, the young detective constable looked crestfallen.

'I know you can't tell me everything about this case, but it smacks of a missing protected witness to me.' He stopped to look at Cornelius for confirmation who in turn hoped he didn't look as impressed as he felt. Statton continued.

'That being the case, unless she had a job lined up for her, she'd have struggled to find work. She wouldn't be able to produce references, as she has no identifiable work history, so, I thought it was worth a stab at contacting some local employers who aren't overly fussy about whom they employ. I know a few, so I started at her address and worked outwards. It was a case of third time lucky, the woman who answered the phone said they had someone called Pippa working for them for about a month, but she stopped coming into work about three weeks ago. I think she was about to tell me more, but there was a loud outburst of Polish in the background and the phone went dead.'

Statton waited for his pat on the back. It never came. Cornelius wasn't sure if Statton had told him the whole truth, but this was a good lead and he wasn't going to question the source of it just yet. A visit to Slowik Foods was in order.

The journey to the western end of Fishponds Road should have only taken ten minutes, but an accident on Muller Road snarled the traffic for a mile radius. Statton was rapidly learning that the detective inspector was not at his best when stuck in traffic. He had an extensive repertoire of insults he levelled at drivers who he thought weren't following the Highway Code and judging by the frequency they came out of his mouth that constituted about half of them. Statton became genuinely concerned that DI Cornelius was likely to have a minor heart attack if his stress levels didn't drop in the next five minutes. His relief was palpable when they eventually arrived at their destination.

Slowik Foods was located on a side street which ran adjacent to a slip road for the M32. It was a two-storey square monstrosity of a building that looked as if it had bullied its way on to the road which otherwise consisted of residential houses and one takeaway specialising in Turkish food. It was only the unsightly presence of the M32 on the other side of the road that stopped it from winning the ugliest structure in the area award.

Cornelius parked under the shadow of the motorway slip road which left them the briefest of walks to Slowik Foods. Statton's hope that he wasn't going to be out in the cold rain for long was short lived, as they struggled to find their way into the wholesalers. A weathered plastic sign above a faded blue fire exit indicated they were at the right place, but the access to what roughly constituted a drive was blocked by two six-foot iron bar gates with barbed wire deterring anyone from climbing over. They tried banging on the fire door to get the attention of someone inside but to no avail. Cornelius was reluctant to give notice of their arrival, but had little option, so he rang the number on the battered sign. A gruff voice answered with a simple hello. Cornelius identified himself and asked for someone to let them in, before the phone went dead.

It took a further five minutes of banging on the fire door and repeated attempts to ring the telephone number before a short stocky man with an overly large round head and a soup-straining moustache came hobbling towards the gates, keys in hand. Cornelius was about to tell him he was on the verge of getting a warrant to take his fucking business apart when the hobbler gave him a warm smile and apologised profusely in broken English.

'I so sorry, sirs, could not finds bloody keys. Not good keeping two fine policemen waiting, sorry – come in, warm inside. I get kettle on for you.'

The use of the word kettle had an instant calming effect on both officers, and any thoughts of early aggressive questioning temporarily vanished at the thought of a mug of steaming coffee. They followed the hobbler into the building and were immediately taken aback. Expecting the inside to match the outside in terms of dilapidation and grime, they were surprised to find a warehouse that was spotlessly clean, well lit, tidy and organised. Two men and a woman, busily packed boxes into metal crates, while a forklift driver loaded wrapped pallets of clearly labelled boxes on to high shelving. Cornelius's knowledge of safe working practices was reasonable from his time as the station health and safety representative, and as he walked through the warehouse he couldn't see a hint of bad practice. It was a well run operation, although it seemed to have low staffing levels.

The hobbler led them into a windowless office at the far corner of the warehouse. The light green walls were mostly covered in white boards which detailed delivery dates and stock rotation codes for the month ahead. The board which declared itself to be the staff rota had been wiped clean.

Without asking what they wanted, the hobbler spooned instant coffee into two matching mugs, poured on boiling water and passed the drinks over to the grateful hands of his visitors. He walked over to his old grey office desk and slumped into his padded chair which responded with a loud farting sound.

'Sorry I so slow, bad leg from old car accident. I am Rafael Slowik, how may I help you today?'

Cornelius had already decided to let Statton do most of the talking; he wanted to observe the way Rafael Slowik responded to the questions. His colleague waded in without any prelude.

'Do you recognise this person Mr Slowik?' he handed over the mug shot of Pippa.

Rafael Slowik reached over and took the photo, removed his glasses and carefully studied it.

'I have bad eyesight, much easier to see up close like this.' He stared intently at the photograph for a minute before passing it back. 'I do not know this person – sorry.'

'Her name is Pippa Hobbs, have you employed anyone by that name recently?'

'I employ lots of people here, lots come and go.'

'Please answer the question, sir.'

If he was hiding anything, Cornelius thought he was doing a reasonable job. Slowik didn't look in the slightest bit flustered; he was almost apologetic.

'Sorry, I cannot remember. When I say I employ lots, I do not always see them all. Katyana, she do all paperwork.'

Statton made a deliberate and theatrical show of flipping out his notebook and consulting its contents.

'Um, would that be the lady I spoke to this morning? The one who said a person called Pippa worked here until three weeks ago and suddenly stopped coming?' He sat back and decided to try his senior officer's trick of saying nothing else until the interviewee cracked. It didn't work.

'I not here, sorry,' he said, accompanying this with a shrug of his shoulders.

'It sounded like your voice I heard in the background, sir.' It was a lie, but it triggered the briefest of twitches on the face of Rafael Slowik. Cornelius decided to apply some pressure.

'Mr Slowik, we aren't interested in your employment practices or how many illegal immigrants you have working for you or, indeed, how many of them you bundled into your cellar while you kept us waiting outside for five minutes.'

Rafael Slowik opened his mouth to protest but Cornelius put his hand up to cut him off.

'We are trying to trace a missing person who may have worked for you. Now, I passed three sets of security cameras on my way here and there's a fourth at the end of this road. I can easily check those cameras, and if I find this woman appears in the first three but not in the fourth it limits her destination to this street and apart from a small takeaway, you are the only employer here. I'd rather not go to the trouble of doing that, but if I do – and I have good reason to believe she did work here – I promise you I will come back mob-handed and any illegals here will be handed over to the relevant authorities for deportation. While we are at it we will also prepare a nice big heavy book to throw at you for all manner of illegal work practices. Now, would you like to look at the photograph again?'

Rafael Slowik leaned forward, picked up the photo and went through the motions of studying it again.

'Ah, her hair different in this one. Sometime she call herself Phil, sometime Pippa, I got confused you see.'

Cornelius could see; Pippa introduced herself to him as Phil, and the change in hairstyle was striking enough to make Slowik's previous denial just about plausible. He knew it was likely to be less than twenty-four hours before he had to come clean about knowing her and was planning the same defence.

Statton took back control of the conversation. 'When was the last time you saw her, sir?'

'About three weeks ago. One day she here, next nothing. Shame, she a good worker.'

'Did you try and find out what happened to her?'

Agitation crept into Slowik's voice. 'They all do it, make it very difficult to run business. If I chased all people who stopped working for me with no notice I do nothing but chase after them. They have no respect!' His voice rose and his cheeks flooded with colour.

Cornelius couldn't tell if he was becoming agitated over his unreliable staff in general or whether it was specifically Pippa that was the cause. Either way he planned to look deeper into Slowik when he returned to the station.

'When was Pippa's last day?'

Rafael Slowik appeared to be wondering whether or not he wanted to answer the question. Eventually, pulling out a bulky ledger from a drawer underneath his desk, holding it upright so his unwanted guests couldn't see the contents. He scanned the pages until he found what he was looking for.

'Here, last Thursday in January, that was the last day she come here.' He paused, and Cornelius knew more was coming.

'I would ring her, Pippa was nice person, but she said she never have phone. How many people like her not have phone? Even old man like me have one. That may be why man come calling for her once, said it was only way to speak to her.'

In an instant Rafael Slowik had the undivided attention of two police officers.

'Man? What man?' said Cornelius.

'I don't know, I did not see him. He left message with one of my staff. I had to write it in my book otherwise I forget it.' He reached back for his large book and flipped through a few more pages, 'Ah, here it is.' For the first time during the interview he looked pleased with himself as he read the message back. 'Please tell Pippa that Lucas called to see her.'

***

Cornelius and Statton returned to the car and the inspector slumped into his seat as dark thunder clouds rolled across his mind. Here it was again – his name – twice in the same day. Like most police officers he didn't like coincidences, and this was starting to look nasty.

Oblivious to the maelstrom inside Cornelius's head, Andy Statton grinned from ear to ear.

'So, butty time?'

Cornelius said nothing; his hands gripped the steering wheel and his knuckles were turning white.

When Statton turned to the inspector and caught sight of his troubled face, his smile faded as well.

'Have I missed something? I thought that was quite a result.'

Still no response from Cornelius, who had made no attempt to start his car. Statton tried a compliment to stimulate a response.

'That was a good line about the CCTV cameras, I didn't think to look for those before we went in.'

Eventually Cornelius broke his silence.

'Neither did I Andy, but Mr Slowik didn't know that. It also means my guess that he hid half his workforce from us was right as well.'

'What made you think that?'

Cornelius fixed him with a stare which suggested he should have worked it out for himself.

'That building is well run, and an organised man like Slowik isn't going to lose his keys; he just told us that to buy time. In a warehouse that size you'd expect to see at least twice the number of people we saw, plus the staff rota had been wiped clean. Add it all together and it was worth a guess to put pressure on him. If I was wrong he'd have happily proved it; it seemed a shame not to use it to our advantage.'

Statton could see his bacon butty slipping away and realised his day was about to get worse.

'Come on, button up that expensive coat of yours, it's time for a walkabout. Let's see how many CCTV cameras there are around here – I want to find out who the bloody hell this Lucas is.'

**

It was mid-afternoon by the time the two men returned to Gloucester Road station, their moods matching the heavy grey clouds that still dispensed rain in short, violent spells. They had been sitting in the car discussing which direction to walk in search of CCTV cameras when Rafael Slowik burst out of his building and hobbled towards them. He'd remembered that Pippa had never received the message about Lucas, as she hadn't shown up for work again. Cornelius wryly guessed this servile behaviour was more about ensuring that he didn't return with an immigration officer in tow. The second gem Rafael Slowik had conveniently remembered was the date of the message. This gave them what they needed to help search for the mysterious Lucas using CCTV footage. As Statton didn't know this was the second time that day Cornelius's name had cropped up, he hadn't made any links between the mystery caller and the inspector sitting alongside him.

Images captured on CCTV could take an age to search through yet offer little help. As it transpired, at least a quarter of the cameras in the proximity of Slowik Foods were nothing more than fakes, designed to act as deterrents. Footage from the real cameras was only kept for two weeks, so anything older than that had already been wiped. Only one camera had any footage from the day in question, but the pictures were out of focus and grainy. Unless Pippa's caller was seven feet tall or four feet wide he would be indistinguishable from any other person that passed in front of its lens that day.

Cornelius thought of a multitude of reasons not to return to the CID offices, but he knew Laverty would want an update. If he was lucky, Karen Liatt would be off licking Rick-with-a-silent-P's arse at Portishead HQ, and with that unsightly image in his head, he made his way back.

A loud cheer went up as he entered the office and any hope of sneaking in, unobtrusively, vanished. Cornelius scanned the five faces staring at him as a chant of 'guil-ty ... guil-ty ... guil-ty' rose up from the CID staff. Even Brawley was smiling.

'What?' Was all he could muster, and before anyone could offer him an explanation, Ross Laverty appeared at his side.

'Afternoon Lucas – fancy a coffee and a chat?' Laverty's amiable expression told Cornelius he was not in for a bollocking. He knew he was the butt of the joke but he was the only person in the room who didn't know why, so he nodded acceptance and followed Laverty to the desk of Rita Sharma.

To squeeze three people around Rita's desk they had to move two boxes of files which smelt like they had been stored in proximity to a cess pit and pull in a third chair that wobbled dangerously when anyone dared to sit on it. When they were all seated, Laverty began.

'Rita has been viewing the CCTV from Broadmead in the hope we can find something out about the severed finger.'

He nodded his head in the direction of the computer monitor. Rita grinned as she clicked the image on the screen in front of her.

'We know the finger was found on a bench at about 17:00, and thankfully one of Broadmead's cameras has a reasonable view of it. The picture is not overly clear, but if you look there ...' Rita pointed to a tiny portion of the screen where the pixilation had turned white, 'you can just make out the package on the seat.'

'Are you sure that's it?'

'Oh yes – look at this.'

She scrolled along the timer slider and the screen changed. A woman who looked to be in her early sixties was sitting on the bench, rifling through her shopping bag. Her Dalmatian sniffed and pawed at the white object that lay in the far corner of the seat; she kept pulling the dog away but it persistently went back to the item which held its fascination. The shopper eventually hauled her dog clear and held it on a short lead with her left hand and with her right she tugged at one corner of the package. Although the image was still grainy, something clearly fell out on to the seat. The shopper leaned closer to look at the mysterious object before it disappeared from view under a large pile of puke.

During his years in the police, Cornelius had been hardened to all kinds of disturbing imagery and appalling smells. The one thing he had never mastered was the sight of someone being sick and he felt his stomach flip over as the shopper emptied her partially digested lunch over the severed digit.

Laverty spotted the change in pallor and smiled. 'It gets better, show him, Rita.'

'Starting from when the finger was discovered, I went backwards to see when it had been placed there. If we go back to 16:00, it's still there – back to 15:15 and it's not there. This is where the fun starts.'

Cornelius looked at his colleagues. Rita Sharma was clearly enjoying herself, but the smile on Laverty's face had not made it as far as his eyes, which were focused on Cornelius rather than the screen.

'Shoot forward to 15:25, nothing. On to 15:33 and look what has appeared!' Rita tapped a few more buttons on her keyboard. 'Now let me run the eight minute clip in real time.'

Cornelius said nothing; he already knew what was coming. He also knew who the finger belonged to.

***

'I'm listening.'

Laverty sat back in his chair in the tiny office where a portable heater did its best to make up for the inefficiencies of a heating system installed over 50 years previously. His elbows rested on his desk with his palms pressed together as if in silent prayer. A noisy commotion played out in the main office but he didn't acknowledge it. He guessed Cornelius had a confession to make and he wasn't going to allow himself to be distracted.

For Cornelius's part, any kind of distraction would have been welcome. He'd planned to come clean about Pippa the following day. He would say that he had been confused by her radically altered appearance and that he was just waiting to see if his number appeared in her telephone record to be absolutely sure that she was the same woman he had known. It was a weak excuse; the truth was that he desperately wanted to investigate the disappearance of a woman he had grown fond of and he did not want to be thrown off the case because of his connection with her.

Now, everything had changed. Someone calling himself Lucas had visited Pippa's employer – most likely the day after she disappeared. And now, there was CCTV footage from Broadmead Shopping Centre showing Cornelius sitting on the same bench where a severed finger had turned up. There he was, checking his mobile phone for messages – no odd package visible, then for the next three minutes, the view of the bench was obscured by a group of students. Cornelius's recollection was that they were all pissed and arguing about which pub to go to next. By the time they had dispersed, Cornelius had also gone, and barely three feet from where he had perched his backside, a small white package had appeared. It remained untouched for the next ninety minutes before being decorated with semi-digested lunch.

Rita Sharma had playfully punched Cornelius on the arm and asked him if he had any more appendages he wanted to scatter around the city. Laverty stared at him with raised eyebrows, inviting him to comment. Cornelius hadn't seen Rita's expression when he solemnly asked to speak to Laverty in private but would have bet his month's salary that her jaw would have been halfway to the floor as they walked away from her desk.

'I don't think it's a coincidence – the finger I mean.' He couldn't look Laverty in the eye. The day's events crashed down on him, and nothing made any sense.

'I worked that out as soon as I saw you look at the monitor, you'd be a crap poker player Lucas. What is it you are not telling me?'

Confession time – again. Cornelius decided to precede his painful admission with a diversionary statement.

'I think you'll find that the finger belongs to Pippa Hobbs.'

Whatever Laverty may have been expecting, that wasn't it. He didn't say anything but behind his thick rimmed glasses his eyes virtually doubled in size. Cornelius followed up with a lie designed to cushion the blow that was coming.

'Earlier today, I realised that I knew Pippa Hobbs.' He could see Laverty was on the verge of blowing his gasket, so he held up his hand, attempting to stop the tsunami heading his way.

'She looked completely different from the photo we were given; I had to be sure before I side-tracked the investigation. Besides, it wouldn't …'

Laverty had already heard enough, 'Don't you dare say it wouldn't have made any difference!'

He pounded the corner of his desk with his fist causing the remnants of his coffee to leap out of its mug.

'For goodness sake Lucas, if you had the slightest suspicion you should have told us.'

'I was planning to, just as soon as I had confirmation from the phone records, but there have been some developments today. And now with the Broadmead footage … I think I'm involved in this somehow.'

Laverty contemplated what demeaning punishment he could hand out to his inspector, while wondering how he could protect him if Cornelius really was involved. He let Cornelius run through the whole story, from Mrs Bettie's initial report, through to the message from Lucas left for Pippa at Slowik Foods. Cornelius told Laverty about his relationship with Pippa but made a specific point of saying he'd never shagged her – as if it would atone for his failure to divulge a personal interest.

'That's it – seriously? It's a bit coincidental I'll grant you, but to draw the conclusion that the finger must belong to Pippa is one hell of a leap. The only thing I can see linking all this, so far, is your sodding incompetence.'

'No, that's not it. Manny Thompson has gone missing and would you like to guess who he said he was off to meet just before he vanished?'

Laverty leaned forward and put his head in his hands. When he spoke, his voice was barely a whimper.

'When did you find this little gem out?'

'This morning, the call that came through while you were doing your briefing was Malcolm Williams telling me Manny's daughter was in reception.'

Laverty opened his mouth but Cornelius cut him off.

'And before you bang on about me being incompetent again, Manny has a history of going missing for days at a time. I agreed with Megan that if he hasn't come home by tonight, we officially classify him as missing. When she said he'd told her he was off to see me, I assumed he'd used the first name which came into his head. Add together today's events and it's starting to stink.'

Silence dominated the room. The commotion from the outside office had ceased and Cornelius suspected that if he flung open the door there would be at least three ears pressed up against it. Laverty stared out of the window into the darkening grey skies; Cornelius sat back in his chair, waiting for the verdict. It took two minutes before Laverty snapped out of his thoughtful trance.

'I'll talk to the Super tomorrow; I suggest you keep out of the way until at least lunchtime. I doubt if I can stop her referring it to professional standards though.'

'What about the finger?'

'I don't think we have Pippa's DNA but I'll get the lab on to it, now go home Lucas, and for God's sake avoid the bloody pub will you. You'll need a clear head tomorrow.'

Nodding briefly, Cornelius stood up. He had his hand on the door handle when Laverty called after him.

'If it is her finger, Lucas, you'll have a shit storm heading your way.'

Cornelius didn't reply. He'd already worked that out.

FEBRUARY

This had better work. The morning wind was freezing his nuts off and he could barely feel his fingers. He stomped his feet to aid circulation, it didn't work. The cold was pissing him off but he had to wait, there was too much at stake.

How long had he been sucking up to those stupid, stuck-up bitches? Over a month now? Seemed like fucking ages. Joining them for their weekly Rotary coffee mornings, listening to them prattle on about their boring, shitty lives. Occasionally, they would ask him a question but only to be polite. They were never happier than when they were talking about themselves, their lives, their holidays – and as for their children, does anyone give a shit? He couldn't give a damn about any of it, and pretending to be interested was fucking killing him. He did it because he wanted the attention of one particular person.

She was another stuck-up bitch who considered herself too high-and-mighty to speak to him. There was no way she would engage him in small talk. No, 'so, what is it you do?' or 'do you have any children?' or any of the other brain-achingly dull chit-chat they all loved. She had her set of friends and wasn't interested in talking to anyone else. Introducing himself and trying to open a casual conversation wouldn't work with this one either. If he wanted to talk to her, he would have to make it look like it was on her terms.

Originally, he was going to take her off the street, a quick snatch and grab. Whack her on the back of the head, bundle her into the back of the van and drive away. The whole thing could be done in less than ten seconds, however, he couldn't find any good extraction points on her usual walking routes. The busy streets gave too many opportunities for people to be watching and sticking their sodding noses in. Her house was a fucking fortress as well; there was no way he could break in and take what he wanted. For his grand plan to work, he needed something of hers, so it had to be this way. The change of appearance, the pretence, trying to be noticed without making it obvious; it was all so he could earn a tiny bit of trust.

It had all come to this. Standing like a fucking lemon in the middle of a crappy suburban street, with the 4x4s parked alongside well-manicured gardens and identical houses with starched net curtains. If this didn't work it would be back to square one. All the research would be wasted; the faked photographs, letters and emails would be for nothing – not to mention the time spent creating his persona. At least the other one had been easier; she had already agreed to his suggestion and was on standby. Stupid cow, she had no idea what she'd let herself in for. He'd feel sorry for her if she hadn't been such a freeloading bitch. She'd bought his cover-story hook, line and sinker and thought she was on to some easy money. She'd soon be paying the price for her greed and doing him a huge favour in the process.

He heard footsteps coming towards him from behind; the sound of sensible shoes clip-clopping on the damp pavement. He looked down at the photograph and sheet of paper he had taken out from a brown manila file labelled *Reunion*. The footsteps were getting closer; he turned his body slightly so she could see him and the expression he had been practising in the bathroom mirror that morning.

Almost there, barely three metres away. Don't look her in the eye ...

She walks right past him. Fuck, fuck, fuck.

She stops, turns around and looks at him. 'Hello, you go to the Rotary Club, don't you?'

Just nod and look confused, don't say anything.

'You appear to be looking for something, can I help?'

Bingo.

Eleven

Following instructions had never been Cornelius's strong point, but today he had every intention of heeding Laverty's request for him to keep a low profile; what he hadn't done was to follow the advice about avoiding alcohol. Although he had restricted himself to two pints of Doom Bar in The Flask on his way home the previous night, he had stopped off at his local supermarket and bought a litre bottle of Canadian Club whisky and this morning, his head complained at his lack of self-discipline.

He sat at his kitchen table blowing the heat out of his coffee and pondered his options. The soporific effect of the Doom Bar and the Canadian Club had given him three hours of dreamless sleep. After that, he'd been restless thinking about Pippa and Manny. He'd kicked himself for not immediately declaring he knew Pippa when he was first interrogated at Portishead. However, if he'd said anything, Superintendent Liatt and DCC McCartney would have jumped to all manner of conclusions and he would never have been allowed anywhere near the case. Cornelius felt he owed it to Pippa to try and uncover what happened to her, even if it meant taking a roasting further down the line. Having appeased his conscience on that matter, another thought occurred to him, which would not budge.

He was being watched.

Although the test results weren't back yet, he was convinced the finger belonged to Pippa, and it had been deliberately placed next to him in full view of a CCTV camera. Up until yesterday, Pippa's status as a protected witness had appeared to be the reason for her disappearance. Now, it looked like Cornelius was the cause and he had no idea why.

The kitchen door creaked open and Daniel wandered in wearing just his boxer shorts, his eyes were bleary and his hair resembled an unkempt forsythia bush. He mumbled something in his father's general direction which sounded vaguely like caniavalft, whilst reaching for the kettle. Still happy that his son was at least prepared to communicate with him, Cornelius offered a positive monosyllabic reply, which he thought Daniel would be able to process at this time of the morning. His dishevelled offspring said nothing else and disappeared back to his room leaving Cornelius none the wiser as to which direction he was heading when leaving the house.

In the fifteen minutes it took Daniel to transform himself into a college student, Cornelius decided what to do with his morning. He had an itch to scratch, and he needed the help of a convicted criminal to do it.

***

Her Majesty's Prison Bristol was still referred to locally by its previous name, Horfield. Built during the 1880s, it had a long and chequered past with some notable former inmates. Until 1963 it had been the scene of executions and it hosted major riots in the 1980s and 90s. It housed a population of over 600 category A and B prisoners, as well as those on remand awaiting trial. A large red brick perimeter wall topped with barbed wire and CCTV cameras snaked around the prison complex, separating it from the gentle 1930s bay fronted terraced housing which surrounded it.

Although the prison was comfortably within walking distance of the station, Cornelius did not want to draw attention to himself, so he parked his car in one of the resident-only spaces that surrounded the complex. He'd barely exited his car when an overweight man with an impressive comb-over waddled out of his house, berating him about parking in a resident-only zone. The puce colouring that gathered in his face promptly subsided when Cornelius flashed his warrant card and reminded the man that harassment was an offence. Comb-over man returned inside, grumbling about fascist pigs who could do what they sodding well liked. Cornelius turned his collar up against the cold wind which had whipped up since leaving his house thirty minutes earlier and headed off for his rendezvous.

Checking in at HMP Bristol reception, Cornelius was greeted by a hard staring warden with cropped blonde hair and neck tattoos visible over the top of her uniform, which looked two sizes too big. Her immediate dislike of Cornelius was blindingly obvious; she never uttered even the most standard of courtesies and made him wait whilst she slowly and deliberately took her time. Not that Cornelius minded, he didn't have any other plans for the morning.

Eventually, she called for him to sign the visitor's disclaimer before revealing the reason for her hostility.

'There's a procedure for this you know, you don't just call in when it's convenient to you.'

Cornelius knew this, but he had phoned this morning and called in a favour, earned when he had helped seize a supply of contraband that was destined to be smuggled into the prison. Clearly, the Rottweiler in front of him knew nothing about it.

'Take it up with the family of the man who has disappeared; see what they think of your procedures.' Cornelius replied.

The tattooed guard responded with a stare that could have flattened a heavyweight boxer; Cornelius grinned back, which made her mood even worse. It was a pleasant change when another guard with a genuine smile arrived to escort him through the maze of corridors, intersected with locked metal grills at every turn, and into a windowless but brightly lit room with pale yellow walls. The only form of comfort was a solitary white table and two metal framed chairs, the like of which Cornelius had last seen at his school, thirty years previously.

The shaven-headed occupant of one of the chairs was leaning forward, elbows resting on the table in front of him, examining his fingernails. He didn't look up at his visitor, preferring to study the non-existent debris he was pretending to pull out from under his nail.

'I hope this is going to take a long time, Inspector Cornelius.'

Cornelius lowered himself into the chair opposite and accepted the bait.

'And why might that be, Danny?'

Danny Palmer looked at Cornelius for the first time and grinned, showing an ugly set of yellowing teeth.

'I'm supposed to be on kitchen duty this morning and I fucking hate kitchen duty.' His voice was raspy from five decades of smoking. 'You win the award for being the first copper I have ever been pleased to see. Even having to stare at your ugly mug is better than having to cook for this bunch of tossers.'

Despite himself, Cornelius smiled. 'Always happy to help and I am sure you'll be equally happy to reward me with your insight and wisdom.'

'No, I don't know where he is or what happened to him. Now, what else shall we talk about to help pass the time?'

'What happened to who, Danny?'

'Seriously? Do you think I'm fucking thick? I know why you're here; I knew you'd be coming to see me before you did.'

Cornelius didn't doubt it, but he wasn't going to bite. The minute Megan had started making calls to her father's associates asking if they knew where he was, one of them would have passed the word on to Palmer. Cornelius paused and faked a look of confusion before producing a look of recognition.

'Oh, you mean Manny. Sure, we'll talk about him later if you like. That's not why I'm here though.'

It was a lie but it did the trick and Cornelius was satisfied to see Palmer's smug grin vanish.

'Then what is it you want?' Palmer smiled through gritted teeth.

'What do you know about Pippa Hobbs?' The traces of recognition he'd hoped to see on Palmer's face didn't appear.

'Who the fuck is Pippa Hobbs?'

'Well, she's not your average missing person that's for sure.' Cornelius played Palmer at his own game by examining his own fingernails. 'We think she may have been abducted by criminals. Questions is, who'd have the muscle to do it.'

Palmer leaned forward, glaring at his adversary, and for the first time Cornelius caught a whiff of the stale tobacco on his breath.

'One – never heard of her. Two – not my style.'

If ever a man deserved to be in prison it was Danny Palmer. For more than twenty years his stock-in-trade had been drugs, gambling and prostitution; he had been utterly ruthless in spreading his tentacles across the whole city. It was rumoured he executed his own son after a drugs deal went wrong and he thought his son was trying to take over his empire. No charges were ever brought, but as an urban legend it massively elevated his underworld status.

'You'll be out in what, twelve months? The station's running a book on how long Weasel will last once you're back on the streets. I'm putting a tenner on a month.'

'Perhaps I need to remind you I am a respectable businessman, inspector?' The sneer returned to his face. 'Now, why don't you tell me what you really came for?'

'Ah well, as you mentioned it, care to tell me what you know about your old lackey, Manny?'

'You're so full of bullshit. What's this? Stats week down at the nick? Clear up any outstanding cases by pinning them on the cons instead of getting off your arses and doing some fucking work for a change? Bastards the lot of you.'

Flecks of saliva formed at the corner of his mouth. Danny Palmer's temper was legendary and Cornelius was close to setting it off. He needed him to remain cool for a few more minutes.

'Of course not Danny and, for what it's worth, I don't think you have anything to do with it. You remember Superintendent Liatt?'

Palmer growled under his breath, 'That bitch.'

'I couldn't possibly comment.' Cornelius smirked at the thought he had something in common with the gangster sitting opposite him. 'But if I try to investigate what happened to Manny without talking to the person whose status earned himself a mention at Weasel's trial, she'd roast my bollocks. So, to be honest, I'm doing this more for myself than anything else.'

'Like I said, full of bullshit.' Palmer sat back, rubbed his shaven head and stared at Cornelius. 'Got any fags?'

Cornelius anticipated this question and reached into his pocket to pull out twenty Benson & Hedges he had bought on the way. He slid them across the table without saying a word.

'He's a good man, Manny, came to see me before the trial, but you already know that.'

'Of course.' Cornelius had no intention of admitting the first time he knew of the visit was at the trial. 'How did you manage to get him a visiting permit, Danny? With a record like Manny's there's no way he should have been allowed in.'

'Not my fault they're a useless bunch of wankers here. Manny only wanted to know if he should give evidence against Weasel.'

'Asking your permission, was he?'

Palmer ignored the question. 'I told him I couldn't give a fuck. Weasel was getting off, so it didn't matter either way.'

'And you knew this how?'

Palmer grinned, showing more of his uneven yellow teeth than Cornelius cared for. As well as his temper, Danny Palmer was well known for his ability to brag, although, unlike most of his compatriots, he was usually telling the truth.

'Easy to say after the event Danny, even I could tell you who won the 3.30 at Taunton yesterday.'

'His brief had someone from your nick by the balls, and before you ask, no, I don't know who and I wouldn't tell you if I did.'

Cornelius tried not to look interested. 'Yeah yeah, anyone in the public gallery would have come to that conclusion. You're the one who's full of bullshit Danny.'

Palmer didn't respond, but he was starting to look bored and, kitchen duties or not, Cornelius knew it wouldn't be long before he would clam up. He reckoned he had one last roll of the dice.

'You've got motive, Danny. Weasel would be locked up if Manny's testimony hadn't been ripped to shreds. Let's face it, you've got a score to settle with him.'

'Are – you – not – fucking – listening? He was always going to get off no matter what Manny said. His brief knew about the holes in the case because there's a snitch in your nick. How else do you think he knew about the skag that was nicked from your own fucking evidence room? As usual, you are barking up the wrong tree, inspector. Look, why don't you have a chat with Guy? He might be able to tell you what's happened to Manny.'

Palmer sat back in his chair and folded his arms. The interview was over.

Cornelius nodded and made a point of thanking Danny for his time. As he headed for the door Palmer called after him.

'You might know about yesterday's 3.30 at Taunton, but do you know about Thursday's 2.10 at Newbury? Regents Choice, worth twenty on the nose I think.'

Cornelius didn't reply. He turned away and was escorted out of the building. By the time he arrived back at his car, he'd decided to place a bet. He was pondering what to do next when his phone rang; it was Laverty.

'Where are you?'

Laverty didn't sound happy but it didn't stop Cornelius from antagonising him.

'Following your orders and keeping a low profile.'

'Well don't! Get your arse in here now – we've got a match on the finger.'

***

Cornelius thought about leaving his car where it was and walking to the station, just to piss off comb-over man, but he caught sight of the thunderous black clouds which had assembled over Bristol's rooftops whilst he talked to Palmer and decided to drive the short distance instead.

He wasn't particularly looking forward to meeting Laverty, but he was grateful for the relative silence and calm of the CID office. Only Andy Statton was sitting at a desk, staring at a monitor with his fingers dancing across a keyboard. He looked up but barely acknowledged Cornelius's arrival.

'Don't tell me you're still sulking over that bacon butty, Andy? Anyone about?'

Statton didn't get a chance to reply. A voice boomed from behind Cornelius which made him jump.

'Lucas! About time. My office. Now!'

Cornelius didn't need to look around; he'd recognise Karen Liatt's squawk anywhere. He didn't know what was more annoying, the superintendent barking at him across the office or the smirk that crept across Statton's face.

'Once more unto the breach,' he mumbled but not quietly enough.

'You can cut the Shakespearean crap; you are not in a position to be making wisecracks.'

Without another word the superintendent turned on her heels and walked in the direction of her office. As Cornelius followed, he resisted the temptation to flick a V-sign to the back of her head.

Karen Liatt lowered herself into her chair; the noises that emanated from it suggested the springs were working at full force. Ramming a jammy dodger in her mouth, she pointed at the chair opposite, indicating Cornelius should sit as well.

'The Chief not joining us, ma'am?' He was hoping, with Laverty in the room, he might have something approaching an ally to help him fend off the superintendent.

'I've sent Chief Inspector Laverty out. I need someone competent to oversee an operation.' She paused, reading the only two papers which sat on top of her desk. 'I despair of you sometimes, Lucas.'

'I'd never have guessed, ma'am.' It wasn't the wisest of retorts, and he knew it the moment the words left his mouth. 'However, I would like to point out that without me you'd still be struggling to find the owner of the finger. Let alone link it to our missing person.'

'I haven't told you it is Pippa's yet.'

'No, you haven't, so tell me I'm wrong.'

'Tell me first why you think it is hers.'

He tried not to sigh and delivered the same speech he had given to Laverty the day previously. Liatt said nothing; her attention distracted by a commotion taking place in the car park below. Cornelius chanced a loaded question.

'It was quick for a DNA result, ma'am – the finger I mean.'

Her attention snapped back. 'It wasn't DNA. What we didn't realise until this morning was that we have Pippa's finger prints on file. She gave them so she could be ruled out of an investigation on some stolen gear which was found in Leroy Jenkins's flat. I bet she never thought they'd be used to match her fingers to the rest of her. Anyway, that's why I've sent DCI Laverty off. It's safe to assume she won't be coming back to her flat, so he's overseeing the forensic team to see if they can uncover anything.'

Although Cornelius had always been sure it was her finger, the confirmation it was Pippa's hit him harder than expected. A lump rose in his throat, but he tried not to show it. Before he could fire off any questions, Liatt had a few of her own she wanted to ask.

'Tell me Lucas, is the forensic team likely to find any of your DNA in Pippa's flat?'

'No, ma'am.' Cornelius was grateful for a question he could answer easily.

'And there's nothing else you have conveniently forgotten to tell us?'

'That's it, ma'am. I assume we are treating this as murder now?'

'We are, and it is the only reason I am not referring you to professional standards. We are going to be up to our neck in all kinds of shit until we discover what happened to Pippa, and I need a fully functioning team, which isn't going to happen if you've got that lot crawling all over you.'

'Thank you, ma'am.' It was a heartfelt comment, but the superintendent wasn't about to let Cornelius off lightly.

'Don't even think about doing anything on the Pippa Hobbs case without the express permission of DCI Laverty first – clear?'

He nodded.

'And if you put as much as a toenail out of line you can kiss goodbye to your job. Now get out.'

Cornelius stood up, nodded and made a beeline for the coffee machine, which was out of order. He tried Laverty's approach of giving it a wallop on the side, but either he didn't have the right touch or it had been beaten once too often and it failed to co-operate. Remembering another machine on the floor below, he descended the stairs and made a sharp turn right. In his haste, he missed the bright yellow A-board designed to alert people of cleaning in progress. He crashed into a trolley loaded with mops, brushes and cleaning materials all of which managed to stay upright. The same could not be said for Cornelius who lost his balance, taking with him an empty bucket and a book that had been resting on the top of the trolley.

He ignored the pain in his ankle, hoping no one had seen him hit the floor in such an ungainly fashion. His hope was promptly dashed by the sight of a man in his early-forties standing over him with a mop in his hand. The man put the mop to one side and extended his arm to help Cornelius get back on his feet.

'Are you alright there, sir?'

Cornelius didn't detect the slightest hint of amusement in his voice and was quietly impressed. If he'd witnessed an accident like that, he'd be pissing himself laughing by now.

'I'm fine thank you,' was the only reply he could muster.

He plonked the bucket back on to the trolley and handed the book back to the cleaner. The cleaner looked marginally embarrassed taking the book back.

'I only read this during breaks, Mr Cornelius.'

'I'm sure you do.' Cornelius looked at the coffee stained cover which had seen better days. 'Hmm, *Injured, remade*, is it any good?'

'Oh yes, it's the tale of a mountaineer who overcomes a serious accident to resume his passion for scaling the world's highest peaks. You can have it when I've finished reading it, if you like.'

Before Cornelius could politely decline the offer, he realised that the cleaner knew who he was.

'Are you Neil by any chance?'

The cleaner managed to look startled and worried at the same time. 'Yes sir, I'm Neil. Neil Stokes.'

'It appears we have a mutual friend, Neil, Elizabeth Bettie?'

'Oh Elizabeth, yes I know her,' he mumbled. 'We play bingo together. She's a nice lady, talks a lot but nice.'

Cornelius couldn't decide if Neil was achingly shy or whether he remembered that as well as recommending him, he also described him as cranky. He didn't want to add to his embarrassment but wasn't going to pass up on the opportunity to ask a question that had bugged him.

'What made you give her my name, Neil?'

'Oh, I hear what people say here Mr Cornelius,' his quiet tone was barely audible. 'You have a reputation for not letting people down and Elizabeth, well she has had some bad experiences with the police in the past, and I thought you may be able to help her. Sorry if I ...'

Cornelius didn't hear the rest of Neil's words. Sergeant Malcolm Williams was hollering at him from the far end of the corridor. Cornelius offered the briefest of apologies to Neil and scuttled off in the opposite direction to the sergeant. Either Williams had work for him or he was after sponsorship for his latest foreign holiday, masquerading as a charity bike ride. Cornelius wasn't interested in either and headed back to his desk, minus the coffee he had come for.

***

Cornelius spent a fruitless ninety minutes trying to clear though a mass of mundane paperwork which had built up around his desk during the last week. Not for the first time, he casually entertained the idea of opening his email, choosing the *select all* function and hitting *delete*. In reality, he couldn't concentrate on anything other than the events which were unravelling around him.

Pippa had probably been murdered, Manny Thompson was missing and Cornelius's name was cropping up everywhere. Because of his own actions, he was half an inch away from getting the boot, and he seemed to be pissing more people off as each day passed.

Liatt had warned him not to get involved with Pippa's case, but she hadn't said anything about Manny. Cornelius looked up from his desk and saw Andy Statton still, evidently, trying to avoid speaking to him. It was 2 p.m. and he hadn't been out for lunch yet. Time to get the moody detective constable back onside.

'C'mon grumpy, put your coat on.'

Statton looked up with a quizzical expression.

'We're off to the zoo, and if you promise not to have a face like a slapped arse all morning I'll buy you that butty.'

'The zoo?'

'A trip to see a primate in his natural habitat.'

Twelve

Situated off Whitehall Road, The George Inn had only one review on Trip Advisor which described it as *the scariest shit hole in Bristol*. The external red brickwork was faded and cracked, and the barely legible hanging sign had been there since the 1970s. A nicotine yellow ceiling competed with a threadbare, beer-stained carpet and a selection of faded, cigarette-scarred melamine table tops for the grubbiest internal feature.

Cornelius briefed Statton on the way, so he knew what to expect, but it didn't stop him from wrinkling his nose when he walked in the door. Cornelius had been in before and knew two police officers would be as welcome as a fart in a spacesuit, but it was the best place to start looking for his quarry. He strolled up to the bar and spoke to the only customer who sat on one of the rickety stools watching an episode of *Murder she Wrote* on the television.

'Good afternoon Guy, fancy seeing you here.'

Guy Dart, better known as Guy the Gorilla, turned his six-foot eight inch frame to face Cornelius. It was a few seconds before Guy realised who had spoken to him, then he turned back to the television and the pint of Thatcher's that sat before him without saying a word.

'Now now, Guy, you know how this works. Either we have an amicable chat here or I have to go through the rigmarole of trying to squeeze you into a squad car, so we can converse in the affable surroundings of the station. Tell you what, I'll even throw in another pint.'

Normally, he wouldn't have offered as Guy would be morally obliged to refuse anything from the police, but today he was the only customer in the bar so bravado wasn't an issue.

Guy eventually nodded at the scrawny barman who Cornelius doubted was old enough to be serving. Another pint of cider appeared on the bar and Cornelius handed over a tenner and waved away the change. He needed some co-operation and thought it might help.

Not wanting the scrawny one to overhear anything, Guy pointed to the far corner of the bar. He levered himself into one of the chairs and Cornelius and Statton sat opposite. Even sitting down, Guy matched Statton's height. He turned to the DC, leaned into him and spoke with a menacing growl.

'Him I know all too well,' he flicked his thumb in Cornelius's direction, 'but 'oo are you?'

Without flinching, Statton pulled out his warrant card, offering it for inspection. Guy barely glanced at it before turning his attention back to Cornelius.

'I'm guessing this ain't a social call, so whadda you want? Or are you still pissed off 'cause you weren't able to frame Mr Weavell?'

Guy was just about the only person in Bristol to use Weasel's full name, because his main profession was being Weavell's enforcer, and they didn't come much bigger than Guy the Gorilla. His height was complimented by broad muscular shoulders and trunk-like arms which were fully covered in tattoos. An atrophic scar travelled down the left side of his face, starting at his temple and ending at the jaw, but no one knew how he'd acquired it. If Guy had had a different upbringing, he would have made a world-

'So, why do you think Danny Palmer reckons I should be chatting to you?'

Guy's nostrils flared.

'Cause 'e's a stirring little shit that's why. 'E was pissed off I wouldn't mind for 'im when I was in 'Orfield a few months back. I was only in for four months an' I wanted to keep my nose clean.'

'Not many people say no to Danny Palmer Guy or at least say no and continue with a happy and healthy life.'

'Your point being?'

'My point is that you declined to help him, yet here you are, drinking cider in the afternoon with all your fingers and toes intact. Are you sure you haven't been moonlighting for Danny?'

Cornelius caught sight of the muscles tightening in his trunk-like neck. Only a brave few challenged Guy the Gorilla and normal police procedure for questioning him involved going in mob-handed with a taser on standby. Mixing Guy's temperament with alcohol was akin to mixing nitro with glycerine and giving it a good shake, so he hoped Guy retained a degree of sobriety.

It took a moment, but Guy composed himself and his muscles relaxed slightly.

'No, I ain't been moonlightin' and in case you 'adn't noticed, I've been keeping out of trouble since working for Mr Weavell.'

Cornelius threw his hands in the air. 'You're not long out of Horfield, Guy! Or did you go in there for a holiday?'

'I was framed for possession Mr Cornelius – say what you like about me but you know I don't do drugs.'

Cornelius did know – that was why he'd baited him with the question. He had been surprised to hear about Guy being busted with two grammes of heroin on him. Weasel used it to control his prostitutes, but he never let Guy carry it on him – he couldn't afford to have his prize enforcer done on any kind of drug charge. Apparently, he went apoplectic at Guy's arrest, but given his previous charge sheet, drugs or no drugs, the courts were always going to impose a custodial sentence. Weasel tried using some other muscle when Guy was inside but no one had the same terrifying impact as the prospect of Guy the Gorilla caving your head in. When Guy was released after three months, Weasel welcomed him back to the fold and his old job of scaring the shit out of people. Cornelius wasn't overly bothered whether Guy had been framed or not. A spell inside Horfield was deserved for all the heads he had busted and not been convicted for. He steered the conversation back to the topic at hand.

'So, you have no idea where Manny is?'

'No, I don't. If I know Manny 'e's off shagging some bird and 'e's keeping 'er away from that maniac daughter of 'is.'

'Maniac daughter? What, Megan?'

Guy slugged his cider again, enjoying the moment of knowing something the coppers in front of him didn't.

'You lot are thinking with your dicks again – you see a fit woman and think what you'd like to do to 'er – not what she might do to you.'

'What do you mean, Mr Dart?' Statton was inquisitive on more than a professional level, and the fact he spoke for the first time since his earlier chastisement was not lost on the enforcer.

Guy looked at Statton and grinned, showing off a gleaming set of teeth that he hadn't been born with.

'See what I mean? Lover boy 'ere's soft on 'er. Take my advice, Sonny Jim, stay away from 'er.'

Statton blushed slightly but tried to carry on as nonchalantly as possible. 'I wouldn't dream of it,' he lied, 'but if there's a lead we should be following, then we need to know.'

'Megan's got a real temper on 'er. She's just as likely to take your 'ead off with a twelve inch spanner as she is to smile sweetly at you. Oh, she loves 'er dad alright, but she's given Manny a black eye before and I wouldn't put it past 'er to whack 'im in a fit of rage. She could easily store 'is body in one of 'is lockup's 'e's got around the place.' Guy grinned again. 'I reckon she's got the pair of you wrapped around 'er little finger.'

Cornelius hadn't even thought of Megan as a suspect, and he couldn't decide whether Guy was telling the truth or whether he was deliberately stirring it up to deflect attention away from his boss. Guy wasn't going to divulge anything else today, so Cornelius slid another tenner over the bar to cover two more drinks and the two officers left.

They were barely six feet from the pub door when Statton complained about the stale smell lingering on him. He sniffed his jacket and moaned about the time it would take to get the odour of the George Inn out of his clothes. Cornelius barely listened to the whingeing; he was processing the conversation they'd had with Guy. The big man's response to the revelation that Manny was missing seemed to be genuine, which suggested that if Weasel was behind it, he hadn't told Guy. Then there was Megan; was she the quiet psychopath that Guy described? He had hit a nerve when he said the two officers were thinking with their dicks. Cornelius had been blinded by Megan's good looks, and rebuked himself for not considering her as a suspect earlier.

They walked the short distance back to the car and Cornelius had just started the engine, when the daylight vanished. The two men looked up to see Guy's enormous frame standing over the car. He rapped hard on the glass making the car move. Cornelius lowered his window with some apprehension, only to see Guy looking just as worried.

'Can I 'ave another word please?' the cocky arrogance of their previous conversation had gone.

'Of course.' Cornelius tried not to let his surprise show. 'Here or inside?'

'Back inside, it's freezing out 'ere.'

Resisting the temptation to say that standing in the late February winds wearing only jeans and a tee shirt can have that effect, Cornelius exited the car, followed by Statton.

'Not you, Sonny Jim – this is between me and your guv'nor 'ere.'

Statton said nothing but looked to Cornelius for guidance, who nodded briefly before following the big man back inside the pub.

Ten minutes later Cornelius returned to a disgruntled DC who made a point of not asking why he had been excluded from the conversation. For his part, Cornelius didn't notice the sulk, he was still slightly surprised about what Guy had asked him to do. It seemed that for all the bulk and muscle Guy the Gorilla possessed, he still had a heart.

Thirteen

The grey skies which had gripped Bristol for the last month lifted overnight, and now a piercing low sun burned holes in the retinas of all eastward facing drivers. Sitting at his desk, Cornelius tried and failed to adjust his eyes to the office's ineffectual strip lighting. He was mulling over whether he should make an appointment to see the optician, when a red file landed in front of him with a theatrical thump, almost decanting his second coffee of the day into the heart of his computer keyboard. He looked up to see Andy Statton, grinning.

'What are you so pleased about?'

Cornelius knew it would have something to do with the papers on his desk, but he wanted the DC to work for the praise he was expecting.

'Some morning reading for you, sir.'

'Oh goody, and there was me wondering what to do with my day. Educate me Andy, what have you found? Is Megan not the angel we thought?'

'I have some info on her, however, whilst I was digging around in the dirt, I thought I'd also take a look at a certain Polish food distributor.'

Cornelius couldn't make up his mind whether to bawl Statton out for doing something he hadn't asked him to or cuss himself for forgetting.

'Go on.'

'Remember the limp?' He paused, waiting for Cornelius to nod a confirmation. 'He didn't get it in a car accident. He had the shit kicked out of him by three men in Stockport seven years ago. It left him with permanent nerve damage in his leg.'

'Okay, so Mr Slowik lied about his injury – I'm not sure I'd want to own up to taking a beating.'

'Maybe, but that's not the good bit – do you want to know why he took a beating?'

'Do tell.'

'Rafael Slowik was stalking a woman – allegedly – it was never proven. At the time he managed a food distribution company in Stockport, and guess what? He took a shine to one of his employees. The victim Lucy Rockett was twenty-five, single, lived alone and didn't have many friends. For two months Slowik pestered her at work, followed her around Stockport and bombarded her with text messages.'

Cornelius straightened in his chair, his curiosity aroused.

'If he was bombarding her with messages there's no allegedly about it; that would be enough evidence by itself.'

'Not if they have come from a pay-as-you-go phone which was never found. Lucy came from a dysfunctional family with an impressive range of convictions from GBH and ABH to theft and receiving stolen goods. When her brother found out about Slowik, he and two of his most eloquent friends took the matter up using the dull end of a tyre lever.'

'Interesting.'

'Slowik was never pursued for stalking mainly because Lucy refused to press charges but also because there wasn't the stomach to go after a man who had already been punished, albeit outside the confines of the law – he had spent two months in hospital. The local police were far more interested in prosecuting Lucy's psychopathic brother, who served two years as a result. Apparently, soon after Mr Slowik came out of hospital, he left Stockport and headed south.'

'Any other previous infractions we should know about?'

'Nothing else I could find in the UK. He moved over from Poland about ten years ago; we'd need to contact the Policja.'

Cornelius assumed the main reason Slowik used illegal immigrants was that they were cheaper; he could pay them less than the minimum wage and they had bugger-all in the way of employment rights. It also meant that his workers were less likely to go to the police for fear of deportation; a handy little situation if you liked to prey on pretty young employees.

'That's good, Andy. Now, what about what I asked you to do in the first place?'

Statton looked crestfallen and Cornelius made a mental note to call into the bakery and get him some *well done* doughnuts.

'Not a great deal on Megan I'm afraid.' He paused before breaking out into another grin. 'Other than an assault charge against her two years ago that was dropped.'

Cornelius knew he should have checked Megan out thoroughly himself, but there was no time to worry about that now – this was a new lead.

'There's the official view and the local gossip. Officially, she was charged with GBH for beating a business associate of her father over the head with a twelve inch spanner. The charge was dropped when the victim withdrew his statement and refused to identify his attacker.'

Cornelius closed his eyes and sighed. Guy Dart had specifically mentioned Megan's violent temper and now it looked like he had been telling the truth. Judging by the eager look on Statton's face, there was more to come.

'And the gossip? Unofficially, of course.'

'The rumour was that the victim was trying to avoid paying Manny for his services. He was having a heated argument with Manny at the workshop when Megan appears spanner in hand and clobbers him. Manny was angry about it and had a go at her, so she gave him a black eye as well.'

'Charming. Why was the victim's statement withdrawn?'

'Danny Palmer's mob waded in. The last thing they needed was for Manny to be in any kind of trouble – he stored too much gear for Palmer. So, they blowtorched one of the victim's testicles and, surprisingly enough, he agreed to drop the complaint.'

Cornelius shivered at the thought; he'd probably have agreed to do the same.

'Okay, we'd better have a chat with young Miss Thompson. In the meantime, it would be a good idea to pass your findings on to the boss.'

'What findings?'

Laverty's voice was low and growly. Statton visibly jumped at the sudden arrival of the chief inspector; Cornelius caught sight of his dark expression and knew he needed to tread carefully.

'Ah, morning, sir.' Cornelius tried to sound more cheerful than he felt. 'Andy's dug up some interesting information on the owner of the food distribution company where Pippa worked.'

Without waiting for a response, Laverty turned on his heels,

'My office inspector – now!'

The ferocity of the command left Cornelius in no doubt of Laverty's mood and he followed him into his office wondering what the bloody hell he had done now.

'Sit.'

'I'm not a bloody dog,' snapped Cornelius.

The veins bulged on Laverty's domed forehead.

'I wish you were; at least dogs do what they're told.' Cornelius opened his mouth to form a reply but Laverty stopped him. 'Karen can't wait to bust you, so when I tell her you have been pursuing a line of enquiry on the Pippa Hobbs case, when you have specifically been told not to, do you know what she will do?'

Cornelius closed his eyes and held his breath, but it wasn't enough to stop a fuse from blowing inside his head.

'That fucking sums it up nicely. You automatically assume I've fucked up. Weren't you listening? Andy was the one who found out about Slowik, and he's done a bloody good job. I had nothing to do with it, not that you give a shit.'

Laverty leaned forward and fixed his unblinking eyes on Cornelius.

'You can cut the self-pity crap. You've not exactly covered yourself in glory recently and that is entirely of your own doing.' His voice took on a mellower tone. 'But, it's a fair comment Lucas. I apologise for jumping to conclusions.'

This unexpected apology took the wind out of Cornelius's sails. He had forgotten Ross Laverty was a fair person who never lost sight of the victims who needed justice.

'There is something else I need to double check, however, and this may be your final chance.' He paused to make sure his comment had sunk in. 'You told Karen you had not been to Pippa's flat. Do you want to change that statement?'

'No, why should I?'

'By going to her flat, I don't just mean inside it. Have you been anywhere near it?'

'Which part of no don't you understand?'

Laverty leaned back and rubbed the dome of his head, something he always did when troubled.

'We have started making door-to-door enquiries at the flats. One of the neighbours has reported hearing a drunk man outside Pippa's flat, shouting.' Another pause and a rub of the head, 'John's gone to take a full statement, but the gist of it is that they heard this person banging on her door, demanding to be let in. Somebody we haven't been able to identify asked him to shut up or they would call the police, to which the man is supposed to have replied that he was the police.' Another pause. 'He identified himself as Lucas.'

The ambient sounds which make up police station life became amplified inside Cornelius's head. He was vaguely aware of Laverty droning on about waiting to see exactly what the statement said but was fixed on the revelation that someone calling himself Lucas conveniently made a scene outside Pippa's flat. His denial about being at the flat wouldn't hold out for long, and if Brawley took the neighbour's statement, he wouldn't have any compunction about leading the witness to give a damning account. Time was running out.

'Lucas!'

'Sorry, what?' his eyes focused back on his boss.

'You know as well as I do, if you've done nothing wrong then you have nothing to fear.'

Cornelius stood up to leave. 'Try saying that to Colin Stag.'

***

Cornelius's dark mood didn't lift for the remainder of the morning. A murder investigation was well underway and he was being publicly side-lined. The gossip machine in Gloucester Road station raged at full pelt as to the reason for his exclusion – most of it correct, which pissed him off even more.

In the absence of having any meaningful work to do, Cornelius cleared out all his remaining emails and was about to start the mammoth task of tidying his desk when he noticed a dog-eared paperback book perched on the corner of it. Neil Stokes had left *Injured, remade* for him to read. Cornelius flipped it open and read the opening paragraphs. Two grammar mistakes on page one eliminated what miniscule interest he had in the biography, and a quick glance of the back page showed that it was printed by a vanity publisher. If Neil paid a quid for the book, he had been overcharged by 99 pence.

Concluding that his productivity in the office was not going to rise beyond sod-all, Cornelius decided to rattle another cage. For this one, he reluctantly acknowledged, he needed a baby sitter.

'Come on young Statton, I think I owe you a doughnut or two.'

Andy knew Cornelius had an alternative motive, but hunger pangs were growing inside him and the mention of food was enough to galvanise him. Cornelius kept his promise and stopped at Jane's Bakery, and Statton perked up, considerably, when Cornelius offered to buy him a bacon sandwich. They returned to Cornelius's car where they sat in silence while they ate. By the time they'd finished, Statton had a contented look on his face, which can only be achieved when hunger is satisfied with stodgy food. It promptly changed when Cornelius told him where they were going next.

'I know this isn't anything to do with me, sir, but should you be going to see Marcus Weavell?'

'What I am doing, is following up a lead on a missing person. It is a matter of coincidence that the person I need to speak to happens to be a drug-pushing pimp I would happily lower head first into an industrial mincer.'

'Not a fan then?'

'Marcus Weavell is a Romeo Pimp, which means he uses charm and flattery to attract the attention of vulnerable girls. He gets them hooked on heroin, which he supplies on the cheap, but in return they have to work for him as whores. He's rarely physically abusive, but with the threatening presence of Guy the Gorilla, they don't give him too much trouble, and if they have any trouble from the punters, Guy wades in and sorts them out. Over the years, Weasel has deliberately kept his operation relatively small to avoid too much attention from the likes of Danny Palmer.'

'You said he brought down Palmer though.'

'It was a classic case of David kicking Goliath squarely in the nuts. We think Palmer was trying to extend his prostitution racket and wanted to operate in Weasel's area. The drugs squad had a tip off about a drop on the edge of Chittening Industrial Estate and arrived to find Danny Palmer staring back at them – he's normally way too smart to get close to the merchandise. Apparently, the look on his face when they uncovered a quantity of heroin in his boot was priceless.' Even now, the thought made Cornelius grin. 'With the volume of skag Palmer had he should have been done for dealing, but he has a seriously expensive barrister who managed to get him off with possession and a five year sentence.'

'So, was it Weasel who stitched him up?'

'Well, Palmer thinks so. And the only reason there hasn't been a hit on Weasel is that Palmer wants him for himself when he gets out. Even with Guy the Gorilla by my side, I would not want to be on the receiving end of that!'

It took 15 minutes in the uncharacteristically light traffic for Cornelius to reach his destination. He eased his car between a gleaming black Jeep and a grimy light blue camper van which looked as if it was being used as a permanent home.

'Why have we stopped?'

'So, we can have a wee break and buy some souvenirs. Why the bloody hell do you think we have stopped?'

'Is this where Weasel lives?' Statton couldn't hide the incredulity in his voice. They were in the middle of a large council estate in the heart of Knowle. 'With all his rackets he must earn a bomb. Why does he still live here?'

'Not everyone is driven by money, Andy. Anyway, can you see the likes of Weasel living in the middle of Clifton?'

They had barely made it to the front door when it opened from the inside. A woman, who could have been aged anywhere between 40 and 65, filled the door frame. Jet black hair, permed into tight ringlets, framed an artificially tanned face, and a comprehensive range of self-administered tattoos ran down the length of her sizeable arms. Her vast frame was adorned with enough gold jewellery to give Fort Knox a run for its money and the facial expression that greeted Cornelius confirmed his expectation that a warm welcome did not await him in the Weavell household.

'You've got a nerve showing your face here.'

'Hello Mary, nice to see you too,' chirped Cornelius. 'Is your husband in?'

'No.'

'Oh, so whose legs are those sticking out from behind yesterday's copy of the Sun?'

'What?'

'Mary, I could see him in the lounge reading his paper as I walked up your pathway.'

'Fuckin' idiot.'

Cornelius didn't know if she meant him or her husband for not making himself scarce at the arrival of the police at his front door, then a voice emanated from within.

'Let him in, Mary, and make sure you offer him a cup of tea.'

Mary shifted her bulk to let the unwanted visitors inside and raised a pierced eyebrow by way of an invitation for a drink.

'Not for me thanks, Mary.' Cornelius knew that his tea would have more than milk and sugar added.

'What about your pet poodle?'

Statton shook his head, thinking the same as Cornelius.

The two officers walked into the lounge which was full of kitsch ornaments and pictures, the majority having a feline theme. The walls were covered in crimson-red flock wallpaper organised in a paisley pattern and there were cream shag pile carpets on the floor. Not for the first time, Cornelius was reminded that money could buy anything except taste.

Weasel sat in an oversized red leather sofa which fully enveloped his slender frame. Pretending to be engrossed in his paper, he only lowered it at the sound of air being expelled from the sofa cushions as his guests sat down.

'I wouldn't make yourself too comfy, inspector, this isn't going to take long.' Mild surprise spread across his face as he looked up. 'Ah, Detective Constable Statton, you've come along for the ride, have you? Or are you here to make sure your boss doesn't do anything stupid with a kitchen utensil again?'

A pair of reading glasses were perched on Weasel's nose, something Cornelius hadn't seen before; age was catching up with the police and criminals alike.

'I'm sure you know why we're here, Mr Weavell, undoubtedly Guy has already told you.'

'Told me what?'

Weasel obviously had no intention of making life easy for his visitor, but Cornelius was spoiling for a fight. Only the presence of Andy Statton held him back from unleashing a full verbal assault.

'So, your pet gorilla didn't tell you we had words yesterday? Bloody hell, Marcus, I'd sack him if I were you.'

'Right now, I'm more worried for my personal safety; if you tell me why you're here I'll happily answer any questions just to ensure you leave my house without assaulting me again.'

Alarm bells rang in Cornelius's head. For Weasel to be this polite meant one thing; he was recording their conversation. He reminded himself to be on his best behaviour and deliberately adopted a soft, conciliatory tone.

'When was the last time you saw Emmanuel Thompson, Mr Weavell?'

'Who?'

Cornelius wasn't going to rise to the bait. 'You probably know him better as Manny.'

'Oh him. Let me think, not since the trial I suppose.'

'No contact at all?'

'None.'

'You didn't feel any need to speak to the man who gave evidence against you? Ask him why he did it?'

Staring at Cornelius over the top of his reading glasses, a thin smile came over Weasel's face.

'Why would I do that? I'm not a vindictive man, inspector.'

'Do you know why I am asking?'

'Not at all. Mr Thompson and I are merely former business associates. I don't know what trouble he's in, and to be honest I'm not interested. Now, if there is nothing else, inspector, I have other important matters to attend to.' To make his point, he reached for the paper.

This exchange was going nowhere, and Cornelius decided it was time to lob the grenade that Guy had given him.

'Before I go, Mr Weavell, there is one other matter.' Cornelius tried to sound as nonchalant as possible. 'We are investigating a number of missing persons, and recently your name has been linked to one of them. She is a sex worker and goes by the name of Tracey Devine.' He flipped open his pad as if to remind himself of the details but the specifics were still firmly etched in his memory. 'Let's see, she was 5 feet 4 inches tall, slim with brunette hair usually shaped in a bob, and she was last seen in this area about a year ago. Does that ring any bells?'

Weasel's head remained buried in his paper, but Cornelius noticed a brief stiffening in his arms at the mention of Tracey.

'Mr Weavell? If this is inconvenient I can either come back at another time or we can arrange to discuss this at the station.' This was crap of course but Cornelius was mindful that his words were being recorded and he had no intention of giving Weasel any ammunition on which to base a complaint.

Lowering his paper, Weasel gazed at Cornelius over the top of his glasses.

'Firstly, none of the ladies I work with are sex workers; they are professional escorts who operate within the law at all times.'

Statton started to laugh but managed to restrain himself so that the noise which came of his mouth sounded like a stifled snort.

'What did you say her name was?' Weasel made a good job of sounding interested.

'Tracey Devine, although we don't think that was her real name.'

Weasel gently folded his paper, placed it on his lap and stared off into space as if in deep thought.

'Ah, yes, come to think of it I do remember giving Tracey some work a while ago. One day she told me she was returning home and wouldn't be available for work anymore. I wished her all the best and never saw her again.'

'Did she say where home was?'

'To be honest, Inspector Cornelius, I can't remember. As you say it was almost a year ago. I think she came from the London area but I can't be sure.'

'Do you know her real name, sir?' said Statton.

'I only knew her as Tracey I'm afraid.' If Weasel had been unsettled by hearing her name, he had now fully regained his composure and was answering the questions with comfortable ease.

'Don't you have any employee records you can check?'

'Technically, I don't employ anyone, Detective Constable Statton. I act as an intermediary, introducing girls to clients. They are responsible for their own tax affairs, so I don't need to keep records of that nature.'

This time it was Cornelius's turn to stifle a laugh. 'You weren't upset at having one of your girls leave you?'

'Why would I? I don't operate fixed-term contracts, so any girls I deal with are free to come and go as they please.'

Cornelius was almost impressed to hear Weasel talk like a consummate businessman rather than the drug peddling pimp he was, but he knew that nothing else would come from this conversation.

'Thank you for your time, Mr Weavell, if you hear anything from Mr Thompson or recall any information about Tracey, will you let me know please?'

'Of course, inspector. Good day to you.'

With the charade over, Cornelius and Statton gratefully exited the Weavell household. They had barely made it to the rusty gate when they heard Mary call after them.

'Wait, I wanna word with you, Cornelius.' The tone of her voice suggested it wasn't going to be limited to just the one word. 'You've got a fuckin' nerve comin' here after what you did to my husband.' Her voice was unnecessarily loud – a performance for the benefit of the neighbours who would have spotted them entering the house fifteen minutes earlier. 'He's done nothing wrong and all you do is come here and accuse him of all kinds of shit that you can't pin on anyone else.'

She lunged at Cornelius with a half-hearted slap of her palm against his chest. Cornelius dodged her, but there was just enough contact to feel something being stuffed into his jacket pocket.

'And don't fuckin' come back.' Her tirade over, she turned around and waddled back into the house.

Statton stared at Cornelius, 'Are you letting her get away with that? Assaulting a police officer?'

Cornelius said nothing and walked back to the car. Statton followed shaking his head.

Once seated in his car, he reached inside his pocket and dug out the note that Mary had clumsily put there. He unravelled the crumpled paper and read the hastily scribbled contents aloud.

Tracey's real name is Kelly Ann Jones, and nobody knows what happened to her.

'There's a surprise,' he said, 'it seems there's a soft side to Mary as well.'

'What do you mean – as well?'

Before Cornelius could respond, his phone rang.

'Time to go, Andy. Manny Thompson has been found.'

MARCH

It was time. He intended to savour every delicious, beautiful minute of it – after all, he'd earned it. He'd already decided to keep her alive for at least a few months. There were several scenarios to play out and she was fit enough to endure it. If she decided to try anything stupid, like a hunger strike, he'd simply tighten the chain mechanism to keep her secure, ram food into her mouth and block her airways until she swallowed. The thought of it made something stir in his groin and he mentally added a session of force feeding to his planned itinerary, regardless of whether she had eaten or not.

From the corner of the room a tiny light changed from red to green telling him the batteries were fully charged. He loaded them into his camera and changed the setting to video. Slinging the camera over his shoulder, he picked up a tripod, a tube of lubricant and a hand paddle he'd fashioned from a hardwood cheeseboard bought from a charity shop. Before reaching the stairway, he stopped to look at the wall clock and did a quick mental calculation. Three hours should be enough for the first session.

The cellar light wasn't bright enough to provide the illumination needed for filming, so he plugged in a portable LED work light and set up the tripod. He was in a good mood, whistling a tune he'd heard earlier on the radio and smiling at the timing of it. Quite what Britney Spears had had in mind when she sang *Hit me baby, one more time* he wasn't sure, but it had a sweet significance now.

With all his props in place, he turned to Alisha hoping to see the terror in her eyes. Instead, her head was tilted back and away from him. It didn't occur to him that anything might be wrong until he noticed her arm, which flopped over the side of the bed, the back of her hand resting on the stone floor twitching with random spasms. He edged closer, until he got better view of her face which leaned against the grimy wall adjacent to the bed.

Through the slits of her flickering eyes, all he could see was white sclera. Her open mouth sagged to one side and a pool of saliva had formed on the sheet beneath her chin. He looked down and realised it wasn't just her arm convulsing, it was her whole body.

She looked like she was OD'ing, but, surely, she couldn't be? He glanced down at the chains and remembered he hadn't tightened them when he last left her, thinking she deserved a limited amount of movement. Had she taken some drugs? Was she having an epileptic fit? He leaned over to check her breathing.

In that instant, her arms shot up and she grabbed the sides of his head, pulling him towards her. He tried to pull his head away but her nails had sunk into his flesh, and his movement backwards only served to deepen their penetration. Just as the agony from her claws kicked in, there was another searing pain as she sank her teeth into his right ear. His scream was deafening as her incisors sliced through the cartilage. With her teeth locked into their target, she let go of one side of his head before quickly stabbing her nails into another part, dragging the flesh away.

He swung his left fist at her head. It missed its target and hit the bed frame instead, smashing his knuckles against the cold hard iron. His second punch bounced off the top of her head but the third attempt connected with her cheek bone and his ear was released from her jaws. He yanked his bleeding head back and took another swing at Alisha. His punch crashed into her upper jaw and she released the grip of her left hand. She still clung to his head with her right hand but her nails were losing their anchoring, and with a swift thrust of his right arm he tore her away and fell backwards, out of her reach.

'You bitch! You fucking, fucking, bitch!' he screamed. Blood streamed out from his damaged ear and an incandescent rage engulfed him, fuelled by the violent, stinging pain and the sight of Alisha, who glared at him with a rebellious, blood-soaked grin.

'You think you can do this do me? Do you?'

He leapt back on to his feet and moved towards her, ready to beat her unconscious. He drew his fist back, but before landing a blow he caught sight of the defiance and strength in her eyes. She needed something else to teach her a lesson, and he had just the thing.

Within five minutes he returned to the cellar. Alisha was still smiling; she hadn't even bothered to try and wipe away the blood on her face. This antagonised him even further.

Shaking with anger, he tightened the chains so that she could barely move, before grabbing her arm and applying a tourniquet. The smile on her face gave way to fear and he felt a brief sense of satisfaction at doing something she wasn't expecting.

'What are you doing?' she whispered. 'Please, no, not that stuff.'

He smacked the veins in her forearm which started to engorge with blood.

'I'm sorry ... I didn't mean to ... please, don't.'

Normally, he would have enjoyed hearing her grovel for her life, but his mind was still clouded by a demonic red mist. He jabbed the needle into her arm with an unnecessary force and injected her with a syringe of Afghan heroin.

Tears poured down her face as the cost of her defiance became apparent. Within seconds, the drug took control and she was lost. A feeling of warmth and well-being collided with a dizziness she had never experienced. All her pain, anger, resentment and frustration evaporated along with the weight of the cares and worries she carried with her on a daily basis.

When the darkness finally came, she wasn't frightened; she gracefully floated into the heart of it. It was a void from which she would never return.

By the time he returned to her lifeless body, the anger which drove him to kill her had been replaced by a simmering resentment and frustration. This wasn't his fault; she had made him do it. Alisha shouldn't be dead yet; the debt was not fully settled. Getting her here had taken months of planning and the stupid bitch had ruined it all. This couldn't be it, there had to be more.

He slowly shut the door to the cellar and climbed the stairs back up to the light, his mind fully focused on what to do next. A new plan was emerging in his head and he smiled as he congratulated himself. All he needed to do was watch and wait – his time would come again.

Fourteen

When Cornelius parked his car on the edge of Leigh Woods, the weak sun was about to disappear behind the horizon, and the stinging night air warned of a hard frost. Cornelius and Statton walked the short distance to an area of the picturesque woodland which had been cordoned off by the police.

Showing their ID's to the young constable guarding the crime scene, they lifted the tape and walked through a hive of police activity. As Ross Laverty saw Cornelius approach, he dismissed the three uniformed officers who were taking his instructions and turned to face his inspector.

'Ah Lucas, I'm glad you're here. You can do it.'

'Do what?'

'The initial ID. We're pretty sure it's Manny Thompson as his wallet was in his pocket, but we've not been able to confirm it yet. You're the first person on site who knew him.'

Cornelius looked around him, taking in the full topography of Leigh Woods. 'Not the most remote location in which to dump a body, is it? Was he hidden well?'

'Find out for yourself, kit up and get in there. Andy, follow me, I want you taking statements.'

Statton was grateful he'd been spared the main event and given a comparatively easy job. The last time he had attended a murder scene he almost fainted and recycled his lunch over a DI's shoes. The fact that the shoes belonged to Brawley had unknowingly endeared him to Cornelius, but it was an event which made him consider resigning from CID. It was only the calm and reasoning tones of Malcolm Williams that persuaded him to stay.

Cornelius climbed into his protective gear and fixed his mask in place before entering the white tent protecting the crime scene. It took a short time for his eyes to adjust to the bright halogen lights which had been placed in the corners, but finally, they focused on two people hunched over a partially obscured body laid out on the woodland floor. Neither of them looked up.

'I said I would need at least an hour, now piss off and let me do my job.'

'Hello Jo, still full of warmth and charm I see.'

Dr Joanne Scutt looked up; although only her eyes were visible beneath her suit, Cornelius could see a change in expression as she clapped eyes on him.

'Bloody hell, Lucas Cornelius! I thought you had been transferred to traffic ages ago. Why are you in here ruining my crime scene?'

Cornelius grinned. Whilst the pathologist scared the living daylights out of most of Avon and Somerset Constabulary, he knew her bark was much fiercer than her bite. Two years previously he had stopped a car which had been weaving dangerously along Ladies Mile late in the evening. The driver, who had virtually fallen out of the vehicle on to the tarmac, was Jo. Instead of calling for back-up, he'd moved her car to safety before bundling her into his own vehicle and driving her the short distance to his place where he'd laid her out on his sofa to sleep the alcohol off. Jane had given him an ear-bending and a half at the sight of another woman sprawled out in her lounge, but Cornelius recognised a troubled soul when he saw one. He'd not done it to curry favour, but Jo

Scutt never forgot his kindness, despite the sharpness of her tongue when she spoke to him.

'I'm here to do an ID. If it's who we think it is, I've had dealings with him,' said Cornelius.

'Okay, have a gander, but if you touch anything I'll ram this pencil into any orifice of my choosing.'

The pathologist and her assistant moved to one side, giving Cornelius a clear view. Despite the natural deterioration of the body, it was immediately evident it was Manny Thompson.

'I know how much you dislike answering questions before you have the body on your slab, but are there any signs of a spanner-shaped bash to his head?'

'If you know I don't like answering them, why ask?'

'If there is, there's somebody I need to pull in right away.'

She paused for a moment to weigh up her response.

'There are no obvious signs of blunt force trauma anywhere, let alone spanner-shaped ones. In fact, there are no obvious signs of a cause of death at all. The only observation I am prepared to make at this time is that he's not been here long.'

'Do you mean he's not been snacked on by any woodland animals yet?'

'Precisely, but it doesn't mean he's recently deceased. You'll …'

'Have to wait for the report. Yep, I get that.' Cornelius risked one more question. 'Do you think whoever put him here wanted him to be found?'

'That, Inspector Cornelius, is your job. Now, you will please do me the enormous kindness of sodding off.'

Cornelius obliged. One other highly unpleasant task remained and he knew he was the best person to do it.

***

A thin shaft of bright light broke through the curtain and slowly travelled up the face of the sleeping Cornelius. As it hit his eyelids he stirred, although his mind was foggy from disturbed sleep and tortured dreams. The last time he'd looked at the clock it was 4 a.m. and sleep had still not come calling for him. He was feeling pretty sorry for himself when his mind flashed back to his conversation with Megan.

Elliot Chorley had been at the crime scene, talking to anybody who would make eye contact with him. Cornelius was rarely in agreement with Karen Liatt, but when she described Chorley as an odious little shit with the morals of a sewer rat, he fully concurred. The reporter from the *Bristol Herald* rarely let the truth get in the way of a good story and would have no compunction about breaking the news to Megan about her missing father. He'd also have a photographer on hand to capture the moment for posterity. It wouldn't be long before Chorley worked out whose body was in the tent, so Cornelius volunteered to tell Megan in person about the identification.

His motivation had been two-fold: firstly, he felt a moral obligation to tell her about Manny, especially following their recent conversations, but he also wanted to see her reaction. The revelation of her violent streak changed her status from concerned relative to potential suspect, although the absence of blunt force trauma on Manny's body made her direct involvement less likely. He'd seen enough emotional grief during his career with the police to distinguish the real thing from pretence, and her reaction would tell him one way or the other whether she'd had a hand in his death.

Megan opened the door to her Morley Square house to see a sombre looking Cornelius with a family liaison officer standing discreetly behind him. In an instant, her expression changed and she backed away from Cornelius, putting her hand up in a bid to stop him from speaking. Her legs gave way, reducing her to an awkward heap on the porch floor. The piercing wail that followed would haunt Cornelius for months to come.

Cornelius stayed with Megan and the family support officer longer than he needed to. Laverty told him to go home afterwards and report to the briefing in the morning. However, Cornelius knew if he left Megan's house too quickly, he would be unable to resist the gravitational pull of The Flask and he'd start the following day with a screaming hangover.

Cornelius forced Megan out of his mind and turned his thoughts to his conversations with Guy the Gorilla and Weasel. Guy had caught him off guard when he had asked him to quiz Weasel about the missing girl. Guy's story was that he'd met Tracey Devine when asked to deal with a punter who tried to pay with forged notes. Once he persuaded the gentleman concerned it was in the interests of his, currently, intact limbs to pay with real cash, Tracey thanked him by buying him a pint in his favourite watering hole. They developed a relationship of sorts, but they had to keep it from Weasel who would not have tolerated his enforcer shagging one of his girls for free. One day, when they were sharing a pint of Thatcher's at the George Inn, she told Guy that she had to go away for a few days to see an elderly relative. He never saw or heard from her again. Weasel went nuts when he found out she had disappeared but refused to do anything about it. Guy wanted to report her missing, but Weasel thought she had probably buggered off to whore somewhere else and wasn't going to waste any more time on the pathetic bitch. Going directly to the police was not an option for Guy, so the lovelorn gorilla had to suffer in silence until Cornelius came calling.

He'd made Cornelius promise not to tell Weasel that he'd reported it, something Cornelius happily agreed to. It represented the first step towards having Guy in his proverbial pocket.

Cornelius now knew Tracey's real name was Kelly Ann Jones. She had gone missing at the same time as Jane, and he hadn't been able to get the comparison out of his head. Initially, huge amounts of police resources had been put towards finding Jane. CCTV had been checked, neighbours interviewed and statements taken. By contrast, Kelly had gone missing and no one, apart from Guy, had batted an eyelid. As far as Weasel was concerned, she was nothing more than a commodity and once he realised he wasn't going to make any more money out of her, he'd forgotten her. With no other friends or family to support her, Kelly's disappearance had hardly been noticed. She deserved to be treated the in same way his wife had, yet because of her profession she had been ignored.

With only three hours sleep under his belt Cornelius had to get back to work. Manny had been murdered, Pippa's disappearance was now being treated as murder and he was inextricably mixed up in both of them.

Fighting a desire to pull the covers over his head and stay there for another five hours, Cornelius forced himself out of bed. He looked in on a gently snoring Daniel and decided against waking him. Daniel would probably ask his father to wait whilst he showered and dressed so he could have a lift to college and, today, Cornelius needed to be at the station early.

***

Scheduled to begin at 7.30 the morning briefing was going to be important. With the discovery of Manny's body the day before, work would begin in earnest to catch his killer. Teams would be drafted in from other stations, alongside specialists in forensic analysis – all trying to answer the who, what, when, where and why questions of his death. Some people would have been working all through the previous night.

The bitter wind reminded all who felt it that the respite of spring was still a few months away. Even the short journey from the car to the station entrance was enough to take some of the air out of Cornelius's lungs, causing him to take the stairs one at a time instead of his usual two step approach.

Cornelius quietly entered the packed briefing room. There was an air of expectation tinged with the excitement that accompanies the launch of a major investigation. He did not want a high profile, so carefully chose the furthest seat from the window, at the end of the line of chairs, where clean air was already at a premium.

He scanned the room, checking out the faces of those he knew and those he didn't. About half the people in the room were recognisable, the remainder had been drafted in to help with the murder investigation. He spotted Andy Statton sitting in the far corner of the room. He was one of the red-eyed brigade who had been up all night, but still he would not have looked out of place in a fashion parade. It was not until the superintendent got up to speak that he noticed who was sitting next to her. Deputy Chief Constable Rick McCartney was gracing them with his presence; Cornelius suspected it would be a link to Pippa's case which brought him here, rather than the death of one of Bristol's minor criminals.

The assembled staff duly fell silent as Liatt's charmless briefing echoed around the room. With the DCC sitting in, this would be an investigation which followed the prescribed protocols to the letter. Cornelius's guess about Rick-with-a-silent-P's presence was confirmed early, when the superintendent covered the circumstances surrounding Manny's disappearance and the discovery of his body in Leigh Woods, before moving on to talk about the discovery of the finger linked to a missing person known as Pippa Hobbs, whose disappearance was being treated as murder. There was one obvious question hanging in the room which no one wanted to ask. Eventually, a young DC Cornelius didn't recognise, plucked up the courage.

'Are the two cases linked, ma'am?'

'There is one potential link, however it is quite weak. I don't want people being distracted, so for the moment we are following the standard lines of enquiry.'

One potential link. There it was in three words, the elephant in the room. Cornelius tried not to react, but he could feel all eyes on him. He was the only known link to both cases and rumour had spread fast through the ranks. His discomfort increased as tasks were identified and assigned to teams and individuals. The only person who didn't have a task at the end of it was him, and as the team was dismissed, Karen Liatt looked directly at Cornelius with a sickly sweet expression on her face and said, 'Inspector Cornelius, can the DCC and I have a word with you please – in my office?'

Cornelius grimly followed Liatt and the DCC out of the briefing room and into her office in the CID suite feeling like a condemned man taking the final steps towards his execution. With his back to the glass wall, he could feel a myriad of eyes boring into the back of his head from the office outside. Bets were probably being taken on his fate.

The arrival of Laverty wasn't unexpected; what unnerved Cornelius was the spindly ponytailed man who accompanied him. Dressed in black chinos and a polo-necked sweater, he was in his early twenties and wore Joe 90 style glasses. In Cornelius's youth, glasses like that had been the subject of school ground ridicule – now they were a fashion statement. The young man said nothing, opting to look awkwardly at the floor instead. With his usual impersonal efficiency, the deputy chief constable launched in without any meaningless courtesies.

'Please hand your mobile phone to Ashley,' he said, indicating the man with the Joe 90 glasses.

Cornelius paused, his furrowed brow indicating to McCartney he hadn't got a clue why he should hand over his phone, but the DCC was in no mood to appease his troublesome inspector.

'That wasn't a request, it was an order – pass it over now, please.'

Cornelius shrugged his shoulders, reached into his jacket pocket and tossed the phone at Ashley. He deliberately threw it awkwardly in the hope Ashley would fumble and drop it. The young technician caught it easily, however, and promptly pressed some of the buttons.

'It's locked,' he mumbled, 'what is the PIN number?'

Anticipating a belligerent reply from Cornelius, Laverty interjected.

'Please, Lucas, you know we can break it if we need to, but time is of the essence and it will help you if you assist us now.'

It was a line Cornelius had delivered to suspects more times than he cared to remember; now it was being used on him. Laverty's soft delivery won him over.

'It's four zeros.'

Ashley looked up with incredulity.

'Haven't you altered the default setting?'

Cornelius said nothing and shrugged his shoulders, aware that this grilling had opened with a demonstration of his technical incompetence. Without saying another word, Ashley left the office with Cornelius's mobile phone in hand.

The door had barely shut before McCartney began his inquisition. His aggressive style, along with his short stocky build and broad head had earned him the nickname of 'the Staffie'.

'When was the last time you had any contact with Emmanuel Thompson?'

'Do I need federation representation for this meeting, sir?'

'I don't give a shit! Answer the question!'

Cornelius concluded that co-operation was the best strategy. He didn't want to cause a delay in the murder investigation, although he was equally unwilling to give them a bloody great stick with which to beat him.

'The last time I saw Mr Thompson was at the trial of Marcus Weavell a week ago. At the request of Superintendent Liatt I called to his premises on the Friday, I think her precise words were, "dump any charge you can muster up against him."' He paused for a response to his counter attack but was disappointed not to see a single face wince. He composed himself and continued. 'Mr Thompson wasn't on the premises so we spoke to his daughter Megan who was unaware of his whereabouts.'

The fact that Cornelius now knew Megan had lied was something he intended to keep to himself for now. Laverty scribbled notes whilst Liatt leaned forward, watching Cornelius intently. The DCC continued with the questions.

'Did you send him a text that Friday evening asking to meet with him?'

'No. Megan says that's what Manny told her, but my guess is, he said the first thing that came into his head. I have already discussed this with DCI Laverty, sir.'

If mud was going to be slung around, Cornelius was keen to share in its distribution.

A knock on the door interrupted proceedings and Liatt waved Ashley back into the room. He put Cornelius's phone on the desk and handed McCartney a note, which he glanced at and passed to Liatt expressionless. Cornelius sensed a further darkening of the mood in the room. McCartney fixed Cornelius with a hard glare.

'Emmanuel Thompson's phone was found in his jacket pocket and, as you would expect, it has been examined. A text was received at 17:34 last Friday.' He paused, staring unblinkingly ahead. 'That text was from you, inspector.'

The pressure of the morning had built up in Cornelius's head and, now, he blew.

'That's complete bollocks and you know it!'

Karen Liatt looked as if the corners of her mouth had risen slightly whereas Laverty appeared crestfallen.

'I wish it was.' The DCC handed Cornelius a copy of the report which detailed the message and the phone number it originated from.

Cornelius read it wide eyed.

> *You are in danger, Weasel has put a hit out on you.*
> *Meet me at 9pm at your lockup, I think I can help. LC.*

Cornelius struggled to comprehend the message in front of him.

'Why did you delete that message?'

Now Cornelius realised why Ashley was analysing his phone, he also knew he wouldn't be getting it back any time soon.

'This is crap. Do you think if I had sent it, I would tell DCI Laverty what Megan had disclosed to me?' He shook his head. 'I'm saying nothing else, this is a fucking witch hunt.'

'We're far from finished.' McCartney's voice was menacing. 'You declared to Superintendent Liatt and DCI Laverty that you had never been anywhere in or near the flat used by Pippa Hobbs. Is that correct?'

'Other than when I called there with Andy Statton, yes.' Cornelius knew he sounded like a confrontational teenager but didn't care.

'We have a statement from a neighbour who overheard a man shouting outside her flat asking to be let in. You can read it for yourself.' McCartney handed over a copy of the statement. 'The person clearly identified themselves as Lucas.'

'This is bullshit! If you bothered to read all the information you would see it was me who found out someone calling themselves Lucas also called at Slowik Foods asking to speak to Pippa – I'd be unlikely to report it, if it was me.'

'True, but you had DC Statton with you and he heard it as well. You could hardly fail to report it when he had witnessed it.'

Cornelius was at a loss for words. He stared open-mouthed at the triumvirate in front of him and could see McCartney positioning himself for the final kill.

'There's one other issue. We've had the DNA results back from the search of Pippa's flat. I won't bore you with all the technical details, but some hairs were found in her bedroom which were not hers. The DNA results were run through the database and we had a familial match. The hairs belong to a close relative of Elaine Cornelius – your sister.'

Total silence. Cornelius knew he was beaten.

'Lucas Cornelius, as of …' McCartney reached over to see the watch on Laverty's arm, 'today at 9.05 a.m. I am suspending you from further duty until such time as a formal investigation has taken place regarding the extent of your involvement with Emmanuel Thompson and Pippa Hobbs.'

***

'I should have seen this coming.'

Cornelius sat in his car, in the station car park, staring out into the morning gloom. His passenger was Ross Laverty whose head brushed uncomfortably against the roof of the Smart car.

The DCI had been assigned the task of escorting Cornelius out of the building and relieving him of his warrant card. He'd wanted to talk to his DI but not in the station where tongues would now be wagging in full force. His car was the only place where they wouldn't be overheard.

'We didn't have a choice Lucas, surely you can see that?'

Cornelius's response was vitriolic. 'I saw that I didn't have any support in there.'

'And how, precisely, was I supposed to defend you against DNA evidence that contradicted your assertion that you had never been inside Pippa's flat and a text message sent from your phone to a man who has turned up dead?' Laverty's exasperation was obvious.

Cornelius shook his head, a stoical smile on his face. 'How many times have we heard someone tell us that they are being stitched up and it's nothing to do with them? Now, here I am thinking the same thing.'

'Look, if they do a thorough investigation and you didn't do this, then you will be cleared.'

Cornelius looked at his boss with disbelief.

'You think this is it? Someone has followed me to plant a severed finger by my side at a convenient moment in front of a CCTV camera; they have deliberately shouted my name outside Pippa's flat and left a message also in my name with her dodgy employer. Now hairs from my head have been planted in her flat in the full knowledge it will be searched. All that, so I am suspended for a few weeks before being exonerated? Pippa's dead. I'm sure of it, and when she turns up you will find something that links her death directly to me and the same will go for Manny when his post-mortem report is complete.'

Laverty puffed his cheeks out. 'I'll do what I can for you Lucas, but if I were you, I'd find some legal representation – I think you are going to need it.'

***

It took every fibre of Cornelius's being not to leave the station and return home via The Flask. Part of him needed to undertake his own investigation away from the constraints of police rules and regulations, the other part wanted to drink himself into oblivion.

Sobriety and reason won, and now he sat in the peace and quiet of his home with a thunderously black coffee for company, pondering his next move.

It was pointless challenging the DNA, Elaine's was on the system following her arrest two years ago for assaulting a bar manager who refused to serve her. The brewery who owned the bar had a zero tolerance approach to violence and pursued a full prosecution. In the end, she was given a penalty notice for being drunk and disorderly, but her DNA had been taken and added to the national database. There were hardly any other living relatives in their family, as both their parents were single children, so it was a 99.9% certainty that the hairs found in Pippa's flat would belong to Cornelius. The question was, how the hell did they get there?

The details of Manny's case fought uncontrollably in his head, distraction only coming when his personal mobile phone buzzed. He rarely had it on during the day, as the only people who ever contacted him on it were Elaine and Daniel. This message was no exception; it was from his sister, and it looked like she was pissed.

Whv U ben up 2 thn. Hop its no u ben tlkd abt lol.

When she was sober all her messages came through in unabbreviated text – the more unintelligible the message – the higher her level of alcohol consumption. Cornelius looked at the clock: Midday. *Sounds about right for Elaine* he thought.

With a growing sense of unease, he fired up his laptop and opened his browser. Typing *Bristol Murder* into Google, his eyes fell on to the first result from the *Bristol Herald's* website. He clicked on the link and a picture of Manny Thompson's smiling face came into view along with the headline:

Body of local criminal found in Leigh Woods

Cornelius quickly scanned down the page looking for a particular name and, sure enough, there it was – Elliot Chorley.

'Bastard!' spat Cornelius.

'Who's a bastard?'

Cornelius jumped and turned around to see his son standing behind him filling the kettle, his limited state of dress suggesting college wasn't on the day's agenda.

'What are you doing here?'

'I live here.'

With no stomach for a fight, Cornelius ignored the comment and went back to the news story that was now trending on the *Herald's* website.

Chorley had found out that the police were linking the murder to another missing persons report and that a senior police officer was linked to both cases and had been suspended pending a full investigation. Cornelius was on the verge of putting his fist through the screen when he became aware of Daniel, staring over his shoulder. Daniel quietly read the story and said nothing, simply turning around and returning to his coffee. Suddenly, he came to an abrupt halt and span around to face his father again.

'Oh shit. Is that why you're home?'

Cornelius closed his eyes and briefly visualised grabbing Elliot Chorley by the scruff of his neck and ramming his pudgy face in a large steaming pile of dog shit.

'It is, and you'd better sit down. You need to know what's going on ...'

Fifteen

Cornelius blew the steam off his first coffee of the morning and mulled over his course of action for the day ahead. The conditions of suspension forbade him from contacting anyone connected with either Manny's or Pippa's case, and if he needed to talk to any serving police officer he had to go through Laverty first. He suspected that his only welcome communication would be his resignation, but he didn't plan to give them the satisfaction. He'd contacted the Police Federation who had agreed to represent him, and his main task for the morning was to submit a report to them, detailing the developments of the last seven days.

Cornelius hadn't fully prepared himself to tell Daniel he'd been suspended from duty, and their impromptu conversation hadn't gone terribly well. He'd been on the verge of telling his son that the missing person was Pippa, when Shagalong Charlotte came bursting in through the kitchen door. Her state of dress or rather the lack of it, explaining why Daniel wasn't at college. Although she looked surprised to see Cornelius, she wasn't embarrassed about being seen in her tee shirt and pants and sat herself down at the table next to Daniel. The sight of his son's braless girlfriend staring inquiringly at him added to Cornelius's sense of discomfort.

It was bad enough that the *Bristol Herald* was on the verge of publishing a story about Manny's death and Pippa's disappearance, but if Shagalong got hold of the full story, anything the *Herald* could do would pale into insignificance. The college was a breeding ground for all sorts of scurrilous gossip about the students and their parents, and with the power of social media at their fingertips the story would spread like wildfire – and mutate in the process.

Cornelius had suggested to Daniel that they talk later in the evening; Daniel had shrugged in vague agreement and disappeared back to his bedroom with Shagalong in tow. That was the last time

Cornelius had seen Daniel, but he knew he would return at some point – probably in search of food or money.

Cornelius was on the verge of switching on his laptop when a sharp rapping noise reverberated around his kitchen. He cursed, audibly. Cornelius usually locked his front gates at night and wasn't expecting any callers. Silently berating himself for forgetting to lock up properly, he opened the front door to find Andy Statton standing there, grinning.

'What are you doing here?'

'Thought you could do with some support.' He held up a bag of doughnuts. 'Do I get a coffee to go with these?'

Cornelius stood to one side to allow his unexpected visitor in. 'Has Laverty sent you?'

Statton's smile vanished and he looked genuinely hurt. 'No, he didn't. I'm not happy with how you've been treated.'

'Do you know how much trouble you are going to be in if the DCI finds out you are here?'

'Tough. The Hobbs investigation would be nowhere without you. I'm not here to give you backhand intelligence, I just wanted you to know you still have some friends at the station.'

The young perfectly-dressed detective constable stared at Cornelius, his chin jutting out, inviting him to challenge his remark. For his part, Cornelius wanted it to be true and not just an exercise in fishing for gossip. One question still troubled him though.

'I thought I locked my gate last night, is the stress getting to me or have you vaulted over the top?'

Statton broke out into a wide grin again. 'Yeah, it's locked, but it's only a six-foot wooden fence. You must have scaled a few of those in your time?'

Cornelius was forced to concede he had and for the first time, he began to relax.

'This is appreciated, Andy. Now, let's get the kettle on – that doughnut has my name on it.'

***

Andy Statton hadn't stayed long with Cornelius, not daring to be out of circulation for too long in case he needed to justify his whereabouts. He brought the day's printed edition of the *Herald* where the story about Manny's killing made page three; it had been kicked off the front page by an article on immigrants getting housing priority over local residents. Cornelius scanned the lead story before deciding it was scaremongering drivel, written by the insidious hand of Elliot Chorley. He flipped to page three and was relieved to see no additional content to what had been published online the previous day. It was only a matter of time before his name became linked to the story, but he had a little time to play with before the ignominy of being publicly identified as a person of interest.

Statton shared as much of the previous day's developments as he could. He estimated that productivity in the station dropped by half in the hour following Cornelius's suspension as people energetically speculated on his fate. As far as Statton knew, there had been no other significant progress in either case and they were still waiting for Jo Scutt's full report to be made available. Fifteen minutes after vaulting over Cornelius's fence, he exited by the more traditional method and headed back to the station to continue with the mundane work surrounding a murder enquiry.

Writing reports was one of Cornelius's pet hates and something he referred to as a necessary evil. It wasn't so much their construction he disliked; it was their inevitable destruction as they were critically dissected by the top brass or – even worse – defence lawyers. They would all be looking to see what was missing from the content, rather than focusing on what was included. Hoping a third injection of caffeine would fire up his neural pathways, he refilled his mug and switched on his laptop, readying himself for a battle with his memory as he attempted to recall, chronologically, the events leading up to his suspension. His email folder bleeped to tell him that messages awaited his attention. The majority of his personal mail usually consisted of nothing more than a collection of spam, occasionally interspersed with progress reports from Daniel's college. Today, one particular email caught his eye – it was from *Youbet*, the online gambling site where he'd placed a bet on the horse Danny Palmer tipped him off about earlier in the week. Going into a bookmaker in Bristol was never a viable option; the chances of at least one punter recognising him were too high, so he needed the anonymity of the internet. He'd even played safe by avoiding the high profile UK based gambling sites just in case Palmer's tentacles reached that far. *Youbet* was a US based firm which offered bets on virtually any horse race in the world.

Cornelius's eyes widened as he read the content of the email. Regents Choice had come in first in the 2.10 at Newbury on the previous day. Before the arrival of the email he'd forgotten about the bet he'd placed in a drunken state on Tuesday night, but the message confirmed his account had been credited with £550, the product of a £50 bet at 10-1 odds plus his stake. The obvious joy of winning a sizeable chunk of cash was tempered by the knowledge the tip off had come from a notorious gangster and he'd gambled on a race that, in all probability, had been rigged. Danny Palmer had been showing off and he'd gone along with it. God help him if Palmer ever found out.

Sixteen

The whisky had done its job and Cornelius's mind was locked in deep slumber when reality crashed into his dreams and a thunderous sound filled his head. His bleary eyes focused on the clock next to his bed and the bright green digits told him it was 6.45. Sleep ebbed away, leaving room for a headache and the realisation that someone was pummelling on his front door. He put on his dressing gown to preserve some sense of dignity, threw two paracetamols down his throat and headed downstairs to bollock the pea-brained idiot who was beating down the door.

Through the frosted glass, he could see that the person on the other side was about to bang on the door again, and he flung it open just before the fist connected.

The legacy of three oversized tumblers of Canadian Club from the previous night interfered with some of his cognitive processes, but he quickly realised that the person standing in the cold grey drizzle was Andy Statton. Unlike the day before, he didn't have a supersized grin on his face; today, he carried a grim expression.

'Andy, what the fuck? You can't keep leaping over my fence like that …'

'Sorry sir, but can you open your gates please?'

'What?' The effects of the whisky fell away rapidly but not fast enough for him to fully process Andy's request.

'There's a team waiting to come in, they have a warrant to search your house. They will smash through your gates if you don't open them.'

For the second time in twenty-four hours he stared open-mouthed at his junior officer, and he felt the reality of the situation like a prickly rash breaking out all over his body. Determined to face down the intruders in a state of dress, he lobbed the gate keys at Statton and ran up to his bedroom to put on his clothes.

Fully dressed, he descended the stairs and promptly caught site of the dark suited Ross Laverty walking into his entrance hall, a stream of sober faced officers following in his wake.

'I'll dispense with the usual morning greetings because I know what response I'll get from you. Do you need to see the warrant or can we get on with our job and leave here as soon as possible?'

'Too fucking right I want to see that warrant.' He snatched it out of Laverty's hand and read the contents, hoping to find an error. 'I don't suppose you want to tell me precisely what grounds you have for bursting in here like this?'

Before Laverty had a chance to reply, Cornelius was distracted by a disgruntled yelp coming from upstairs. Daniel had quietly returned at some point during the night and was now reacting badly to the arrival of strangers in his bedroom. Cornelius hoped Shagalong wasn't with him, recording the moment to broadcast on social media later.

Cornelius returned his attention to Laverty. 'Well?' he barked. 'Don't I get any kind of explanation?'

In all the time he had known Laverty, he'd never seen him look as uncomfortable as he did now.

'Please, Lucas, don't make this any more difficult than it needs to be. You, of all people, know we don't do this without good reason.' He paused, working out how to best continue. 'New information has come to light and I'm afraid it means we need to search your home for potential evidence.'

Cornelius became belligerent.

'Fine, search away. You know as well as I do that you won't find a bloody thing.'

Here, at least, Cornelius was confident. While someone had been able to plant his hairs in Pippa's flat, the security at his house meant that no one could break in easily, they would have to be invited inside. He mentally checked off the people who had visited his house in the last two months and could only come up with Daniel, Shagalong, Elaine and Pippa – unless Daniel had invited anyone in without telling him; he would have to find out once this bloody charade was over.

For the next thirty minutes Cornelius sat in his lounge in steaming silence as various aspects of his life disappeared out of his door in polythene bags to be forensically analysed by people he was probably on first name terms with. A detective Cornelius didn't recognise, appeared in the doorway and asked to speak to Laverty, who was babysitting Cornelius in embarrassed silence whilst the search took place. Laverty lifted himself out of the Chesterfield sofa, that Jane always considered hers and moved to talk to the DS in the doorway.

Cornelius strained his ears; he could see Laverty's expression darkening with each word. The DCI turned to face Cornelius, his voice close to apologetic.

'We need to gain access to the land behind your sheds, Lucas. Before we go clambering over fences and shed roofs, is there an easier way?'

A public footpath ran along the eastern perimeter of Cornelius's property, separating it from a block of sixteen flats, opposite. Cornelius's boundary was marked by a sturdy six-foot fence, in front of which was a dense leylandii hedge which had grown well in excess of 20 feet tall. In front of the leylandii, Lucas and Jane had erected a potting shed and a storage shed, connecting the two buildings with a simple roof and using the space underneath to store wood. The buildings ran the full width of the garden, so if an intruder managed to scale the fence and drop down into the hedge, the sheds blocked their path. Now, the search team wanted to gain access to this area.

Laverty broke into Cornelius's train of thought. 'Lucas, is there any way through?'

A dark sense of foreboding built inside his head. 'No,' he mumbled. 'The only way is over the external fence, I'd ask Andy Statton to do that if I were you, he's more than capable.'

Cornelius slumped back into his sofa, powerless to do anything except wait.

Two minutes later, Daniel was escorted into the lounge by one of the WPCs and asked to wait with his father. A painful silence hung in the air as Daniel struggled to comprehend what was unfolding around him and the only sounds were those of the police combing their way through the house.

Barely ten minutes later, the DS appeared at the doorway again to give Laverty the latest update. This time his back was turned, so Cornelius couldn't read his expression, but when he looked around his face was ashen. He took two steps forward, closely followed by the detective sergeant. Laverty's voice was low and calm.

'It's over, Lucas. We've found the body.'

Whatever Cornelius had been expecting, this wasn't it, and he remained seated – unable to speak. The stunned silence was eventually broken by Daniel.

'Dad, what's he talking about?'

Cornelius smiled thinly; it took the discovery of a corpse in the back garden for his son to call him Dad.

A state of quiet resignation came over Cornelius. 'I warned you something like this was coming Ross.'

He turned to stare solemnly at his son.

'It might not seem like it now Daniel, but everything will be fine.' He wanted to add, I promise, but right now he doubted that his future would be anything but fine. 'These gentlemen will want to ask you some questions soon, answer them honestly and go to Charlotte's when you have finished. It won't be long before the press come calling here and I don't want you getting caught up with them.'

Cornelius turned back to Laverty; it looked as if his eyes had moistened slightly. 'Is it her?'

He nodded gently. 'There's a finger missing.' Ross Laverty drew a long, painful breath. 'Lucas Cornelius, I am arresting you on suspicion of the abduction and murder of Freya Louise McAndrew, also known as Pippa Hobbs. You do not have to say anything but …'

The rest of Laverty's arrest statement was drowned out by the sound of Daniel's wail.

***

Cornelius had been in plenty of police cells in his lifetime but never as a prisoner. The humiliation at being led out of his own home in handcuffs, gave way to despair as he arrived at Bath Road Police Station and was unceremoniously dumped in a cell. His transition from suspended officer to detained suspect had been processed discreetly and fairly. The staff at the station clearly didn't know how they should treat their new detainee, but he'd been offered food and a cold drink which he had declined.

With nothing but four grey walls to look at, Cornelius spent his first few hours of incarceration lying on the bed, deep in thought. The custody sergeant passed on a message, saying Daniel had been driven to his girlfriend's and planned to stay there for a few days. With the immediate concern of the welfare of his son dealt with, he was free to focus his mind on his own predicament.

Pippa's body had been disposed of in his own garden, the final act in a macabre drama which had been playing out for months. The question now, was when did it start? He must have been followed for the perpetrator to know about his relationship with Pippa and also where to dump her body. No matter how hard he tried to remember, he'd never been aware of anyone trailing him but then he hadn't been looking.

It would have been relatively easy to hide the body in Cornelius's garden. The public footpath running adjacent to his house was quiet and badly lit. Once the body had been lifted over the fence it would have been easy to dig a shallow grave under cover of darkness in an area of the garden which was private. If the search team bothered to look over the fence it would be easy to see the disturbed earth. All that was needed was a trail of breadcrumbs to lead them there.

Whoever killed Pippa probably used her keys to access her flat and leave his hairs in there, knowing they would be found by a forensic team if they were given a reason to search it. What better way to direct them there than to cut off her finger and leave it in a public place? It was an act that neatly pointed suspicion directly at Cornelius.

***

Two hours later Cornelius was guided from the solitude of his detention cell into a remarkably bright interview room which stank of disinfectant. He tried not to let his heart sink when he saw that his solicitor, who had been hurriedly arranged by the Police Federation, looked barely old enough to be out of law school. Lynda Culvert was a petite blonde woman with a tailored grey pinstripe suit and a natural pearl necklace. She'd reviewed the evidence against him and catalogued all the potential errors she could use to help secure bail. Lynda was exactly the type of lawyer he had come to detest as an inspector, as this clinical dissection of procedure and law had, all too frequently, allowed suspects to return to the streets when they deserved to be under lock and key until their trial. Today, he was bloody grateful she was on his side, and the irony of the situation was not lost on him.

Lynda listened carefully to Cornelius as he methodically detailed the events leading up to his arrest, furiously scribbling notes as he talked and nodding in agreement with his analysis. What she didn't seem pleased with, was Cornelius's instruction for her to keep quiet during his interview and only interrupt if she witnessed any glaring errors. He'd spent all morning working it out; he didn't know who was behind it all, but he was ready to face his inquisitors.

One hour later, Cornelius was called back into interview room three where he caught the first sight of his interrogators; McCartney, Liatt and Laverty had reassembled to conduct his first interview under caution.

Cornelius plonked himself in his chair with as much gusto as possible, looked around the room and blew his cheeks out.

'It's a bit warm in here, can we open a window?'

Ross Laverty gently closed his eyes when he realised his inspector planned to be pugnacious.

Deputy Chief Constable Rick McCartney levelled a cold eye at Cornelius before going through the usual preliminaries. This time he was more observant of the correct protocols and Cornelius wondered if he knew that Lynda Culvert intended to take him to task for not responding positively when he asked if he needed federation representation during his suspension.

Formalities over, McCartney fired his opening shot.

'Earlier today, we conducted a search, under warrant, of your home address, during which the body of a female aged approximately 35 to 45 years old was discovered in a shallow grave located within the perimeter of your property. Can you please tell us how you think the body got there?'

It was a little earlier than expected, but the DCC had given him a chance to deliver his prepared opening statement.

'I wish to state, categorically, that I had nothing to do with the abduction or death of the person purported to be found at my address. Furthermore, I had no direct part in the death of

Emmanuel Thompson. I believe there is a deliberate plan by a person or persons unknown to implicate me in these crimes.'

It was the same line he'd heard countless times when interviewing suspects and it sent a clear message: I'm not going to admit to anything and it is entirely down to you to prove my involvement.

Cornelius sat back in his chair and stared directly at each of his interrogators in turn, challenging them to commence their questioning.

The bulk of the questions came from Rick McCartney, although his former uncompromising and aggressive style of inquisition had been replaced by a more measured approach, probably because their conversation was being recorded and there was a sharp legal mind on standby ready to pounce on any irregularities. Cornelius was starting to gain a whole new appreciation of suspects' rights.

For two hours, the questions came thick and fast and Cornelius parried each one away with cold hard facts. He admitted concealing he knew Pippa; it was a mistake but done with good intentions. He pointed out the absurdity of leaving the finger of his murder victim on a bench in the middle of Broadmead on a Sunday afternoon. He said he had never been in Pippa's flat, but given the contact he had had with her, it would have been quite easy for a few of his hairs to be transferred on to her clothing and end up inside her home. He also raised one issue that had been quietly eating away at Laverty all day. Why would he, an inspector in the police, make such a bad job of disposing of a body, when he knew ways to hide a corpse which would make it impossible to find? Digging a shallow grave in his own garden made no bloody sense at all.

Cornelius anticipated every question they fired at him and had answers or theories for them all. Lynda Culvert kept to her word and sat quietly by Cornelius's side, wishing that all her clients were this adept under questioning. It was not until they moved on to the subject of Manny Thompson that Cornelius was caught off guard.

Karen Liatt took over from McCartney; she looked highly unimpressed. Cornelius hadn't helped matters by suggesting they have a biscuit break; Liatt had glared at him, McCartney didn't flinch and Laverty was forced to suppress a smile. The superintendent was poised with the forensic report on Manny's death. Lynda Culvert protested that she had the right to review its contents before proceeding, but Cornelius wanted to carry on and she acquiesced to her client's wishes. Liatt began.

'Emmanuel Thompson died from a massive overdose of heroin that had been injected into his left arm. He ...'

'He's left-handed,' chirped in Cornelius.

'What?' His attitude riled her.

'You heard. I thought I'd mention it, in case you were entertaining the thought he'd OD'd.'

'Yes, thank you for that inspector, we had been thinking Mr Thompson administered his own overdose and then made a point of hiding under a bush in Leigh Woods just to confuse us.'

For his part, Cornelius was happy to let her know that he wasn't intimidated.

'Just being thorough, ma'am, carry on.'

Liatt paused just long enough to show he'd got under her skin.

'The heroin in his body was unusual due to its purity. The concentration was similar to the heroin stolen from the evidence room at Gloucester Road station.'

Karen Liatt sat back in her chair and waited for the implication to sink in. So that was the reason for the search warrant. He could see from the corner of his eye his solicitor bursting to speak; he rested his hand on her forearm and gently shook his head.

'Thank you for sharing that, ma'am, but I'm yet to hear a question.'

'Well, you seem to have a theory for everything. I'm curious to hear what you have to say about how a batch of heroin stolen from the station you are based in, ended up in a man whose last known contact was with you.'

Lynda Culvert had heard enough and exploded. 'This is a ridiculous fishing exercise with no proof whatsoever to link this to my client. I shall be writing to the chief constable to say that ...'

Lynda Culvert did not get the chance to elaborate. The interview room door opened and a nervous blonde man in his mid-thirties poked his head in. He'd barely opened his mouth when the DCC barked fiercely at him.

'I said no interruptions under any circumstances – which part of that wasn't clear?'

'Yes, I know sir, but this is extremely urgent.'

McCartney sighed theatrically and formally suspended the interview. He slammed his pen into the table and stormed out of the room with the intention of giving some poor sod a good verbal kicking for having the temerity to override his orders.

The four remaining people in the interview room sat in uncomfortable silence for several minutes until McCartney reappeared. The demeanour which helped earn him the nickname of the Staffie had gone; he was now more akin to a Labrador suffering from separation anxiety. Without making eye contact with anyone in the room, he declared the interview would remain suspended and proposed that questioning would resume in one hour.

Cornelius took the opportunity to consult with his solicitor, although all she did was to compliment him on his handling of the questions. She tried to ascertain the reason for the sudden suspension but found herself stonewalled. With nothing further to be achieved, Cornelius returned to his cell. Whatever the reason for the suspension of the interview, he hoped the outcome would lead to his exoneration. In the belief his accusers would soon be eating humble pie, he dozed off on the rock-hard cell bed.

The hour deadline came and went and was followed by another hour and a half of inactivity. Lynda Culvert created merry hell, demanding an explanation for the delay but found herself blanked by a custody sergeant claiming he knew sod-all.

Eventually, Cornelius was ushered back into the interview room. The absence of Rick McCartney had Cornelius hoping he had opted out of having to apologise for Cornelius's unnecessary arrest and detention.

The two remaining senior officers looked grim and it was obvious that neither wanted to break whatever news they had. As the senior of the two, Karen Liatt spoke first; her usual bluster was replaced by a more conciliatory tone.

'Lucas, I need to remind you that you are still under caution, however, for the moment we are not formally restarting your interview, thus as I am sure you are aware, whatever is said now will not be admissible in court. Are you happy we proceed?'

A puzzled Cornelius glanced at Laverty to try and read any signals he may be giving off, but he looked blankly at the floor. He turned to his solicitor who replied by saying that it was entirely up to him.

A sense of unease slowly crept up his spine. 'Okay – carry on.'

'The body which was found in your garden – we have established that it's not Pippa.'

Cornelius stared wide eyed at the superintendent, his mouth unable to form any words.

'A full forensic and DNA test is well under way, however, we have been able to refer to dental records and we are sure we know who the deceased is.'

Cornelius became acutely aware of two pairs of eyes boring in to him, ready to gauge his reaction.

'It's Jane.'

'Jane?'

'Your wife, Lucas. Your wife Jane was buried in your garden.'

Seventeen

The four stark walls of interview room three closed in on Cornelius as his mind struggled to contain the bombshell tearing his world apart. He stared wide eyed and disbelievingly at the superintendent and the detective chief inspector, but their expressions didn't change and were still achingly sombre. He could hear voices – Karen Liatt asking him if he needed water, his solicitor demanding she have time with her client, but the loudest sound was the roar of his own thoughts telling him this was not happening. He put his hands up, blocking the faces of the people talking.

'Quiet!' he yelled.

His mind was void of reasoned thought. Looking around the room he became aware of the sweat tricking down his forehead. His palms were clammy; his breathing shallow. He tried to stand up but felt lightheaded. The strength had left his legs; dizziness was setting in.

Liatt and Laverty could only stare at Cornelius. They hadn't been sure how to play this and were clueless as to the best way to proceed. Lynda Culvert took control.

'My client is in shock; he needs to see a doctor.'

The police officers nodded in agreement and quietly shuffled out of the room leaving the solicitor holding Cornelius's hand. Cornelius insisted he did not need to see a doctor but compromised by allowing a first aider to look at him. He knew there was bugger-all they could do, but it helped buy him some much needed peace and quiet. He returned to his cell, lay down, closed his eyes and blocked out the sounds of drunken accusations of police brutality coming from the adjacent cell. He attempted to process the revelation that it was his own missing wife who had been discovered in his garden and not Pippa as everyone had assumed. Laverty told him that a finger was missing, so how could it be Jane? It was almost a year since she had gone to Turkey and disappeared; how had she ended up as a corpse – and buried right under his nose?

Nothing made sense. All he had were questions, and the people who had the answers were sitting in a comfortable office upstairs. He banged on the cell door and demanded to see his superior officers. The custody sergeant had been on the verge of telling him to shut the fuck up when he spotted Lynda Culvert glaring at him from a corner of the custody suite.

Forty minutes later, the same three people who had witnessed Cornelius fall apart were confronted by a man with fire in his eyes. Reassembling in the same stiflingly hot interview room, Karen Liatt had barely started her speech about the admissibility of any comments made before Cornelius cut her off.

'Do you think I give a shit? Record away to your heart's content, here, let me do it for you.'

He lunged for the recording device before Laverty reached across the table, grabbing his arm.

'That's not necessary, Lucas. We'll make this as formal as you want.'

Laverty began the recording and had barely finished running through the legal formalities before Cornelius went on the attack.

'Why haven't you arrested me for Jane's murder?'

'Should we?' the words were barely out of Liatt's mouth before she regretted saying them.

'Don't fuck with me – ma'am.' He said, using her title with as much contempt as he could muster. 'You know as well as I do this is nothing to do with me.'

'It has everything to do with you, Lucas, and that's the problem. As I told you earlier, we are still waiting for the full results of the post-mortem and forensics, however,' she paused for a breath and searched for words that were least likely to inflame Cornelius further, 'at the moment, we don't know how long she has been dead.'

'She was supposed to be in Turkey, not buried in her own garden.' Cornelius's anger blinded him to the crassness of his words. 'What killed her?'

'We don't know yet.'

'When was her finger removed?'

Both of the senior officers felt uncomfortable. The discovery that the body was Jane Cornelius and not Pippa Hobbs as they expected, had thrown the whole investigating team into a flat spin. Cornelius didn't know it, but these were the same questions the DCC had fired at them twenty minutes earlier before storming off and demanding they sort out the whole bloody mess.

Before they could answer any further questions, Lynda Culvert cut in.

'Unless you plan to arrest my client for the murder of his own wife, I assume you will be releasing him immediately?'

Liatt never took her gaze away from Cornelius.

'Your client, Miss Culvert, will be released on bail later whilst we continue our investigations. He will be asked to attend an identity parade on Monday, and all other restrictions regarding his suspension still apply. However, we request that your client makes a statement regarding the circumstances surrounding the disappearance of his wife.'

Cornelius didn't need to look for approval from his solicitor. He had played out the circumstances behind his wife's disappearance in his mind so many times, they were etched into his brain. The police already had statements from him that were taken at the time and would carefully compare the two for any discrepancies, but Cornelius knew there wouldn't be any.

For the next hour and a half, Cornelius painstakingly detailed everything he knew about the events of a year previously and everything he had done to try and discover what had happened to Jane. The air grew thin in the interview room, as Cornelius delivered what was almost entirely a monologue. His recollection of the detail was so precise that neither Laverty nor Liatt had any meaningful questions to ask, and nine hours after his arrest on suspicion of Pippa's murder, he was released on bail pending further investigations.

Walking out of Bath Road Police Station into the dying February light, Cornelius took a lungful of cold air, realising for the first time how oppressive the atmosphere had been inside the station.

Switching on his mobile phone, he was slightly surprised to see six text messages appear on his screen. He hoped one would be from Daniel, checking to see if he was okay but was disappointed to see they all came from Elaine. He made the mistake of opening the most recent text first only to see that it was nothing more than a collection of seemingly random characters which presumably meant something to Elaine before she started on her second bottle of wine. He scrolled back to the first message in the hope she had at least been sober when she first contacted him.

Lucas, OMG, just rd the heralds nws. R U ok?

The remaining texts were all variants of the same question, each message less intelligible than the previous one. For a moment he considered ringing her, but a conversation would be pointless until she sobered up. It didn't take a huge leap of logic to work out what the *Herald* had printed. Elliot Chorley had named him as the suspended officer in the Hobbs and Thompson enquiries, and it was only a matter of time before the whole of Bristol heard the latest developments.

Eighteen

It was gone 9 p.m. when Cornelius arrived back at his house. He had hoped Daniel would be at home, but when he opened the gates he saw that none of the lights were on and the house was clad in darkness. At least there were no press camped outside, and Cornelius was grateful for small mercies. Either they hadn't got hold of the story yet or they'd got bored waiting for Cornelius to come back. He would need to check the news, but right now his priority was finding his son.

In keeping with Daniel's normal practice, he wasn't answering his mobile. Text messages were usually more successful, but he had not replied to any of those either. He might still be at Shagalong's house, but Cornelius didn't have a clue where she lived, and he had thrown away the number she had given him a few months previously because he couldn't think of one conceivable reason why he would need to ring her. On the other hand, Daniel might have gone out for the night. Cornelius tried to remember the names of bars and clubs he had mentioned, but he rarely shared any information about his social life with his father, and looking for him amongst the nightlife of Bristol would be hopeless without some idea of where to start.

The house had never felt the same without Jane, but now Cornelius faced the stark realisation that the hope they had clung to for the last year was gone forever. Jane would never come back and the house seemed like nothing more than four walls – an empty shell. The years leading up to her disappearance were not a sea of domestic bliss, but a police officer's life is rarely conducive to a harmonious marriage. Cornelius always suspected Daniel was the only reason Jane had stayed with him, and yet they had spent some very happy times together.

When Daniel reached his mid-teens, their family life had become increasingly disjointed. Jane blamed Cornelius's work, whereas he thought the problem lay with the marriage itself. He'd never have believed he'd miss her nagging him to get a proper job or the stilted silences when he'd done something wrong and she refused to discuss it with him. But miss her he had and now the darkness in his heart matched the gloom inside his home.

He opened the front door and went to disable the intruder alarm, only to realise it had not been set. Given the day's events he probably should have expected it. He made his way through the spacious hallway, the sound of his footsteps reverberating off the walls was disproportionately loud. Just before he opened the door to the kitchen he froze at the gentle creak of a chair leg moving, fractionally, across the tiled flooring on the other side. In an instant, his weariness disappeared and adrenaline had full control. No signs of a break in were visible at the front of the house, but with the alarm off it was possible to enter via the back, even if it did mean levering your way through some heavy duty door and window locks. He looked for something to defend himself with but could find nothing other than a battered old umbrella which had been left by the door. Armed only with a desire to break the legs of whoever was topping off the worst day of his life, he flung the kitchen door open, flicked the switch and flooded the room with light.

Bracing himself for a struggle, he was thrown by the sight of Daniel sitting at the kitchen table. His unkempt hair framed a face as hard as granite staring directly and unblinkingly at his father.

'Daniel! You scared the shit out of me!' Cornelius's heart was pounding its way out of his body.

'Why are you sitting here in the dark? I've been trying to ...'

With an almighty roar Daniel launched himself at his father.

It was a career hazard to be on the receiving end of an assault for Cornelius, and years of living with that expectation sharpened his reflexes. However, the sight of his own son attacking him was completely disabling, and he stayed rooted to the spot. In three short steps Daniel was upon him and only then did Cornelius see that his son had a long, cylindrical weapon in his hand. Daniel swung it sharply, and the white marble rolling pin that had once been Jane's most prized kitchen utensil caught Cornelius on the side of his head. Pain and light exploded inside him and he reeled backwards with only the kitchen worktop keeping him on his feet. A burst of adrenaline stopped him from keeling over completely, and he could see Daniel coming at him again, arm extended to deliver a second blow. This time Cornelius was ready; he lurched to the right and slammed his fist hard into Daniel's ribs. Daniel yelped with pain and slumped sideways losing his balance. Cornelius leapt at him, crashing them both to the floor blasting the wind out of Daniel's body as he landed on top of him. For the second time his son cried out in pain and from the corner of his eye Cornelius saw the rolling pin spinning across the kitchen floor, well out of reach.

Daniel's lack of combat experience was apparent, as he had no way of shifting his father. Cornelius lifted himself off his son and grabbed his arm, locking it firmly behind his back. For the first time Daniel spoke, his blubbing words coming through a sludgy mix of tears and snot.

'You killed her, you killed her.'

It was just three words repeated, but it caused Cornelius more pain than the marble rolling pin smashing into his head. He eased his grip slightly but was in no mood for a repeat performance.

'Daniel, in a minute I am going to let go, but before I do you need to listen carefully, understood?' He waited until Daniel nodded, his face still pressed to the floor. 'I had nothing to do with mum's death. I didn't know she was dead until earlier today and that is why I have been trying to contact you.'

'Liar!' Daniel struggled again so Cornelius tightened his grip.

'Calm down and think this through carefully, do you think if I killed your mum I'd bury her in our own garden? I might make mistakes but I'm not so bloody stupid as to do that. If it was me, I'd have made sure she'd never have been found. Right now, somebody is doing their best to screw up my life and they are doing a damn good job of it. What is worrying me more than anything is that you could be targeted next. I have no intention of letting that happen but for me to protect you, you must help me.'

He paused until Daniel nodded and then slowly eased his grip. When he was sure that all the fight had left Daniel, he let go, helped his son to his feet and guided him to a kitchen stool.

'It was a nice touch using her rolling pin, she would have appreciated it.'

Daniel snorted a brief laugh spraying phlegm over his father.

Cornelius looked at his son's face closely and saw his eyes were red and puffy. It was obvious he'd been in a state of distress for some time.

'How did you find out?'

'Some reporter, he was waiting at the gate when I got home.' Tears trickled from his eyes again.

'Did this reporter look like a greasy version of the Michelin man?'

'Who?'

Cornelius kept forgetting about the generation gap which existed between them.

'Was he an overweight gentleman, with jet black hair and a bad complexion?'

'Yeah, that's him.'

The side of Cornelius's head throbbed, exacerbated by the knowledge Elliot Chorley had found out it was Jane's body in the garden and had broken the news to his son. At this precise moment, he couldn't think of a death painful enough for Chorley.

'Was Shaga ... was Charlotte with you?'

'No, I only came back to pick up some things, I ...' His words were broken by the sound of a text message arriving. He looked at his screen. 'That's her wondering where I am.'

'Good, tell her you're coming now, and I want you to stay there as long as possible – but ask her not to broadcast it at college or on Facebook, I need you to keep a low profile for a while.'

'Why?'

'I wasn't kidding when I said you may be in danger, but it's your choice. Stay at Charlotte's or with Elaine.'

Daniel didn't need to answer; he quietly disappeared to his room to pack.

Nineteen

Cornelius wasn't sure where his Saturday night ended and Sunday morning began. He had delivered Daniel to Shagalong's the previous night and planned to return home to plot the untimely demise of Elliot Chorley. It was not until he looked for his laptop that he remembered it had been seized and felt a twinge of embarrassment at the knowledge his colleagues would find out his background wallpaper was a picture of his childhood favourites, Tom and Jerry. Mild embarrassment gave way to a full blown cringe when he realised they would also see his internet browsing history. Whatever the *Bristol Herald* was publishing about him would have to wait until morning.

Unable to do anything else that night, he opened a bottle of Canadian Club and sat on the Chesterfield sofa. He stayed there all night, alone with his thoughts. To start with his thinking had been reasoned and precise, as he carefully considered his options and thought about what he should do next. As the whisky took over, his mind became darker, and thoughts of a systematic approach to finding Jane's killer were slowly replaced with plans for violent revenge. At some undeterminable point he stopped thinking altogether and passed out.

His watch said 5 a.m., but the darkness outside gave no clue as to whether his timepiece was correct or not. For a few moments, he struggled to comprehend his whereabouts. He was still wearing the clothes he had been interrogated in, and he was slumped in the same sofa as the night before. Rubbing his eyes, he cursed as he sensed the pain of the spectacular multi-coloured bruise which had developed overnight on his temple, and a quick sniff test confirmed he stank of sweat and whisky. Once he had fully processed his state and location, he went for a cold shower in a bid to return himself to something resembling normal.

An hour later he stepped out into the freezing morning air and walked briskly in search of the Sunday papers to sober up. It was too early for the supermarkets but the newsagent in Stoke Lane, barely a mile away, would be open. In the twenty minutes it took him to reach the shop, any remaining cobwebs had been blown away and his mind had sharpened up to the task ahead of him. He was still wondering how to deal with Elliot Chorley as he entered the tiny shop, his eyes immediately falling on piles of Sunday papers, all ready for public consumption. The *Bristol Herald* favoured attention grabbing headlines. 'Body found in cop's back garden' was printed in bold across a picture of his colleagues carrying bags of evidence out of his house. Cornelius had been named, but thankfully no photograph had been published. Any sense of relief rapidly vanished, however, as he read the full article. It declared in sordid tones that the body was believed to be the missing wife of Detective Inspector Lucas Cornelius and that he had been arrested and questioned. It was truthful and misleading at the same time; unsurprisingly, it was all written by Chorley. Cornelius scanned the rest of the day's papers with increasing dismay. The juicy story had made it on to the front page of four nationals.

Cornelius had no intention of handing over any money that may end up in the *Herald's* coffers, and he confined his purchase to a loaf of sliced bread and a pint of milk before exiting the newsagents and making a beeline back home. It wouldn't be long before the braying bastards of the press and the local gossips would congregate outside his house, and he wasn't ready to run the gauntlet just yet.

Four hours into his self-imposed barricade, his phone sprang to life indicating the arrival of a text message. 10.30 a.m., way too early for either Daniel or Elaine to be contacting him. He read the message and immediately chose to ignore it, thinking it was a scam from one of the eight reporters who had pitched up outside his house. Cornelius cursed out loud at the thought that one of them had his personal number and was trying to ambush him, so they could fire off their moronic questions. He'd locked the gates when he'd returned from the newsagents, and none of the reporters would dare scale his fence just for the fun of knocking on his front door. The second text came through from the same person twenty minutes later, and when he saw the sender called him a lazy, workshy git, he realised who JS was and happily agreed to meet for coffee.

Wearing a thick black parka with a heavy hood to hide his face from the cameras, he opened his gates so he could drive out. Cries of 'Did you kill your wife, Mr Cornelius?' started immediately, but he ignored the scrum. It took all his self-control not to thump the balding, overweight cameraman who viciously elbowed a diminutive female correspondent, so that he could get a better camera angle.

Thirty minutes later, he had lost the three reporters who'd tried to tail him and was sitting in a dark corner of a bistro on the edge of Clifton Village. Only one young couple were there, and they ignored each other in favour of their smart phones. Cornelius thought the scarcity of customers was hardly surprising given the price of the coffee – not that value for money was a concern today.

Jo Scutt looked up from her copy of the *Herald* and grinned.

'I don't know whether to thank you or kick your sorry arse from here to Bath.'

Cornelius said nothing but raised an eyebrow to invite further comment.

'You've certainly kept me busy, and that keeps the mortgage company off my back, but what the bloody hell have you got yourself into?'

Before Cornelius could answer she spoke again. 'Oh, and sorry about your wife and um, whatever else I should be saying at this time. Now, be a good boy get me a coffee will you, white with more sugar than is healthy for me.'

He couldn't help but smile. Being so close to death deadened the capacity for sympathy in most pathologists, but Jo could take emotional indifference to a whole new level.

Cornelius ordered two coffees and a slice of carrot cake for Jo without asking if she wanted it and briefly filled her in on the circumstances of his arrest before getting to the question that had been intriguing him since her message arrived.

'Why did you want to see me? Don't you know how much trouble you could get into?'

Jo was tucking into her cake and didn't look up. 'Are you going to tell anyone I'm here?'

'Of course not.'

'Well then. I thought you might appreciate some honest information, rather than waiting for that dreadful superintendent of yours to give you an edited version of the facts. She wasn't best pleased when I gave her my preliminary report last night, as it didn't fit in with her nice theory. She was even less pleased when I called her staff wholly incompetent at crime scene management – but that's another story …'

'Her nice theory?'

Jo Scutt's prolonged gaze suggested she considered him to have learning difficulties.

'The theory that you killed Jane?'

'So, you don't believe it?'

'I believe what the science tells me. Not all the results are available yet, but what I can tell you is that the body hadn't been in your garden since the time of her death.'

'I'd already worked that out, Jo.'

'I'm sure you had smart-arse, but now there is proof – not just your discredited word for it.'

Her words stung, but Cornelius knew she was right.

'The microbial and chemical composition of the soil around her body show that she had been there for about a month.' Jo lectured with clinical efficiency and little regard to the emotional turmoil that Cornelius was going through.

'For the next bit I am going out on a limb; I think she had been dead for some time before she was moved to your garden, but her body had been kept in a freezer. I'll know for sure in a few days.'

Cornelius couldn't bring himself to look at Jo, a lump was rising fast in his throat but he had more questions.

'What about her finger?'

'Removed just before burial.' Her voice was utterly matter-of-fact in tone, oblivious to Cornelius's pain.

'What killed her?'

'I'm not sure yet, but that reminds me, did she self-administer any intravenous drugs, medicinal or recreational?'

Cornelius smiled at the thought. 'She hated taking paracetamol, let alone anything involving a needle.'

'Hmmm, she had a puncture mark in her brachioradialis.'

'Her what?'

'Sorry, forearm to you.'

She put her cake fork down and pointed to the inside of her arm.

'It looks like she was injected with something, but it's going to be a bugger to work out what. Frozen bodies play merry hell with the forensics.'

Cornelius had one last question about Jane. He dreaded the answer but needed to know.

'Had she been ...'

He paused, struggling to find the words that afforded her memory some dignity. 'Was she ...'

Jo spared him the agony of finishing the question. 'There were no signs of sexual abuse, Lucas.'

She thought better of telling him she hadn't found any signs of sexual activity in the months leading up to her death.

Cornelius puffed his cheeks out with gentle relief. It was one less trauma Daniel would have to deal with. He decided to change the topic.

'What about Emmanuel Thompson?'

'What about him?' Jo's attention returned to her carrot cake.

'He had a massive OD of heroin.'

'Correct.'

'Manny didn't do drugs, he hated them. There's no way he ...'

'Tasered. Didn't they tell you?'

With her usual efficiency, Jo anticipated the question about how Manny had been incapacitated and provided the second reason for the search warrant. She watched as his expression changed and rolled her eyes in exasperation.

'They didn't, did they? Unbelievable ...'

Not for the first time Cornelius's own policing practices were coming back to haunt him. Sometimes it was important to hold back information from the suspect in the hope they would incriminate themselves by contradicting known facts. Now he was being kept in the dark, and it was fucking annoying. He continued to quiz Jo about the findings but she wouldn't commit herself to anything more than she had told him already, so he offered her another coffee which she declined. Cornelius was about to peck her farewell on the cheek when he felt her freeze and remembered just in time she didn't like being touched. He stepped out of the café on to the Clifton pavement and the ice cold wind reminded him he needed to keep a low profile. He lifted his hood over his head and returned to his car deep in thought.

Lucas Cornelius was finally unravelling what had been happening to him; stopping it from going any further would be an entirely different game.

Twenty

It had been four weeks since Cornelius ran an identity parade for a flasher apprehended on Durdham Down. One of the men they drafted in for the line-up asked him in all sincerity if they would need to drop their trousers when the witness came into the room. Cornelius managed to keep a straight face when replying but only just.

Today, he was the suspect on parade and Laverty insisted on officiating. Much to Cornelius's appreciation, Laverty kept the number of station staff present to a bare minimum, to help preserve what was left of his dignity.

His day had begun badly when he saw the *Herald's* front page. They were still running the story of his arrest, and this time they included a photograph of him, dug out from their archives. He'd had his photo taken five years previously alongside a group of grumpy looking school children as part of an initiative with the City Academy. A cropped version of this photo stared back at him from the newspaper – showing the *Herald's* readers what a murder suspect looked like.

Cornelius looked at the volunteers who had assembled to help with the line-up and was pleased to see that by and large they were similar in age, weight and size to him. He didn't want to make a significant fuss, but if he had been six inches taller and ten years older than everyone else he would have insisted they be changed for something more representative. Nodding his agreement to Laverty, he took his place in the line-up and stared ahead, wondering who the bloody hell was about to come through the door.

The sound of irregular footsteps travelled up the corridor that led to the stifling hot subterranean room used for identity parades.

Cornelius's mind was racing at full pelt, wondering who would be called to identify him when Rafael Slowik limped in.

In cold and sombre tones, Laverty told Slowik he should look carefully at all the people in the line-up, and if he saw the person he had seen following Pippa Hobbs, he must identify him by the number on his card.

Slowik had a history of stalking some of his young and vulnerable employees, and now here he was being called into an identity parade as a potential witness. He must have been questioned about Pippa Hobbs and admitted tailing her, but he'd seen somebody else following her as well – and that's why he was here.

Rafael Slowik nodded. He carefully and systematically made his way down the line, staring enquiringly at each person. When he came to Cornelius, his expression changed. This was the person who had threatened to ruin his business if he didn't co-operate in helping to identify Pippa. He frowned and turned his gaze to Laverty, whose expression remained resolutely dispassionate. Cornelius felt uncomfortable at the sight of the stocky, heavily moustached man staring at him for a disproportionate amount of time; not until Slowik moved on to the next person did he realise he had been holding his breath whilst under scrutiny.

Having taken a dutiful amount of time examining the line-up, Slowik limped back to his starting point and looked to Laverty for further instruction.

'Mr Slowik, have you seen the person here today that you saw following Pippa Hobbs?'

'Yes, yes, I see him today.'

Cornelius tried to stick with protocol by staring directly ahead, but his eyes strayed to the left to try and see Laverty's reaction.

'Please identify him using the number on the card he is holding.'

'No.'

Incidents which ruffled the chief inspector during an identity parade were rare but this one hit the mark.

'I beg your pardon?' he said, his voice not rising beyond an undignified splutter. 'Either you have seen him or you have not Mr Slowik; it is important you are honest.'

'I know. I have seen him here today, but he not here in this room. I saw him as I was coming into station.'

Four of the ten heads in the line-up were unable to maintain their forward stares and gawped open-mouthed at Rafael Slowik. For Cornelius, not looking was the easy bit. He needed all his self-discipline to refrain from grinning like a Cheshire Cat.

***

'Now do you believe me?'

Laverty leaned back in the plastic chair, rubbed his head and tried not to make eye contact with Cornelius. At Laverty's suggestion, Cornelius had met him in a grubby café off the south end of Gloucester Road. He'd used it before to meet with informants and trusted the owner to keep anything he saw to himself. The press were digging for information and someone was leaking details to the *Herald* – he had no intention of making it worse by speaking to his inspector inside the station.

'Lucas, you know damn well if you were me you'd have taken the same decisions, and ... by the way, what happened to your head?'

'That's not what I asked and don't try and change the subject.'

Cornelius wiped the grease from his chin and took another bite of his bacon butty. For the first time in two days he felt hungry and his body welcomed the hot, stodgy food.

'C'mon Ross, you know as well as I do this whole thing stinks. You don't have one shred of evidence that will hold up in court and ...'

'Apart from your wife's body being found in your back garden?' As soon as the words were out he regretted it. 'Shit, sorry, Lucas. Finding out about Jane has thrown us.'

Cornelius wasn't about to let on he knew about the initial report from Jo Scutt, but it gave him an excuse to fire another question at Laverty which had been gnawing at him.

'It pisses all over the investigation which concluded she'd travelled to Turkey of her own free will though. What has Brawley had to say for himself about that?'

'Lucas, you are still under suspension; you know I can't answer that question.'

Laverty had gone back to head rubbing again, a sign he was carefully mulling over his next comment.

'I can tell you that we have opened up multiple lines of enquiry which involve you – but as a victim rather than a suspect.'

If he thought that statement would mollify Cornelius, he was mistaken.

'Multiple lines of enquiry? What am I, the bloody press?'

'Okay okay,' Laverty held his hand up in submission. 'We have reopened the file on Jane's disappearance and yes, your favourite inspector will have to account for himself.'

Now it was his turn to ask a question which bothered him.

'What is it with the two of you anyway? You don't make a good job of disguising your dislike of the man.'

Cornelius stared out the window at the passing traffic. The pain of Jane's disappearance rose within him again and although he had talked about it at length during his interrogation, he'd avoided commenting on the official investigation conducted by Brawley – largely because he didn't have any proof of the allegation he was about to make.

'You remember I went out to Turkey in search of Jane?'

'Yes, against my advice in case you need reminding.'

Cornelius briefly smiled, remembering the rant Laverty delivered at the time and how his face turned a light shade of purple when Cornelius declared he needed a holiday, saying he'd heard Turkey was nice this time of year.

'Well I'm pretty sure it was Brawley who rang the local police and told them I was not there in an official capacity. It screwed up any chance I had of running a decent investigation, and I think he was worried I would uncover something which contradicted his findings.'

'For what it's worth, Lucas, there are a few other red faces about that, including mine. We downgraded the investigation when we thought Jane had left of her own free will. It had all the hallmarks of a woman who'd had enough and run away.'

Giving apologies was not one of Ross Laverty's strong points; he needed to reassert his authority.

'You need to keep your head down, avoid the press and let us get on with it.'

'Are you reviewing my old cases, to see who might be behind this?'

Laverty nodded.

'You'll need my help, Ross. No one else knows enough about their backgrounds.'

'You can't be seen at the station Lucas, you know that.'

'Let me come in in late, when everyone has buggered off home.'

'I'll think about it.'

Cornelius chanced one more question. 'Are you planning to ask Mr Slowik to do an e-fit of the person he claims to have seen following Pippa Hobbs?'

Laverty's expression indicated he wasn't going to respond to the question. He stood up and put his coat on, preparing himself for the drizzly rain which had just started coming down.

'Just leave it to us, Lucas.'

Lucas Cornelius nodded and smiled back. He had no intention of just leaving it to them.

Twenty one

Cornelius had two people to talk to and anticipated that neither of them would be particularly pleased to see him. He would need a bit of luck and patience, but with a failed identity parade under his belt he felt buoyed, as he set off in search of his first victim.

An intrinsic part of police work is surveillance, and Cornelius hated it. He theorised that his brain was not wired to be inactive for long periods of time, but surveillance demanded just that. Positioning himself a safe distance from the house, he passed the time by doing some research for his next task. He was about to make a call on the pay-as-you-go mobile he had purchased for cash earlier in the day, when he saw his target leave her house. She climbed into her outlandishly large 4X4 and reversed out on to the main road causing the driver of a Mini to swerve and blast his horn. Cornelius watched as she gave a V-sign and mouthed her response.

The size of her vehicle made it easy to follow from a distance, and only two miles into her journey, she pulled into a large supermarket with plenty of parking available.

Leaving his Smart car on the periphery, he quickly scribbled a note before following her into the supermarket. The jet black permed hair, tattooed arms and abundance of gold jewellery gave her a distinctive appearance, so keeping track of her was simple. Cornelius wished all the people he had kept under surveillance were this easy to follow, although he reminded himself it was his picture which had been plastered all over the front page of the newspapers, and he was the one who needed to keep a low profile.

He followed discreetly and waited until she buried her head deep into the meat counter. Then he took his opportunity, left the note in her trolley and quickly withdrew back to his car.

He wasn't sure if she would take the bait or not, but he'd phrased the note in such a way that she wouldn't be able to show her husband – and to anyone else it would mean bugger-all. After an anxious thirty minutes, and on the verge of giving up hope, his passenger door opened and Mary Weavell squeezed herself into the seat next to Cornelius.

'What the fuck are you doin' leaving me notes? Why should I wanna speak to a killer like you?'

'Thank you, Mary.' Cornelius wondered if his media status as number one suspect had influenced her decision to meet him. 'I promise you this is nothing to do with Marcus, but I do want to find out what happened to Kelly Ann.'

'That's bollocks; you've been kicked off the force. I do read the papers you know. Marcus thinks it's fuckin' hysterical.'

Cornelius bit his lip to stop himself from losing his temper.

'If you think that, why are you here?'

Mary pondered the question. She'd responded to Cornelius's note with a mixture of curiosity and anger. Why had she agreed to meet a discredited policeman? Even talking to the police was anathema to Mary. Cornelius helped her out.

'How about this, I tell you why I'm asking and what I want to do. If you don't like anything I say, you get out of the car and we will both deny this meet ever took place. Deal?'

Mary's eyes were fixed ahead, watching a young mother try and load up her car with provisions, slowed considerably by her young child's insistence on helping. Eventually she nodded.

'Okay, despite what you have read, I haven't been kicked off the force yet, but I am in a bit of trouble.'

Mary snorted. 'A bit? You're looking at life, mate.'

He had to explain why he wanted to track Kelly down and struggled to believe he was about to share his thoughts with the wife of a man he wanted to see behind bars.

'It is a bit of a long shot, but Kelly Ann went missing about the same time as my wife. It is probably a coincidence, but I want to track her down and rule out a connection. If I find her, I'll let you know she is safe and well, but I have no idea where to start, so anything you can tell me may help.'

'Why can't your lot do it?'

He'd anticipated the question but didn't want to answer truthfully. Firstly, the police didn't know about Kelly; she hadn't been officially reported as missing. Secondly, the fact that Kelly was a prostitute, meant only cursory checks would be done in the absence of a formal missing persons report, especially since his colleagues were knee deep in a double murder investigation. Finally, if a link existed, he wanted to be the one to find it. Cornelius answered Mary's question by playing on her prejudice against the police.

'Because the lads at the station are busy trying to nail me for something I haven't done, Mary and, besides, I'll be more thorough. I'm the one with the most to lose.'

'Marcus won't know we've spoken?'

'I promise.'

Silence reigned in the car while Mary pondered whether she should talk to Cornelius or not. It took her two minutes to decide.

'I liked Kels; she was a good girl. Marcus went nuts when she went missing but wouldn't do fuck all about it. Even that fuckin' great lump with the muscle didn't give a shit, and I think Kels was soft on him. She told me she had to go somewhere for week or so, and she was going to get paid well for it. I thought she was plannin' to mule for someone, so I tore her off a strip coz that's a bloody mug's game. Anyway, she promises me on her mother's life she weren't doin' that but wouldn't say what she was doin' or where she was goin', only that it were abroad.'

'Did you believe her?'

'Yeah, she seemed excited about the trip.'

'You never saw her again?'

Mary Weavell wiped something from the corner of her eye before shaking her head.

'Marcus told me she returned to her home in London,' said Cornelius.

Mary gave an irritable snort. 'He never had a clue where she came from.'

Cornelius phrased his next question carefully.

'Kelly said she promised on her mother's life?' he waited for Mary to nod confirmation. 'Do you know where her mum lives?'

'Why do you want to know?'

'So, I can ask her myself.'

'Good luck with that, she may have promised on her mum's life but they'd fallen out and hadn't spoken for years. Her name's Daphne and she lives in Crawley, I don't know anythin' else.'

Mary put one tattooed hand on the door handle indicating she was about to go.

'Remember, if you breathe one word to Marcus that we've spoken, I'll personally rip your nuts off.'

'Fine, but you'll have to get to the back of the queue.'

Cornelius couldn't be sure, but it looked like Mary almost smiled as she left his car.

Twenty two

It was 7.30 p.m. when Cornelius wandered into the CID office. Laverty had called an hour earlier and given him the terms. He had to come now or not at all. With an empty office, he could work quietly without being seen. Secondly, he needed to have somebody with him and, lastly, he must not access any information other than what he was there to review. Cornelius happily agreed and asked that Andy Statton be the one to join him. He didn't tell Laverty the reason he wanted him was Statton's fingers were far more dexterous and could dance over a keyboard at twice the speed of his.

The CID office still stank of a madras curry which someone had brought in for their lunch. A mixture of turmeric, coriander, cumin, cinnamon and chilli hung in the air, ungraciously reminding Cornelius his lunch consisted of a solitary ham and pickle sandwich. Andy Statton was already there waiting at his desk; he'd even bought the coffees. His monitor displayed the front page of the police national database.

'Evening, sir, pleased to be back?'

'This is strictly a one-off, Andy. I am the best person to review my old case files to see if there is anyone who has a big enough grudge against me to frame me. I need to compile a list, and then you have to escort me out of the building.'

Statton knew that of course. Laverty lectured him at length about why he was there and what would happen to him if he let Cornelius do anything else.

'Do we need to do a search though? Aren't there two obvious suspects?'

Cornelius sipped his coffee. At this time of night he would rather have a pint of Doom Bar in front of him, but it would have to do.

'You are referring to Danny Palmer and Marcus Weavell I assume?'

Statton nodded.

'Palmer has the ability to orchestrate this, but he doesn't have a specific grudge against me. I put one of his henchmen away a few years ago, Calvin Marks, but that's about it.'

'You put Calvin the Cutter away?'

'I did. Calvin has been in and out of prison since he hit puberty, but for him it's more of an occupational hazard. He's not one to hold a grudge; if there is somebody he doesn't like he slashes them there and then.'

'What about Weasel?'

Cornelius nodded. 'Weasel's a candidate for sure, but he doesn't have anyone he could call on.'

'He has Guy the Gorilla at his beck and call.'

'Guy?' Cornelius coughed as his last dribble of coffee shot back up his oesophagus and tried to head down his trachea instead. 'Guy's way too thick. He'd have left a hefty set of evidence leading right back to him. No, unless Weasel has contracted someone to frame me, it's not going to be him.'

Statton sighed and looked at his TAG Heuer watch.

'I was hoping we could save ourselves some time. I've got a date later.'

'Lucky you,' said Cornelius. 'We'd better crack on with it then.'

***

Two hours, four cups of coffee and half a packet of chocolate digestives later, they had a list of suspects fitting the criteria set by Cornelius. They were looking for someone with a history of violence; that condition alone removed at least half of the cases Cornelius had worked on. Secondly, Cornelius needed to have had a significant role in their conviction or apprehension; that ruled out five more names. Lastly, they needed to have been out of prison for the previous six months at least; that left them with three potential suspects.

Cornelius clicked on the first file, and a photograph of the shaven head of Peter Fitzavon stared back at him.

Big Pete was born ugly and he went downhill from there. Nobody would have looked at Mrs Fitzavon's baby and cooed with genuine delight. His square face framed a large forehead and a bulbous nose which occupied more space than it should have done. By the time he was fifteen, tattoos of spiders' webs had appeared on his arms and neck, and he spent his seventeenth birthday in court receiving his first conviction for GBH.

Cornelius first came into contact with Pete when he moved to Bristol to escape the unwanted attention of a Glaswegian mobster called Dougal Mullins. He suspected Big Pete of skimming the takings from the sales of crack cocaine made from his fleet of ice cream vans. Rather than try and persuade Mullins it was own son who had been helping himself to the money, Big Pete packed up his few belongings and headed south. His desire to start a new crime-free life lasted seventy-two hours after his arrival in the city. Darren McCormack, a regular of the Pike and Musket in Wells Road made the mistake of calling him a clumsy jock after Big Pete accidentally knocked half an inch of beer out of his glass. As far as Cornelius knew, Darren still had to have his food liquidised for him.

Cornelius led the hunt for Big Pete and tracked him down to a bedsit in Knowle. When the police had tried to restrain him, the taser had failed to fire. Pete had head-butted the officer holding the faulty taser and sent his colleague sprawling with a ferocious right hook. Cornelius had thrown a dustbin at his legs to stop him from running away, and Big Pete face-planted the concrete pavement beneath him, knocking out three teeth and damaging his retina in the process. It had been the beginning of his campaign of vilification against Cornelius which included raising a formal complaint of assault. The grounds for his complaint were always flimsy, but Big Pete didn't help himself by declaring at his trial he was going to skin the bastard copper, who'd arrested him.

Big Pete had been sent down for seven years but released on licence two years previously. He'd moved to Bridgwater, 50 minutes away on the M5, and managed to stay out of trouble since.

The second person on the list was Brendon Pike. His profile showed a man who was unremarkable in almost every aspect of his life. He was an accountant for a Clevedon firm specialising in the manufacture of food packaging. Brendon had been married to his wife for ten years; they had two daughters, a detached house in Nailsea and a Dalmatian called Sebastian. He was a member of the Clevedon Players and appeared to be a devoted father who spent his weekends taking his girls to gymkhanas. However, when he wasn't living his perfect suburban life, Brendon Pike had an alter ego. After his trial, he described his other life as a hobby; the judiciary referred to it as rape and false imprisonment.

Cornelius was a fresh-faced detective sergeant based at Bath Road station. One Saturday morning he interviewed a distraught mother who stormed in, demanding her daughter's boyfriend be chemically castrated and locked up for the rest of his life. It didn't take long to find out that Gemma Moreton's boyfriend was innocent of any crime, but it started an inquiry that mushroomed into the largest rape investigation of the decade. A total of 14 girls aged between 15 and 21 were identified as probable victims of Brendon Pike.

Pike's father was a wealthy fund manager and paid for the services of Hugo Chester, a London-based lawyer whose colossal ego drew him to high profile cases, often with celebrity clients. Chester's demolition of the DNA evidence presented at Pike's trial subsequently triggered the biggest review on the handling of forensic evidence the country had ever seen. It also helped ensure his client was only convicted of three of the ten rapes he was charged with.

Although Cornelius had not led the case, he was the one who had chased and caught Pike as he tailed a 17 year old girl through Bedminster Down one damp February evening. From that point on, Pike blamed Cornelius for ruining his life. Cornelius still had the letter Pike sent him, giving the graphic details of exactly what he planned to do to Cornelius as soon as he was released, and nobody had bothered to tell Cornelius that Pike had been out of prison for 18 months, having served ten years of an 18 year sentence.

The third suspect on the list chilled Cornelius to his core – Ivor Millington. Just reading the name unsettled him, even after five years. Millington was a former detective inspector, based at Gloucester Road Police Station. Conservative estimates for the number of bribes taken by Millington were close to a million pounds; the majority of the money coming from three gangsters who controlled Bristol at the time. The internal investigation also concluded that at least 17 wanted criminals escaped arrest because of his tip offs, and four innocent men went to prison thanks to Millington's fabricated evidence.

Cornelius had suspected for some time that Millington was crooked, and one evening he pick-pocketed an unregistered pay-as-you-go phone from Millington's jacket. It didn't contain much information, but it was enough. There were two calls to a Clifton drug dealer, one hour before he was due to be arrested. As damning as the evidence was, it had been acquired illegally. Consequently, Millington was not charged, but he was suspended from duty pending a formal enquiry. That evening, Ivor Millington walked out of his detached house in Long Ashton, never to be seen by his family again.

Cornelius had been credited with finding the missing inspector, although technically it was Millington who found Cornelius. He broke into his house, armed with a twelve inch hunting knife, a roll of duct tape and a ball of polypropylene twine. Two factors went Cornelius's way that night. He was uncharacteristically sober; and both Jane and Daniel were away at a wedding in Shropshire. Millington may have been the most corrupt officer in the history of Avon and Somerset Constabulary, but he wasn't an accomplished house breaker. Cornelius heard Millington snaking his way up his stairs and confronted him on the landing. The fight that followed was the most brutal Cornelius had ever been in, and he still bore two scars where Millington's knife punctured his ribcage and thigh. Cornelius never knew how much damage he inflicted when he swung Jane's precious Jennine Parker bronze statue at Millington's head, but it saved Cornelius's life. Millington staggered out of the house, trailing blood and drove away in the stolen Nexus he had arrived in. Cornelius lost so much blood he could only crawl to the phone, dial 999 and wait for help. Five years after the event, Ivor Millington still headed the National Crime Agency's top ten list of most wanted fugitives.

'Any thoughts, sir?'

The question startled Cornelius. Reviewing the files had stirred up some unwelcome memories and he had become engrossed in his own reflections.

'First thing tomorrow, Andy, we need to start tracking these two down,' said Cornelius, pointing to the pictures of Fitzavon and Pike.

'And by we, I assume you mean ...'

A polite knock drew both men's attention away from their work.

'Excuse me please, sir, is it okay if I vacuum in here now?'

Neil Stokes was standing in the doorway with a battered Henry vacuum cleaner by his side.

Cornelius looked at his watch and stretched the muscles in his back, the cricking sounds reminding him of his age.

'Give us five minutes will you, Neil? We're almost done here.'

'In more ways than one. What are you two ladies doing in here this time of night?' Inspector John Brawley barged past Neil and stood adjacent to the desk. He looked directly at Cornelius and broke out into a triumphant grin. 'Aren't you suspended, Lukey?'

Cornelius didn't hide the scowl on his face which made Brawley grin even more. He looked at the monitor and his eyes twinkled with delight.

'Tut-tut Lukey, looking at old files when you should be at home, watching porn.'

Cornelius felt his blood pressure rise, but it was the good manners of Andy Statton which prevailed.

'We're reviewing old case files, and we've just finished.'

'Yeah, right. Your grubby little secret is safe with me.' Brawley bit down loudly on the apple he was holding – the crunching sound grating on Cornelius's nerves. Without being invited, he lowered himself into the seat opposite Cornelius and Statton and leaned back, his legs unnecessarily far apart. He looked at Cornelius but gestured towards Statton.

'Have you told *Young Hearts* here about the Parfield Principle?'

Statton ignored the Candi Staton reference; he'd heard it all his life, not once finding it amusing. He glanced across at Cornelius, looking for a hint as to how to respond.

Cornelius quickly weighed up his options, deciding that if he told the story, at least Statton would hear the truth instead of the colourful and inaccurate version which Brawley preferred to recount.

'About four years ago we were called to the Bristol Royal Infirmary to see a suspected victim of domestic abuse. Her injuries were so bad the domestic abuse team referred it to CID. I was on duty and arrested her husband, a thirty-six year old former military policeman called Donald Parfield. During the investigation, we discovered he was having an affair with a sixteen year old girl.'

'Okay,' Statton paused, wondering how to phrase his follow up question. 'Creepy but not illegal. Was there relevance?'

'Oh, there was relevance. The girl had mild learning difficulties, and she looked more like a twelve year old. I was convinced he had an interest in vulnerable underage girls, so I checked his internet history. He had a subscription to a Ukrainian website specialising in sexual violence towards young girls; as soon as I saw that, I applied for a search warrant and seized his computer. Three separate external hard drives were found, all of which were encrypted. Back then we couldn't force him to divulge the passwords, and we weren't able to break the encryption either. Without access to the files, we didn't have enough evidence to prosecute. Shortly afterwards, his wife turned up at the station and withdrew her statement that it was Parfield who had beaten her black and blue. I had little choice but to let a violent paedophile back out on to the street.'

Brawley looked like he was enjoying himself. 'Tell him the best bit Lukey.'

'There is no best bit. Donald Parfield worked at Summerville Middle School as an IT technician and posed a potential threat to the pupils. I visited the school and warned the Head about the risk Parfield posed. The school should have taken the sensible step of quietly removing him, while we monitored his activities. However, a school governor let it slip to one of the parents that Parfield was a suspected paedo and within an hour, a mob of parents turned up outside Parfield's house, wanting to beat the crap out of him. By the time we arrived they'd broken every downstairs window and were about to torch the place. Once his long-suffering wife found out about his internet activity, she finally snapped and threw him out. In the space of four days he was homeless, unemployed and shunned by everyone he knew, but in the eyes of the law he remained an innocent man.'

'So, he blamed you for tearing his life apart.'

'He did, yes.' Cornelius sighed deeply at the memory.

'Did?'

Brawley had no intention of allowing Cornelius to answer that question.

'Three weeks after Lukey walked into Summerville School, Mr Parfield threw himself off the top of the cliffs at Ash Cove. A witness stated he bounced off the cliff face twice before landing head first on the rocks below.' Brawley emphasised the point by mimicking the fall with his right hand. 'It was just as well the tide took him out, he would have been a real mess.'

Despite himself, Statton's curiosity had been piqued. 'So, what is the Parfield Principle?'

'That the police should name and shame the offender and let the public decide on the punishment. Lukey's theory was that it would save taxpayers a fortune in trial and incarceration costs.'

Cornelius's patience ran out. 'It's not my theory,' he growled. 'Now why don't you fuck off and die?'

The grin returned to Brawley's face, showing a mixture of artificially whitened teeth and partially chewed apple. 'Later, Ladies,' he chirped, as he sauntered out of the office, whistling *I fought the law*.

'Wanker!' Cornelius mumbled.

The silence was broken by Statton. 'We might be barking up the wrong tree you know, sir. What if the culprit is right under our noses?'

Cornelius didn't reply, he had been wondering the same thing.

Twenty three

Elliot Chorley was not a happy man. He had planned to get out of Bristol for the night and had reserved a hotel room in Birmingham along with two hookers who were happy to cater to his unusual tastes. It would cost him a small fortune, but he'd made a packet on the back of the Cornelius story, so he'd decided to treat himself. Now, he'd had to cancel his plans which pissed him off, but unless he kept his mole happy there would be no more scoops like the ones he had been getting recently. His mole had been content to pass information to him and hadn't even asked for any money. Now, he was being offered something to prove once and for all that Inspector Lucas Cornelius was a cold blooded killer and the prospect of uncovering a murderer at Avon and Somerset Constabulary overrode his sexual needs.

The first message told Chorley to go the eastern park gates in Greystone Avenue at 11 p.m. and wait for further instructions. The fine drizzle clung to his face and created the illusion of light fog against the orange glow of the street lights. It was 11.10 p.m. and Chorley started to think he had been conned. As he contemplated the best way to take it out on the stupid bitch in the office who organised the meet, someone came at him from out of the gloom. Without saying a word, a note was thrust into his hand and the dark figure disappeared down the street at speed.

Chorley rolled his eyes at the cloak and dagger approach but perked up at the thought that it may be a high ranking officer taking necessary security measures. With rising anticipation, he scanned the printed note which told him to head to Pen Park Road and follow the footpath into Fonthill Park and set off through the cold drizzle.

He turned off the residential street and headed down a narrow footpath between the large red brick terraced houses into the new soulless development which bordered Fonthill Park. Hazy street lights cast black shadows in every direction that Chorley looked, but he didn't need to search the darkness for long. A dim lamp in the park highlighted the stranger's silhouette as he leaned against a wooden fence on the park's periphery. Chorley strolled towards the figure, hand outstretched.

'Elliot Chorley, good to meet you at last.'

The mole had his head covered by a thick hood, and a scarf wrapped around his face ensured only the eyes were visible. In the split second it took Elliot Chorley to realise he had been duped, a fist slammed into his solar plexus exploding the air out from his lungs and sending a searing pain through his body. Unable to speak or straighten up, he opened his eyes just in time to see a knee coming towards his face. It connected directly with his nose and this time he screamed in agony as bone and cartilage crashed together. The force of the impact sent him flying backwards and he landed in a bloodied heap on the cold wet grass. He tasted blood as it flowed out of his shattered nose, down the back of his throat and into his mouth. Gloved hands delved into his pockets, and he felt his wallet and smart phone being taken.

Through bleary tear filled eyes he could just make out his attacker turning to leave, when he paused, turned back and kicked him hard in the crotch. As his pain rocketed, his body declared enough was enough, and he passed out.

***

Sitting on a bench in Monks Park, Cornelius stared out into the gloom knowing he should feel at least some guilt. The objective had been to acquire the phone, and he had considered a mugging to be the best way to do it. What was wholly unnecessary, was going back to kick Chorley in the balls. He tried to convince himself he'd done it for Daniel, to pay him back for the callous way Chorley had broken the news about Jane. In reality, he did it to quell the anger which had built up inside him and it was nothing more than pure revenge for the mauling he was getting in the papers.

It was an ambitious plan, and Cornelius was banking on the fact that whoever was feeding Chorley information was doing it anonymously. The call to Chorley's office was made on a pay-as-you-go mobile purchased earlier in the day, and that phone was now lying smashed to bits in a bin on the edge of St Werburghs. He had asked Chorley to move from one meeting point to another so he could watch the reporter from a distance and make sure he was alone, and he'd deliberately kept him waiting to gauge how nervous he was. Chorley would remain calmer for longer if somebody was watching his back, but it had taken barely ten minutes before his body language revealed him to be getting twitchy.

The outer clothes Cornelius had worn were now packed into a polythene bag and stuffed in his rucksack ready for incineration in his wood burner; he could not run the risk of them being subjected to forensic analysis. The wallet contained £200 in cash and in the morning, he would split it and leave donations in the charity shops run by the Children's Hospice and the Bristol Refugee Centre – the latter being the charity most likely to be one of Chorley's pet hates.

Cornelius's main prize was to access the contents of Chorley's phone. No sooner had he left Chorley lying on the ground, than he turned the phone off; he didn't want the tracker to be used on it – not yet. The challenge now, was to break into it. Any kind of retina or fingerprint recognition would scupper his plan, and he was pleased to see it was a simple four digit PIN – all he had to do now was break the code in less than ten attempts – after that the phone would lock down completely.

Elliot Chorley had a publicly accessible Facebook account which he used as a vehicle to promote himself and satisfy his vanity, by publishing professionally taken photographs of himself along with links to articles written by him. Cornelius scanned the page, marvelling at the man's ability to publicise himself and justify his vitriolic writing, but his vanity also led Cornelius to the information he was after – Chorley's date of birth.

Beginning with what he considered to be the most obvious choice, Cornelius entered the month and year in four digits and when that didn't work he changed the order around. With each failed attempt, he moved on to another numerical combination based on Chorley's birth date. On his ninth attempt he entered Chorley's year of birth in reverse order and the phone sprang into life. Cornelius punched the air and congratulated himself at the same time. With a broad grin on his face he navigated his way through the options until he reached his ultimate goal.

Elliot Chorley's list of contacts.

Twenty four

It wasn't the kind of deep dreamless sleep that Cornelius longed for, but for the first time in days he woke feeling he had managed a few hours rest. The case against him was developing small holes which Lynda Culvert would convert into large gaping ones. Laverty had conceded the possibility he may be a victim of a set-up – even though he remained the main suspect. Topping it off was the glorious knowledge that Elliot Chorley would have woken today in a considerable state of discomfort.

Wondering whether he needed to pack for one night or two, Cornelius was throwing some clothes into a holdall when he heard a familiar knock. He ambled down the stairs and flung the front door open, before heading for the kitchen, knowing Andy Statton would happily follow him without the need for doorstep niceties.

'Glad to see you are still doing a passable impression of Dick Fosbury.'

'Who?'

'Never mind.' He smiled to himself as he flicked the kettle on, knowing the young detective constable would be logging on to Google as soon as he returned to his car. 'I assume this is another unofficial visit.'

'Er, no. The DCI asked me to come and see you.'

'Really?' Cornelius looked up abruptly. Statton was developing the same uncomfortable expression he had worn when he asked Cornelius to open the gates and allow the search team in.

His colleague stumbled. 'I ... I have to ask you where you went after leaving the station last night.'

Cornelius expected the question but managed to feign just the right amount of surprise to keep Statton on his toes. 'Oh, I see. I was here, why?'

'You didn't go to The Flask?'

'Andy, in case you hadn't noticed I am the social pariah of the moment. Can you imagine the fallout if I had my photo taken enjoying myself down the pub? The press would have a field day. *Killer cop boozes while his hard working colleagues search for evidence.* That assumes my old drinking buddies would even want to be seen with me. I ...'

Statton put his hands up. 'Okay, point made. It's just that someone mugged Elliot Chorley last night and he is alleging police collusion.'

Cornelius broke into a grin in the knowledge his colleague would be expecting it. 'Oh, what a shame, I trust he was badly hurt?'

'A broken nose, with abdominal and genital bruising. DCI Laverty had trouble not smiling as well, but he wants to be sure it was nothing to do with you.'

'I didn't have anyone with me, Andy. But if you check any of the CCTV cameras from last night you'll see me heading straight home, and if you can get a trace on my mobile, you'll find it was here – and you know I don't go anywhere without it.' He had deliberately left his phone at home and used Daniel's bike to travel by back-roads and footpaths after dark. 'Did he have anything taken?'

'Wallet and phone; both were recovered from a park nearby. Cards and money were missing and the phone was locked down. The mugger tried to access it but ran out of permitted attempts.'

Cornelius managed to maintain an impassive expression. He had removed the credit cards from Chorley's wallet as any self-respecting mugger would. Plus, it would be inconvenient for Chorley, as he would need to cancel them all and have new ones issued. For the same reason, he deliberately locked the phone down once he found what he was looking for. He'd left it switched on, so that it could be tracked and he had partially hidden it by placing a lump of dog shit on top. He felt a twinge of disappointment that his final flourish went unreported.

'I'm afraid there's nothing I can add, Andy, but good luck with tracking down the guilty party and when you do, buy them a pint on me. Any other developments this morning?'

For the next twenty minutes the two men talked about Cornelius's case. Statton confirmed that Rafael Slowik had admitted to stalking Pippa, but when he revealed he'd seen somebody else following her, his status promptly changed from potential suspect to witness. His failure to identify Cornelius in the line-up and his assertion that he had seen Pippa's other stalker elsewhere in the station had been the source of extensive speculation. Slowik had been ushered away from the identity parade and spent the next few hours with the e-fit team. Statton wasn't able to report on much else, as he had been tasked with tracking down Peter Fitzavon and Brendon Pike. So far, his initial enquiries hadn't yielded anything interesting, but as he left Cornelius's house, he reassured him it was his priority for the rest of the day.

***

Cornelius threw his holdall into the back of his car and flung his gate open to find his exit blocked by a large black Mercedes. He thought the press had given up waiting for him, but now the bastards had taken to deliberately blocking his gates. With unconcealed fury he yanked at the Merc's door and in an instant realised the driver was no reporter.

'Good morning Inspector Cornelius or should I say former Inspector Cornelius.' Calvin Marks grinned, showing off his gold crowned front tooth.

Cornelius recognised him immediately. Calvin the Cutter was one of Danny Palmer's trusted associates and his appearance was an unwelcome development. The fact that the heavily tattooed psychopath stayed sitting in his car was of some comfort. Determined not to be cowed by his presence, Cornelius spoke with as much contempt as he could muster.

'Calvin, I thought you were still inside, when did you get out?'

Calvin Marks had no intention of answering the question.

'I have a message for you from Mr Palmer.' He waited to be sure he had Cornelius's full attention. 'He says he looks forward to seeing you as a guest at Horfield sometime in the near future and is expecting you to pay him back for the financial advice he gave you recently.'

He flicked the remnants of his cigarette at Cornelius before bringing the car to life and gently pulling away. Watching him leave, a new leaden weight descended on to Cornelius's shoulders.

'Brilliant. Just fucking brilliant,' were the only words he could muster.

Twenty five

The worrying thing about Calvin's visit was that Danny Palmer now considered Cornelius to be in his debt because of the racing tip he'd given him. The question was, how did Danny know Cornelius had taken the tip seriously and placed a bet? He hadn't been in to the bookies; he'd placed the bet online. Normally, it would have stayed between him and his internet service provider, however his laptop had been seized and analysed as part of the murder investigations, so it would have come to light then. As a one-off transaction it wouldn't have raised any eyebrows at the station, but Palmer obviously had a contact there who was feeding information back to him. Cornelius kicked himself – once Palmer thought you owed him something, he never let go until he had his payback.

With over two hours of driving ahead of him, Cornelius had plenty of time to take stock of his situation. The forensic report on Jane was unlikely to exonerate him on its own, and a significant number of questions remained unanswered including how she came to be buried in his garden. Jane's passport had been used when she left the country but there was no record of her coming back. CCTV recorded her at the airport, seemingly untroubled and travelling alone, and the footage from Turkey showed her meeting someone at Adnan Menderes – but after that the trail went cold. The missing finger appeared to be a ploy to alert the police that something significant had happened to Pippa and to put Cornelius in the frame at the same time. In Cornelius's mind, it was a clumsy approach, and he knew if it came to court a barrister would easily rip apart any suggestion that he deliberately or accidentally left it on the bench in Broadmead. So why remove Jane's finger as well? And where was Pippa's body? Then there was Manny Thompson. Manny had been lured by a text he believed to be from Cornelius. He'd been tasered and injected with a lethal dose of heroin. His body was stored for a few days before being left in the woods where it would soon be found. How had the text had been sent?

The message, originated from Cornelius's phone, which meant someone at the station had sent it.

Cornelius presumed that whoever sent the text message was the same person leaking stories about him to the press. Elliot Chorley had been given intelligence about the case as it developed, and the press were baying for Cornelius's blood, condemning him before he'd even been charged. The search of Chorley's phone had been interesting but not conclusive. Most of his contacts had code names, so Cornelius had looked at his call history instead. Two numbers had occurred repeatedly over the previous two weeks. One was a landline belonging to the city housing department; the source behind Chorley's immigrants getting preferential housing story. The second was a mobile number which Cornelius made a note of. He didn't want to ring it yet for fear of spooking whoever it belonged to, but it represented a good lead and with luck Chorley would be thinking that his phone had not been compromised, even if it had been abandoned and covered in dog shit.

He'd been so engrossed in his thoughts he hadn't noticed the traffic grinding to a crawl as he approached the M25 turnoff. The next thirty miles were the slowest and most frustrating of his journey, but eventually he exited the orbital motorway and headed south on the M23.

The journey took 55 minutes longer than expected, and he pulled up at a nondescript whitewashed travel hotel on the edge of Crawley whose primary trade was to cater for travellers catching early morning flights from Gatwick. Not that he was interested in having a relaxing stay; he just needed a bed for the night as he was unlikely to achieve his objective in a single day.

He had to find Daphne Jones in a mass of 109,000 people with nothing but her name to start him off. His grumbling stomach reminded him he needed some sustenance first, so he bought a lukewarm pie and an overly large packet of crisps in the garage opposite the hotel before heading for his first stop, the library in Southgate Avenue.

Cornelius made a beeline to the information desk where he asked for a copy of the electoral register and found a quiet booth in which he could study it. It was his first time outside of Bristol since becoming vilified in the press, and whilst some national papers had run the story, Cornelius wasn't sure if they had printed his picture. The last thing he wanted was for someone to identify him as that bloke who's in the news, so to help maintain some kind of anonymity, he pulled a dark woollen hat over his head. Scanning the people around him, he saw one student deeply engrossed in one of the largest books he had ever seen and two scruffy men casually flicking through magazines – their main task for the day was to stay warm and dry. Wondering if he was being paranoid about being spotted, he eased his hat off and scanned the register, hoping Daphne Jones had not opted to remove herself from it.

An hour later, he had identified four Daphne Jones's living in the Crawley area and, armed with their addresses, he sat down at a computer with internet access. Working on the assumption that Kelly probably developed her drug habit when living at home, he started by trying to find out which of the addresses were in areas of high social need. He cross-checked the postcodes against the Indices of Multiple Deprivation and seeing that one address was in a particularly deprived area, he decided to make it his first point of call. He managed to find telephone numbers for two of the addresses but only intended to use those if he had to, preferring to see people face to face.

His first stop was a block of thirty flats in Broadfield. Squeezing his car on to a patch of grass adjacent to the flats, he made his way through the misty rain passing a line of tightly packed cars and two sofas which had been abandoned in one of the bays. The flat he was after was on the third floor and the stairwell leading up to it smelt of piss and disinfectant. He climbed the plain concrete steps, found the flat he was looking for and rapped on the faded yellow door. No answer. Cornelius raised his hand to knock for a second time when the door opened barely an inch – any further movement being restricted by a security chain.

'Yes?' A diminutive voice came from behind the door.

'Mrs Daphne Jones?'

'Yes.'

Cornelius couldn't see the woman, but the tone of her voice suggested she was at least seventy and probably too old to be Kelly Ann's mother. Hoping it may be her grandmother he carried on anyway.

'My name's Lucas and I am trying to track down somebody called Kelly Ann Jones, do you ...'

Before he could say anything else, the door quietly shut and for a minute he thought she might be releasing the security chain to let him in. The door didn't reopen, however, so Cornelius decided to move on.

His second address was in Juniper Road where the door was flung open by a young teenage girl who was more interested in her smart phone than the stranger at the door. All his questions were met with monosyllabic answers which seemed to suggest that Daphne Jones was the girl's mother but that she was out and would be back later. Cornelius resisted the temptation to deliver a lecture about opening the door to strangers, especially when she was on her own, and thanked her instead. She grunted some kind of acknowledgement and shut the door on him.

There was no answer at the Deerswood Road address and realising it was about the time people would be coming home from work, Cornelius wondered whether to stay for an hour in the hope that someone would appear. The final address was in Charlwood, barely a few miles away, so he decided to call there next and if he drew a blank he would come back.

Finding the address in Charlwood proved to be more challenging. His satellite navigation told him he had reached his destination, but he couldn't see Tauntfield House. He stood in a sporadically lit main road, hoping to stumble across a local dog walker who could direct him. In the distance, the soft warm lights of the village pub flickered gently, calling Cornelius. There would probably be somebody in there who could help him, but he didn't want to announce publicly that he was looking for a local resident. He also didn't trust himself not to have a quick pint first, then try and talk to Daphne Jones whilst stinking of beer. He strolled down a dark lane which ran at a right angle to the main road and passed a walled garden with a tightly clipped privet hedge topping it off. A car whizzed past and, helped by its headlights, Cornelius saw a plaque embedded in the wall. There was just enough light for him to see the word *Tauntfield*.

Large double gates straddled a driveway leading up to an imposing Georgian house; whatever difficulties this household may have, money was not one of them. The glow of lights inside pierced the evening darkness enough to allow him to navigate his way up to a solid oak front door and a cast iron knocker moulded into the shape of a cherub, which produced a thunderous knock.

The door creaked open and a thin faced woman with long brunette hair tied in a ponytail stood in the doorway, staring at Cornelius over the top of purple reading glasses. He guessed she was in her mid-fifties; she was casually dressed but elegant at the same time.

'Good evening, my name is Lucas and I am a private detective. I am trying to track down Kelly Ann Jones who I believe came from this area. Do you know anyone by that name please?'

Cornelius tried for charm, but it didn't seem to be working. The woman stared at him expressionless, and from somewhere deep inside the stylish house, he heard another young female voice.

'Who is it, Mum?'

Daphne Jones never took her eyes off Cornelius. 'It's no one, darling,' and then she mouthed two words to him.

'Go away.'

***

Cornelius returned to his car in a troubled state. Doorstep rejection was commonplace in police work, but the dismissive look Daphne Jones had given him played on his mind. He was so engrossed in his own thoughts that a sharp rapping noise on the car window caused him to jump. He lowered the window to see a girl with thick brown glasses and a dark grey and blue chullo hat, staring at him expectantly. Her quick and breathless voice broke through the cold evening air.

'Did you just knock on our door?'

Cornelius nodded. She pointed through the darkness in the direction of the pub.

'Meet me there in one hour.'

And without any further comment, she ran back towards Tauntfield House.

The Halfway Inn was a 17th century country pub with low oak beams darkened by years of log fires and cigarette smoke. The flagstone floors ensured all the tables and chairs were wonky to varying degrees. Apart from the portly landlord, the only other punters were three men standing by the bar. They looked to be in their mid-sixties and quite possibly constituted part of the pub's furniture. A large German Shepherd provided a trip hazard for the remaining free space at the bar but no one seemed bothered by his presence. The ability to make one pint last an hour was not part of Cornelius's make up, but he had no intention of drink-driving, so he opted for a shandy on the basis he could have two and still get behind the wheel. He plonked himself into a red leather Chesterfield positioned in front of a large inglenook fireplace, its dancing flames throwing out a reassuring heat.

Exactly one hour after first scaring the shit out of him, the young girl in the chullo hat lowered herself into the seat next to Cornelius and gave him a weak smile as an introduction. He offered to buy her a drink, hoping she was over eighteen, but she shook her head. It soon became clear she had questions for him and didn't want to waste unnecessary time.

'Do you know where Beanie is?' Her voice was breathless.

'Beanie?'

'Sorry, I mean Kelly.'

Cornelius's heart skipped a beat and he hoped his sense of anticipation wasn't showing.

'You need to help me out here young lady. At least tell me who you are and I'll tell you what I know.'

'I'm Marie, Beanie is my older sister. We haven't heard anything from her in about 18 months. Mum ...' she paused trying to find the right words, 'Mum struggled with her behaviour and they had an almighty fight about three years ago. I think Beanie nicked some of her jewellery to pay for ...'

She paused again, this time unable to find the right words. Cornelius decided to help her.

'It's okay, Marie, I know she had an addiction and I know what it can do to families. Whatever happened, it wasn't Beanie's fault; heroin rips lives apart and leaves a trail of chaos in its wake. To answer your first question, no, I don't know where she is, but I'm trying to find her.'

Marie stared directly at Cornelius, her eyes moistening rapidly. 'Why are you looking for her?'

Cornelius thought carefully before opting for the partial truth. 'She's gone missing, and she disappeared about the same time as someone close to me. I want to see if there's any connection.'

'I haven't even seen her in two years, she came back to try and patch things up with Mum but it ended in another row. Do you know where she's been since then?'

'Bristol, but I need to tell you she has been missing for a year. Nobody reported it at the time she disappeared, which is why it has taken this long for me to start making enquiries.'

He didn't want to tell Marie her big sister worked for a pimp who didn't care what happened to her.

'She may have moved on elsewhere in the country, and that is what I was hoping you would be able to tell me.'

Marie shook her head, dejected.

'Why didn't your mum report her missing?' His voice was soft, not wanting to sound accusatory.

'Mum said she'd made her bed and she must lie in it. She probably thinks Beanie's in trouble again and you're here to claim some kind of debt; that's why she shut the door on you.'

'She doesn't know you're here?'

Marie snorted a laugh but didn't answer.

Cornelius sat back in the comfortable chair and sighed. He'd found Kelly's family yet was no further forward. He wondered if he was on a wild goose chase when a thought occurred to him.

'Marie, do you have a photo of Beanie?'

Marie reached inside her coat pocket for her phone and without saying a word swept her way through an endless album of photos. Eventually she held the phone up and Cornelius could see two girls grinning at the camera, both blissfully unaware of the trauma that would eventually tear their lives to shreds.

'It was taken not long before she left; it's the last photo I have.' She did her best to stifle her sobs.

Cornelius gestured for the phone, 'May I?'

Marie passed the phone to Cornelius and for the first time he looked closely at Kelly Ann – Beanie to her sister – Tracey to Guy the Gorilla – and nothing but a piece of tradable meat to Weasel. Her smiling face beamed out, beautifully framed by a cascade of blonde curls. Cornelius put two fingers on the screen and zoomed in on Kelly's face. In an instant, his throat went dry and a bead of sweat formed on his temple.

He'd found the connection he was looking for.

Twenty six

It was 6 a.m. when Cornelius started up his car and waited for the engine to generate enough heat to clear the frost from his windscreen. It had been quite late by the time he'd left Charlwood the night before and whilst he'd entertained the idea of heading straight back to Bristol, he had not relished the thought of another three hours driving, so had opted for an early night.

He'd stayed in the pub and talked to Marie about her sister for a while the previous evening; Kelly's tale was the same as countless others who fell into the sinister web woven by heroin. For an entire decade her life had been defined by a recurring cycle of addiction, abstinence and relapse – and she had sold her body with all the risks that entailed purely so she could feed her addiction.

By the time he returned to Bristol, Cornelius had little recollection of the journey home. His mind had been fully occupied by Jane, Kelly Ann and drugs. He was now pretty sure Kelly was dead and had an idea about how her murder was linked to Jane's. His theory made sense, but he didn't have a shred of evidence to support it and so he had no intention of telling Laverty just yet.

What he wasn't quite sure about was the role drugs had played in the sorry tale. Manny had been given an overdose, Jo Scutt had suspicions about a puncture mark on Jane's forearm and Kelly was an addict. Pippa's body had yet to be found, assuming she was dead, but he couldn't rule out the idea that she may have been a user and he simply hadn't realised.

With a torrent of questions swirling in his mind, he decided he needed some help from a local primate.

***

Trying to see Guy the Gorilla before the afternoon was futile. His line of work kept him out late into the night so he rarely surfaced from his pit before lunchtime. However, Guy was also a creature of habit, and Cornelius knew he could be found mid-afternoon nursing a pint of Thatcher's at the George Inn.

The rain hammered down in sheets as Cornelius eased himself into one of Bristol's most insalubrious drinking establishments. Deliberately keeping his head covered by his coat hood, he took the few short steps to the bar where Guy was perched ungainly on a bar stool, fully engrossed watching Angela Lansbury trying to solve the riddle of the murdered dentist. He didn't flinch at the arrival of a dripping wet punter by his side, so Cornelius gently prompted him.

'Buy you another?'

Guy's enormous frame turned slightly, his expression hardening as he recognised the face still partially hidden by a coat hood. His eyes flitted about the bar to see who else was there, resting on a group of three men in the dingiest corner of the bar who were playing poker. He turned to the fresh-faced barman and mumbled something quietly to which the barman nodded agreement. Guy gestured to Cornelius to follow him and exited through the bar and down into a dimly lit cellar which stank of damp walls and stale beer. He sat himself down on one of the empty barrels, his expression showing just how pleased he was that a disgraced policeman had come looking for him.

'What do you fuckin' want?'

'Bloody hell, Guy, couldn't you find somewhere warmer?'

'Don't know that lot in the corner, now what … do … you … want?'

'I think I know what has happened to Kelly.'

'Who the fuck's Kelly?'

Cornelius closed his eyes briefly; he'd forgotten Kelly lived a different life in Bristol.

'Sorry, I mean Tracey – Kelly was her real name. She grew up in Surrey and came here after she fell out with her mother. That was about 18 months ago – does that fit with when you first met her?'

At the mention of Tracey's name, Guy's expression changed, the latent aggression disappeared and was replaced with confusion. As he processed the information he slowly nodded his head. His next question threw Cornelius off guard.

'What d'you mean, was?'

Cornelius immediately realised his mistake. He stalled for a few seconds to work out how to break the bad news to Guy, but it was too late. The big man leapt to his feet, blocking the exit out of the cellar.

'Guy, I don't have any proof, but I think she has been abducted and I believe her disappearance is linked to the murder of my wife.'

If Guy had problems processing the notion that Tracey's real name was Kelly, the thought that she had been kidnapped and may have had something to do with a murder was a step too far. A fuse blew inside Guy's head and he lunged forward and grabbed Cornelius by his coat lapels lifting him off the floor and ramming him against the cellar wall. The impact blasted the air out of Cornelius's lungs, but before he could make any protestation, Guy's snarling face was inches from his.

'Do you think I'm fuckin' thick? You killed your own missus and now you're lookin' for anythin' that'll get you off.'

Cornelius kicked himself for following Guy into a confined space. As well as having a simian nickname Guy also shared their unpredictable behaviour traits, and Cornelius needed to calm him down.

'I'll make a deal with you, Guy; you listen carefully to the whole story without trying to beat my brains out, and if at the end of it you still think I'm lying, feel free to pummel away.'

Cornelius spent another minute pinned against the wall whilst Guy decided whether or not to kill him on the spot. Cornelius avoided staring him down; challenging Guy when he was agitated was never a good idea. Eventually he lowered Cornelius and let go of his coat, but he made sure he was still blocking the exit.

'I'm listening.'

It took Cornelius twenty minutes to explain his theory to Guy the Gorilla. The numbing cold of the cellar barely affected Cornelius as he was entirely focused on selling his idea to Guy and, just as importantly, making sure he kept his limbs from being broken. By the time he had finished, Guy had sat back down on one of the barrels. Cornelius could make a dash for freedom if he needed to, but he reckoned Guy had been persuaded. It was time to put it to the test.

'I know it was a year ago, but do you remember any of the girls ever telling you about a particularly creepy punter?'

'They're all fuckin' creepy.'

He smiled at Guy's response to his badly worded question. 'Fair point, but was there anyone in particular who seemed overly particular about which girl to choose?'

Guy stayed silent, looking straight ahead. Cornelius couldn't work out whether he understood the question or whether he was simply processing it. Eventually he spoke.

'There was one fuckin' idiot who thought 'ee could just come in, look at the girls and walk out again. We'd 'ad a tip off that 'e'd done the same at another club, so I told 'im 'ee had to pay anyway.'

'Did he?'

Guy smiled for the first time. 'Stupid fucker tried to make a dash for it. I took 'im outside and gave 'im a slap.'

Cornelius doubted it was just a slap, but Guy had let something slip and he needed to follow it up carefully.

'Where was this Guy?'

Guy realised his mistake and tried stalling for time. 'Is it important?'

'It could be.'

A resigned look came over his face. 'The Peacock Palace.'

'That's one of Danny Palmer's joints! Have you been moonlighting?'

As quick as a flash the snarl was back on Guy's face. 'If you tell Mr Weavell I'll rip you limb from fuckin' limb.'

Cornelius didn't doubt it, but Guy had no need to worry; this was an interesting snippet that he had every intention of keeping to himself. Besides, it was yet another reason for Guy to be in his pocket. Cornelius barely dared to ask the next question.

'Do they have CCTV there?'

Guy's troubled expression told Cornelius he didn't know how to respond.

'Guy, at the moment I am a suspended police officer and some of my colleagues are looking for a reason to make it permanent. If I am caught reviewing CCTV in a brothel without authorisation I'll be kicked off the force long before any kind of trial can be brought against me.'

'It's not a brothel, it's an adult entertainment club.'

'Whatever. Even if I see something remotely incriminating there's sod-all I can do about it officially. Now do they keep CCTV footage?'

Guy gave the briefest of nods. 'We keep all the clips where there's been trouble.'

Cornelius grinned. 'Get your coat on – you and I are going to an adult entertainment club.'

***

The Peacock Palace was tucked away down a back alley, five minutes' walk from the Watershed, a digital media centre located on Bristol harbour side. The reception was decorated with lime green carpets and turquoise blue wallpaper with a swirling floral pattern. A peroxide blonde woman in her sixties with a red bandeau top two sizes too small was seated behind a black table covered in old coffee mug rings. Before Cornelius had a chance to say anything, she told him all the girls were busy and asked if he could he wait for fifteen minutes. Her heavily made up smile froze when he said he was there to meet Guy and she promptly disappeared into a small office, leaving Cornelius to stare at the faded prints of Indian peacocks hanging on the walls.

Three minutes later the peroxide blonde woman returned looking more relaxed and told him Guy would be with him shortly. Knowing one of Danny Palmer's brothels had Guy on speed dial was a useful snippet of information, and he was still thinking on how best to use it when Guy strolled in, ducking his head to squeeze under the doorframe.

Without acknowledging Cornelius's presence, Guy walked straight through to the office, leaving Cornelius wondering what the bloody hell he should be doing now. It took another five minutes for Guy to reappear in the office doorway, gesturing with his head for Cornelius to follow him.

The room Cornelius assumed to be an office turned out to be a slightly enlarged broom cupboard. It had a cluttered desk barely wide enough for a normal person to sit at, let alone accommodate Guy's bulk. Cornelius squeezed in, reminding himself that the last time he was this close to Guy he had been suspended in the air by his coat lapels, so at least this represented progress. The computer screen showed a folder called *archive footage* and judging by the number of files in it, The Peacock Palace had had its fair share of trouble over the last year. Guy selected the clip he wanted to show Cornelius, and the screen showed a grainy picture, immediately recognisable as the Peacock's gaudy reception.

A man stood with his back to the camera and the receptionist appeared to be showing him the girls available. Kelly wasn't one of them, but given the joint belonged to Danny Palmer, Cornelius wouldn't expect to see her. The girls were doing their best to make themselves look alluring and although there was no sound, he could see the man in question shrug his shoulders and turn to leave. Just before his face came into view, the man was obstructed by Guy's bulky frame, and all Cornelius could see of the mystery man were his arms waving around in agitation. Guy stayed rooted to the spot, blocking the exit of the punter who had come for a look but had no intention of paying for anything. Suddenly, the mystery man darted to the left and made a break for it. Guy took one enormous stride, grabbed his coat and dragged the punter back.

Guy paused the clip and for the first time, the mystery man's face appeared motionless on the screen. Cornelius leaned in to get a better look and felt his blood turn to ice. He stared at the face of the man who killed Jane Cornelius and Emmanuel Thompson and in all likelihood Pippa Hobbs and Kelly Ann Jones – and he knew exactly who it was.

DECEMBER – NINE MONTHS LATER

This one will be the last. He will have his fun, and it will be mission accomplished. After that, he will disappear, the same as last time.

How many people had he stalked over the years? More than he cared to remember and none of them had a clue he was on their tail. Following people isn't difficult. Keep your distance, blend in and know when to walk away – easy. Not this one though. She used counter surveillance techniques. Taking different routes each day, doubling back on herself, turning around and watching who was behind her – occasionally writing down car number plates. She'd almost caught him once; he'd had to make a quick turn into a residential alleyway to avoid suspicion. He was bloody lucky the real home owner wasn't in. After that incident, he changed his appearance with reversible coats and different hats and spectacles. It had taken time, but eventually it had paid off. He knew where she worked and, best of all, where she lived.

The street light that overlooked his van wasn't working; he wouldn't have parked there otherwise. The dirty orange glow from the surrounding lights was enough to pick out his silhouette but not sufficiently bright to pick out the lines on his face. Not until it was too late anyway. Happy that he was close enough to her flat for her to feel safe, he scanned the high-sided industrial units on either side of the street. All the businesses were closed up for the night; no lights were on in any of the windows overlooking his chosen spot. The wig scratched and his scalp itched, but with the flat cap, the walking sticks and the cheap crappy clothes bought the day before from a charity shop, he reckoned he'd done enough to age himself. All he needed now, was for her to be a good Samaritan. He'd seen her do it with her neighbour; the old woman took the piss, but the girl still helped her. He'd have told the lazy cow to fuck off and do her own shopping ages ago.

Two billiard balls in an old black rugby sock were stuffed into his coat pocket; he'd got the idea from a film called *Scum* and had used it many times since. Inside the van was a syringe of freshly prepared heroin which would ensure her compliance until she was safely back in the cellar.

Gentle footsteps drifted through the night air, progressively getting louder. He'd watched her leave work, figured out which route she was taking home and driven ahead. She was right on time; if she'd stopped off *en route* to do some shopping it could have ruined his plan.

Reckoning she was about ten metres behind him, he lifted the large cardboard box up to the rear bumper. He started grunting and puffing, trying and failing to lift the box the last few centimetres to load it into the back of the van. The footsteps behind him slowed down. She was watching. He needed to keep up the act for a moment longer.

'Hang on a minute, sir.' She appeared alongside him wearing a warm reassuring smile as she placed her hands on the box. 'You are going to do yourself an injury in a minute. Here, let me help.'

She was a sucker for helping old people in trouble, just as he suspected.

'Gosh, yes, thank you. It is a bit heavy for me.'

He'd practised the voice for the previous two days, playing back each recording until satisfied he sounded like an eighty year old man. He stood back and let her take the box off him. She didn't look directly at his face, perfect.

'Blimey, this is heavy,' she said, laughing. 'Have you got a dead bod ...'

Pippa Hobbs had just spoken her last words.

Twenty seven

Cornelius burst out of the Peacock Palace and gasped a cold lungful of late afternoon air. Even the normally unsympathetic Gorilla followed him out, firstly wanting to know if he was okay and then what the hell he had seen that made him freak out.

Struggling to speak, Cornelius managed to utter that he needed a pint. Guy offered him one from the Peacock's tiny and, hugely overpriced, bar but he shook his head. He needed sanctuary to help him assemble his thoughts into some course of action, and he wouldn't get that in the club. He told Guy he needed to speak to an old colleague to check something and promised to ring him before the day was out. Without waiting for a reply from the big man, he turned and headed towards a pub off Deanery Road, only vaguely aware of Guy shouting after him, saying something about him being a fucking wanker.

The Masons Arms was an old drinker's pub which had been converted from a Victorian two bedroomed house in the early part of the 20th century. It sold real ale, bags of crisps and smelt of cigarette smoke – despite the ban. Cornelius ordered a pint of Doom Bar and sat in a dimly lit corner to think.

The shock of recognising the person Guy had ejected from the club and beaten up gave way to simmering fury. He had been right under his nose all along, taunting Cornelius without him realising. The text to Manny had come from his phone; the bastard simply took it from his jacket pocket, sent the message and put it back. Cornelius was partly to blame for not changing the PIN code, but he tried to reassure himself that the killer would have got to Manny one way or another.

Pippa had been in the wrong place at the wrong time; the fact she was on the witness protection programme was irrelevant. Her fate had been sealed when she became friends with Cornelius; it was the trigger for a series of events that had been gently simmering since Jane and Kelly disappeared. But there was still one piece of the puzzle missing. Cornelius reached for his phone and called a charity on the edge of St Pauls. Ten minutes later, he had the information that helped him fill in the gaps, but he didn't have one scrap of meaningful evidence to support his theory.

Cornelius took another slug of beer; if he made it through the next 48 hours he would try and give up the booze. Alcohol was his drug of choice just as heroin had been Kelly's; the thought gave him an idea.

The stash of high grade heroin stolen from Gloucester Road Police Station had been used to kill Manny, and it had also been used to frame Guy. The only reason the killer had planted the heroin on Guy, was because Guy had beaten the crap out of him at the Peacock Club.

Now, there was something Cornelius needed to do, and it involved returning to the very building where his nemesis was likely to be waiting for him.

***

Cornelius needed to slip quietly into Gloucester Road station avoiding as many people as possible. He hoped that at this time in the evening, most of his colleagues would have gone home, but with a double murder investigation in full flow, there were no guarantees. A quick tour of the car park told him that Superintendent Liatt and the DCI were not there. It was a good start.

He had just entered the building and turned the corner ready to run up the stairs, when he collided with Malcolm Williams – almost knocking a cup of boiling tea out of his hands. His expression told Cornelius his surreptitious visit to the station may not be as easy and he had hoped.

'Inspector Cornelius, I wasn't told you were visiting us this evening.'

'Communication in this place has always been dreadful,' replied Cornelius. And before the sergeant could respond he shot up the stairs. If Malcolm Williams was going to raise the alarm, Cornelius reckoned he only had five or ten minutes.

Quietly entering the CID office, Cornelius scanned the room. Rita Sharma was the only person he could see deeply engrossed in some CCTV footage on her computer monitor. Just when he thought he might get away with sitting quietly at his desk for a few minutes, she looked up and broke into a wide grin.

'Blimey, look who it is. Hello, sir, what are you doing here?'

'Hello Rita, I was after DCI Laverty, is he in?'

Her expression remained bright and welcoming.

'No, he's at Portishead with the Super – some kind of big pow-wow we underlings are not privileged to know about.'

'Oh, he must have forgotten he asked me to come in.' Cornelius feigned his best confused expression. 'I'll give him a quick ring.'

He pulled out his phone and dialled the number he'd recently put in his contact list. He wasn't sure if it would be answered, but this was one of the few leads open to him. When the sound of a buzzing phone emanated from somewhere in the room it didn't come as a huge surprise. Ignoring the quizzical look on Rita

Sharma's face, he made straight for the desk where the phone was ringing.

It was the desk of Inspector John Brawley.

'Where is DI Brawley Rita?'

He tried to contain the sense of urgency in his voice but Rita sensed that something wasn't right.

'Uh, he left in a bit of a hurry about an hour ago. Sir, do you mind me asking what you are doing?'

Cornelius pretended not to hear. He reached into Brawley's desk drawer and pulled out an old mobile phone with faded numbers and a dirty old case covered in a sticky substance which he hoped was nothing more than a sugar residue.

He scanned the outgoing call list and saw that all the calls had been made to the same number – Elliot Chorley's.

A quick check of the received calls showed a recent call from Elliot Chorley – far too recent for Cornelius's liking. With deepening apprehension, he moved to his own desk, easily finding what he was looking for. Picking it up gently, he placed it into an evidence bag. The almost imperceptible sound of breathing nearby, startled him and caused him to spin around to see Rita standing there.

'Rita, I need you to get this fast tracked for DNA.' He handed her the evidence bag. 'Make sure Laverty gets the results – no one else! Clear?'

She nodded cautiously.

'Now, exactly when did DI Brawley leave?'

'I'm not his keeper, sir, it was about an hour ago I'd say.' There wasn't a hint of apology in her voice and in normal circumstances Cornelius would have admired her for it.

A phone rang in the far corner of the room and Rita Sharma frowned at an unwelcome distraction in the saga that was playing out in front of her. She walked over to the phone but stayed standing so she could keep an eye on the errant inspector.

Frustration was building in Cornelius's head; discovering the phone in Brawley's desk drawer only compounded his problems. Suspecting that the person now talking to DC Sharma could be Laverty or Liatt, he decided to exit the building before he was called to the phone. As he turned to leave his foot caught the waste paper bin beneath Brawley's desk and sent the contents flying across the floor.

Rita's stifled laugh was reassuring insomuch that it told Cornelius that Rita was not talking to one of the hierarchy.

As soon as she was off the phone, Rita offered to help him clear up, but Cornelius was giving a partially screwed up envelope which had landed by his foot his full attention. It was addressed to Detective Inspector L Cornelius.

Whether the document which had been inside the envelope was also scattered somewhere on the floor Cornelius didn't know, but he gathered up all the papers, to make it look like he was putting them back in the bin. However, with his back turned to Rita, he stuffed them into his inside coat pocket and with a wave of his arm he left the office as fast as he could.

***

Cornelius raced back home and sat at his kitchen table with a mass of crumpled and torn paper spread out in front of him.

Thankful that John Brawley didn't use his bin for any food waste, he set about trying to reassemble the assorted papers into their original state. One was particularly easy, a page from the estate agent's section which was included with the Sunday version of the *Bristol Herald* and had been crudely ripped into quarters. The date immediately caught Cornelius's eye; the property page was over two years old. All the remaining pages seemed to be printed copies of emails.

He turned his attention to the screwed up envelope, flattening it out on the table in front of him. Nothing indicated its origin, but when Cornelius held it up to the light he could see indentations in the paper. It looked like a note had been written on a piece of paper with the envelope underneath it; the pressure of the pen having left a ghost impression. With a quickening breath, Cornelius started to decipher the marks. The ridges on the envelope caused by screwing it up were masking most of the words, but Cornelius could make out four of them: All, need, here and look.

He went back to the page with properties listed for sale. One page was for an estate agent that specialised in low grade housing in the city's sprawling estates. The other side was for properties located in the rural areas around Bristol. There were ten properties on the page in total and Cornelius reckoned the link was here. Had Rita Sharma not been watching him like a hawk, he could have checked each property online from the office; all he had now was his phone and the limited internet access it provided. He accessed a property site which gave details of when houses were last sold and for how much. It was the third house on the list which caught his eye. He found it on a map and clicked on the street view. The house couldn't be seen from the road; there was only a narrow lane with a high-sided hedge leading to it.

A perfect place to hide.

Twenty eight

Cornelius sprinted to his car and set off as fast at the Bristol traffic would allow. Ignoring the advice he had given to other motorists during his time with the police, he reached for his phone and called the only person he could think of who might be willing to help him. It was a risk, but he was running out of options.

Barely a mile from the Gordano Services junction, he turned off an unlit road into Failand Lane, a single track road giving access to a few farms and remote cottages. The tight lane was flanked by claustrophobic high hedges and Cornelius hoped he wasn't going to meet any cars coming in the opposite direction. When his satellite navigation proudly announced he had reached his destination Cornelius cursed; other than high hedgerows he couldn't see a thing. Even a car as small as his couldn't turn around in the tight lane so he kept going and barely 100 metres further on, he came to an unmarked turning on the left. It was an unkempt road and the combination of mud and potholes slowed him down to a crawl. After half a mile, the high hedges gave way to a copse, and as his headlights illuminated a straggled line of beech, ash and oak, he caught sight of a break in the trees with a narrow gravel track giving limited access for vehicles. He parked his car on the edge of the tree line and armed with a pocket torch, made his way down the track.

The 19th century farmhouse nestled amongst the trees appeared to be occupied, with mustard yellow lights streaming out of three ground floor and two first floor windows, illuminating the overgrown grounds surrounding it.

Cornelius's heart sank at the sight of the pristine red MG sports car parked at the front. It belonged to John Brawley.

As Cornelius made his way closer to the farmhouse, he could see it was still in the same run-down state that it had been in when offered for sale in the newspaper two years ago. The external rendering was cracked and falling away and rotten sash windows barely held their filthy glass panes in place. The brick paved yard had developed a sweeping undulation over the years, and the sand and cement that originally separated the bricks had long since vanished and been replaced by moss and ryegrass.

Looking for something to defend himself with, Cornelius headed towards the two dilapidated outbuildings next to the house. Easing open the door of the smaller outhouse, he was hit with the smell of damp mould. A sweep of his torch showed all it contained was a rusty bicycle and a pile of logs, so he quietly moved to the other building. Cornelius's suspicion that it was used as a garage was confirmed when he opened the double wooden doors. It housed an old grey Volvo and a white Transit van which, judging by the botched effort at removing the previous livery, used to belong to Chandlers Plumbing Supplies. Both vehicles were clean and looked like they were in regular use, but no heat radiated out from either engine. They hadn't been used in the last few hours at least.

Cornelius caught sight of a few garden implements heaped in the far corner and picked up a wooden handled mattock. He exited the garage and edged his way carefully across the yard. There were no sounds coming from the house, even the woodland adjacent did its best to stay quiet. All Cornelius could hear was the sound of his own shallow breath. Not wanting to go in through the front door, he walked around the house, peering in through any window that offered him a view. An unlit door at the rear of the farmhouse briefly offered him hope, but it was firmly locked, and Cornelius was soon back to where he started.

With no other choice, he pressed down on the aged front door handle; without any resistance it gave way and the door gently creaked open.

The bright hall lights temporarily blinded him, but as soon as his pupils made their adjustments, he saw the sight he most feared. The soles of two feet were just visible on the floor, poking out from a doorframe that led into what Cornelius surmised was a kitchen. He eased forward, cautiously, trying to watch three doorways and a stairwell at the same time – the mattock raised and ready to strike. When he reached the body of John Brawley he knew any attempt at finding a pulse would be futile. The blood oozing out of Brawley's ears told him he was dead. Cornelius checked his mobile phone – no signal. He'd have been surprised if there was – this house had been chosen for its isolation.

The gentle creak of a floorboard alerted Cornelius to someone else's presence, and he swung around preparing to launch himself forward, when he saw that the person in the hallway was holding what looked like a gun in his hand – and it was pointed straight at him.

'Hello Donald. It's been a few years …'

The man Cornelius had seen being ejected from the Peacock Club was staring straight at him, his blank expression giving way to a smile which didn't travel as far as his eyes.

'Well, well. I was right to tell Elizabeth Bettie that you are a tenacious bugger.'

Cornelius remained silent.

'I guess I need to give you credit for finding this place. You caught me in the middle of something though – leaving your DNA all over the joint.' He briefly looked down at Brawley's prone body. 'John was an annoying little shit, wasn't he? I think I've done your lot a favour there.'

Cornelius couldn't tell whether his matter-of-fact voice was a sign of genuine detachment or whether he was trying to goad him into an attack.

'He was so desperate to take the credit for solving your case he fell headlong into quite a clumsy trap. Presumably you found the envelope and its contents?'

Cornelius nodded.

'Damn, your fingerprints were all over that. You weren't supposed to be at the station.' His eyes never left Cornelius, as he weighed up his options. 'When did you realise it was me?'

'You were caught on CCTV being thrown out of a brothel. It took a while for me to work out who Neil Stokes really was. For a dead man Donald, you are looking remarkably fit. I'm guessing you have been in hiding – Turkey by any chance?'

'Aren't you Mr Fucking Clever? But you worked it out a bit too late.'

'I should have worked it out when you left that crappy book on my desk. *Injured, Remade* – it's an anagram of *I murdered Jane*.'

Donald Parfield grinned. 'My little joke; a nice touch don't you think?' He took a slight bow but didn't take his eyes off Cornelius.

'You can alter your appearance Donald, but you can't change your DNA. Your book is being tested at the lab; soon everyone will know you are still alive.'

'I doubt it; I was careful. The only DNA on that book will be from you, the dotty old woman who sold it to me in the charity shop and the book's previous owner. Did you ask for anything else to be tested?'

'Of course,' Cornelius lied. 'Your cover will be blown by the morning.'

Parfield laughed. 'Oh Lucas, you do make me smile. I've been dancing under your nose for months. You even bumped into me, literally, yet you didn't recognise me.'

'You've had plastic surgery.'

'Exactly what your wife said. She believed me when I said it was because of an accident I'd been in.'

The reference to Jane was too much and, gun or no gun, Cornelius pounced, but he didn't move quickly enough and Parfield fired the taser. A blinding pain seared through Cornelius's body as his entire musculature was thrown into an involuntary spasm and he collapsed to the ground.

Incapable of any movement, Cornelius couldn't resist having his arms manacled together and his legs bound by twine. In the time it took for him to regain movement, he was already being hauled by his legs towards what looked like a stair cupboard. When Parfield opened the door and flicked the light switch, Cornelius realised it wasn't a cupboard but an entrance to a cellar.

'Sorry about this, old chap,' said Parfield, 'but there's no easy way to do this and it's going to hurt you more than it hurts me.'

He dragged Cornelius feet first down the steps that led to his lair. The stairs were made of old oak rather than stone, but this was of little comfort as his body pounded against all twelve of them. His thick parka coat stopped any significant abrasions, but his spine felt as if it was about to burst out of his body, and he could feel a trickle of blood oozing out from a cut at the base of his skull.

Lying in an agonised heap, there was just enough light in the dingy cellar for Cornelius to see it had been whitewashed at some time, but its sheen was long gone and the dull walls were now a mosaic of peeling paint, mould and grime. A fold-up wire-framed bed lay against one wall and a chest freezer against the other. Oblivious to the cold touch of the old flagstone floor, Cornelius's eyes focused on Parfield. He had recharged the taser and was pointing it again at Cornelius.

'Brace yourself, Lucas. This is going to hurt.'

As Cornelius's body was immobilised for the second time in 15 minutes, he lost consciousness.

***

Cornelius wasn't sure how long he had been out for, but when he regained consciousness he was no longer prone on the cellar floor but was sitting upright with his back to the wall. His arms were spread out at ninety degrees to his body and manacled to the mouldy wall; his legs were still bound together. He tried to get his mind back into gear, but the residual pain from being tasered and dragged backwards down a flight of stairs impaired his thinking.

His eyes cleared and focused on the empty cellar. Cornelius had no idea if Parfield was still in the house; he strained his ears, listening for any sounds at all, but silence reigned. His gaze fell on the chest freezer opposite, and he realised something was different about it. His thinking was still muddled and he closed his eyes to try to focus his mind. Then it dawned on him. The lid on the chest freezer had been shut when he first looked at it, but during his period of unconsciousness it had been opened. He was looking at the resting place of Jane's body between her murder and being moved to his garden. Jo Scutt's theory had been right. Pippa's body had probably been stored here as well, but if an open lid meant an empty freezer – where was her body now?

The pain in his muscles eased a little to be replaced by a sense of discomfort at his restriction. He pulled hard with his arms, but his shackles were made of cast iron and their fixings were solid. There would be no Hollywood style breakout out by working a chain loose or picking a lock.

Parfield whistled casually as he descended the stairs.

'Change of plan, Lucas, I've had a quick re-think and come up with a cracker of an idea. What I'm going ...'

'Back-up is on the way, Donald.' Cornelius needed more time. 'Even if you kill me now, you'll be caught before you get to your car.'

Parfield took two steps forward and stared at Cornelius like he was an unusual zoo exhibit.

'Call for back-up before you arrived at the farm, did you?' Your phone wouldn't work within a half mile of this place. No one is coming; you are entirely at my mercy.'

'All this because I busted you?'

Parfield never replied, instead he smashed his fist into Cornelius's stomach. A scalding pain ripped through his body, temporarily removing his ability to breathe. Parfield stepped forward and grabbed Cornelius by his chin, yanking his head up and staring him in the eye.

'I was an innocent man. You ... ruined ... my ... life. Bastard!'

Another first crashed into his ribcage, Cornelius was unable to stop himself from crying out in agony. Still gasping for air, Cornelius tried to keep Parfield talking; he still had unanswered questions. Each breath raked his lungs, and flecks of saliva formed at the side of his mouth.

'You're a vile thug who preyed on vulnerable young women. You get close to people, pretend they are your friends, then kill them.'

Parfield leaned in to Cornelius, his breath stinking of stale beer and pear drops.

'I never killed anybody until I met you. You are the one with blood on your hands, not me.'

'Callum Thomas.' Cornelius fired off one of the names that the missing persons charity had given him. Callum was the closest match to the criteria Cornelius had specified. He was age approximate to Parfield and had been reported missing by the Salvation Army two weeks after Parfield's faked suicide.

'You chose him because he was the same height and build as you are. Callum was a homeless man who thought you were being kind. You gave him some of your old clothes and took him for a day out. Ash Cove was a clever choice: there are high cliffs, occasional walkers to act as witnesses and a strong tide that would take the body out to sea. Given your circumstances, suicide was a perfectly reasonable deduction, and you used a homeless man you thought no one would miss.'

It was mostly speculation, but Cornelius hoped Parfield would correct any inaccuracies in his theory.

'Bravo.' Parfield clapped mockingly. 'It's just a shame you're too late, Lucas. How did you know I travelled to Turkey?'

'Call it an educated guess. Question is, why did it take you so long to come back for me?'

Parfield let go of Cornelius's chin and took a step backwards.

'Ten months after arriving in Turkey, I was thrown into prison in Izmir. Inconvenient, but time in prison can be a learning experience. One of my cell mates was a versatile criminal, but he kept getting caught. I taught him how to avoid detection; he taught me breaking and entering, covert surveillance, oh – and abduction. That was particularly useful. Which reminds me, did you want to know what happened to your wife?'

Cornelius wasn't about to give him the satisfaction.

'I know. You found a prostitute called Kelly Ann who looked similar enough to Jane in her face and height. You dressed her up in Jane's clothes and gave her a wig to help with the illusion. She travelled to Turkey using Jane's passport and was fully expecting to come back using her own passport and be paid a handsome sum on her return. Job done. Jane has disappeared in Turkey. Only she hadn't; she was stored in that freezer until you buried her in my garden about a month ago.'

'I'm impressed, Lucas. The whore was a greedy little bitch. She called herself Tracey and believed me when I said I had trouble forming relationships and just wanted friendship from her. Stupid cow, who wants to be friends with a scabby tart like that? I used her to settle an outstanding debt with the Turkish Mafia. She may still be alive, but for her sake, I hope not.'

'How did you get Jane's passport?'

'She gave it to me.'

Cornelius said nothing, quietly shaking his head in disbelief. It did the trick, Parfield carried on talking.

'Getting your wife's trust wasn't easy, but I told her I knew you from school and showed her an old photo I'd fabricated to prove it. That's when I said I'd had cosmetic work following an accident.'

'She believed you?'

'Why shouldn't she? I wasn't asking her for money. I told her I was trying to track you down as I was organising a school reunion and trying to keep it quiet until the last minute. She offered to help, so I gave her cash to reserve a large room at the Royal Hotel and suggested she bring her passport as they would need proof of ID to confirm the booking. She did that to help you have what she thought was going to be a pleasant surprise.'

Parfield's grin was as taunting as it was triumphant; Cornelius wanted to kill him.

'Rohypnol's a wonderful thing, Lucas. She never even put up a struggle when I put her in my car – and we had a lot of fun together before I killed her.'

'You never touched her. If I know Jane, she found a way to kick you in the nuts long before you could put your slimy hands on her.'

Parfield wasn't going to admit that on cold days his ear still stung where Jane had sunk her teeth in.

'I went to great lengths to observe you Lucas, that's why I got a cleaning job at the station.'

'How the hell did you get clearance?' growled Cornelius. 'Even the cleaners are vetted.'

'You of all people should know that it's not what you know but who you know. And I know someone who is adept at creating new identities. By the way, you CID staff should be ashamed of the way you talk to each other, most of the time you behave as if cleaners don't exist. The stuff you talk about is shocking.'

'And you targeted Pippa because she was getting friendly with me?'

Parfield nodded. 'She was more of a challenge; did you know she'd had counter surveillance training? It took me ages to find her flat. You may like to know she was dead before I removed her finger, I gave her some heroin to keep her calm but the stupid bitch was allergic to it. She had an anaphylactic shock in the van on the way back here. Never mind eh? I needed a good excuse to send your lot into her flat. They obviously found the hairs I left there ...'

'Was it really necessary to kill Manny as well?'

'Ah, that was a bit opportunist on my part, and it made life a little more uncomfortable for you. By the way, naughty-naughty for not changing your PIN.' Parfield wagged his finger at Cornelius. 'He'd still be alive now if I hadn't been able to send him a text from your phone.'

'Presumably, it was also you who leaked the information to Tobias McMillan and to the press.'

Cornelius didn't really think so, but he had to keep him talking.

'Oh no, I had no intentions of doing that myself; I recruited help from within the station. The same person who helped me get the heroin out of the evidence room.'

'Who was it?'

'Nice try, but I may need him again in the future.'

'Does it matter? You're not letting me out of here alive anyway.'

Parfield looked at Cornelius and spoke calmly. 'And there was me thinking you were intelligent. I have no intention of killing you, Lucas. I've taken your wife from you, your career and your dignity. You are going to suffer the same way I had to.'

'You know the chances of me going to jail are very slim. The evidence is circumstantial at best; even a half decent barrister will tear it to shreds.'

'Oh, for goodness sake, haven't you been listening? I know you won't be going to jail Lucas, but there's enough evidence to warrant a trial. Yes, the chances are you'll be found not guilty, but that's not the point — it has never been the point. You will forever be known as the man who got away with murder. Your son will always wonder if you killed his mother, you won't be able to work as a police officer again and the public will always have you marked as a guilty man. These, Lucas, are the things by which we are judged.'

Cornelius closed his eyes and realised Parfield was right. Speculation and suspicion was all that was needed to ruin a life. More often than not, the facts were a mere bystander.

He was about to open his eyes when Donald Parfield drove his fist hard into his face. A white pain exploded in his head followed by the taste of blood tricking down the back of his throat. Lights danced in front of his eyes, but he could see enough to know that Parfield was grinning with delight.

'Sorry about this Lucas, but I have to make it look like you had a fight with your old friend upstairs.'

Another fist caught him on the side of his head. With no way of defending himself, Cornelius was entirely at the mercy of the man who was now raining blows on him. Four more punches to his head and through the excruciating pain he felt his consciousness slipping away.

'There, that'll do. Now all you need is a good sleep. When you wake up I'll be long gone, but your colleagues will be here in force. They will be jumping to the wonderfully neat conclusion that you had a fight with Brawley, your injuries rendered you unconscious but John didn't survive. Yes, you'll be found not guilty, but it's another death you'll forever be associated with.'

Parfield rummaged around in a black canvas holdall on the floor. He pulled out a small clear glass vial, followed by syringe which he carefully filled.

'One other thing before I send you off to the land off nod, don't bother trying to find your girlfriend's body. Pippa Hobbs and her missing finger will be yet another unsolved enigma in the mysterious case of the murderous Inspector Cornelius.'

Parfield didn't see the man quietly descending the cellar stairs behind him. It was only when he realised that Cornelius was looking at something over his shoulder that he turned around.

Guy Dart put all his muscle and weight into the fist he smashed into the face of Donald Parfield. In a split second Parfield's internal nervous system collapsed, and he fell to the floor in a complete state of unconsciousness.

'Bloody hell Guy, you took your time.'

'I wanted to 'ear it for myself,' said Guy. And without looking up, he drove his right foot into the rib cage of the man who framed him for drug possession and killed his beloved Tracey.

Cornelius was incredulous.

'You've been up there all that time? You could have saved me from getting a sodding beating!'

Relief at the prospect of being rescued subsided as he guessed what was going through Guy's mind.

'Guy, don't do it. If you kill him now we'll both be in a barrel of shit. As it stands, the bloke you have just knocked seven bells out of will be going to prison for a long time. The chances are he'll end up in Horfield, so all you need to do is speak nicely to Danny Palmer to make his life a complete misery.'

The Gorilla never replied, his eyes stayed fixed on the man lying at his feet. Cornelius had one last trick up his sleeve. 'You'll probably get your drugs conviction quashed as well.'

For the first time, he looked at Cornelius who could see him wondering whether to take this advice or finish Parfield off for good. The thought of Parfield suffering in Horfield as well as him earning a nice compensation payment won out, and he grinned at Cornelius.

'You look a right fuckin' state.'

'Thanks a bunch. Now get his keys out of his pocket and let me out, will you?'

***

Guy the Gorilla disappeared off into the night leaving behind a battered and aching Cornelius in his wake. Cornelius promised Guy there would be an investigation into Kelly's disappearance, but if she had fallen into the hands of the Turkish Mafia, he knew exactly what that would have meant for her. Guy thanked Cornelius for giving him a chance to clear his name. Cornelius's knuckles still throbbed from the hand shake, but he put the pain to one side as he had work to do.

In the boot of Parfield's Volvo, carefully wrapped in black bags, Cornelius found the corpse of Pippa Hobbs and a spade by her side. A large holdall on the front seat held a few clothes, a stash of cash and a one-way ticket to Ho Chi Minh City, for the following evening.

Beneath the driver's seat was the heroin which had been stolen from the Gloucester Road Police Station wrapped in three separate packages. He removed one of them and armed with his torch, set off into the woodland to bury it in a safe place for retrieval at a later date.

With his task completed and story straight, he wandered out to the main road, retrieved his car and drove for a quarter of a mile at which point his phone told him there was sufficient signal to make a call.

He dialled 999 and waited for the cavalry to arrive. While waiting, he pondered who in the station had been helping Parfield. In order to find out he would have to make a deal with the devil.

Epilogue

Three months later

Inspector Lucas Cornelius asked for two days leave which were granted without any dissent whatsoever. Since his reinstatement everyone had gone out of their way to be nice to him and if he was honest with himself, it was starting to piss him off a bit.

He'd not got off entirely scot-free. His failure to disclose his relationship with Pippa and his decision to charge head first into Donald Parfield's house whilst on suspension and without calling for any police back-up earned him an official reprimand. However, the fact he had brought a serial killer to justice easily outshone any blots on his copybook.

The same could not be said for Assistant Chief Constable McCartney and Superintendent Liatt. Their failure to follow proper suspension procedures caused them significant embarrassment and it was officially noted that they failed to authorise lines of enquiry that would have established the innocence of Lucas Cornelius at an earlier date.

The only issue the enquiry failed to answer, was who assisted with the theft of high grade heroin from the evidence room of Gloucester Road station, the lack of appropriate security procedures also being attributed to failures by senior managers.

A trial date had yet to be set, but the indications were that Donald Parfield intended to plead guilty to the murders of Jane Cornelius, Pippa Hobbs, Emmanuel Thompson and John Brawley. His legal team were still wrestling with the question of how to plead to the charge of abduction for Kelly Ann Jones, arguing that, technically, she travelled under her own free will. The Turkish investigation was still on-going, but the last update Cornelius had was that they were examining a shallow grave located outside Manisa. To everyone's surprise, Callum Thomas was found alive and well and living in a squat in Liverpool. The Missing Persons Bureau had taken on the case but had yet to report their findings.

Parfield's claim that he had been knocked out by someone other than Cornelius at the remote farm house was never taken seriously, and the police believed Parfield had sustained his injuries in the struggle with Cornelius alone.

Three weeks later, Cornelius returned to the woodland and retrieved the heroin he had hidden. Giving it back to Danny Palmer stuck in his throat, but he needed information only Danny could give him and it would get Palmer off his back after the saga with the horse race bet.

Sitting in a quiet leafy cul-de-sac in Selly Oak on a warm June evening, Cornelius hoped Palmer was as good as his word. He exited his car and headed for a gleaming white Georgian three storey house which had a plum slate path leading to a black high gloss front door, flanked by two elegant rosemary topiaries.

He walked up to the electronic key pad and tapped in the first of the two five digit codes that Calvin the Cutter had passed to him the previous day. The door gently clicked open and he found himself admiring the interior which easily matched the elegance of the exterior. Cornelius stood in a hallway gracefully lit by a cut glass chandelier and warm light that radiated out from a selection of original oil paintings which had their own drop-down illumination.

He quietly glided over the travertine flooring and made his way to the top floor where he found the second key pad he was looking for. Quietly entering the number, Cornelius eased the door open, thankful that the hinges didn't announce his arrival with a squeak. Once inside, he could hear a swishing and thwacking sound coming from a room at the end of an unlit corridor. The door leading into it was ajar, giving him just enough light to move forward safely without bumping into the rosewood furniture that adorned the generous passageway.

Cornelius was not surprised to find the man he had come to see lying naked on the bed, blindfolded, gagged and handcuffed. The real surprise came in the form of two leather clad women: one holding a whip – the other a black paddle with silver studs. Cornelius recognised them immediately as the two witnesses who provided Weasel with an alibi at his trial.

They stared in open-mouthed horror as Cornelius quietly strode forward with his ID on full show. Without making a sound, he gestured to the women to leave and they didn't need telling twice.

Although Tobias McMillan had minor abrasions on his torso and legs, the size of his erection suggested to Cornelius that he was enjoying himself. That was all about to change.

'Smile for the internet, Tobias.'

A loud, muffled protest came through the barrister's ball gag, and Cornelius grinned.

'Just a couple more pictures ... oh dear, you appear to be going flaccid.'

For one horrible moment Cornelius thought McMillan was about to have a heart attack. He'd only just repaired his reputation and a dead barrister on his hands would have buggered that right up.

The convulsions, however, were McMillan trying to break free of his restraints, but his dominatrix had done a good job of securing him. Cornelius leaned forward and lifted the blindfold off McMillan's head but left the ball gag in place. Tobias McMillan's eyes doubled in size as he recognised the person in front of him holding the camera.

'A couple more, so people can be sure that it is you ...' Cornelius was thoroughly enjoying himself. He slipped the camera back into his pocket and did his best to look stern.

'I'm sure an intelligent man like you, has probably worked this out already, but let me tell you how this is going to work. In a minute, I am going to ask you some questions and you will either shake or nod your head.'

From behind his gag, McMillan could only grunt with fury.

'Now, now, Tobias, my list of demands has already grown by one since I walked into the room, right now it is in your best interest to listen and co-operate. I know a young lady who would happily share these photos on social media and within an hour the whole city would know about that mole on your penis. In fact, I reckon the photos would go viral within a day. I'm also guessing Mrs McMillan doesn't know about your, um, hobby, but that would be the least of your problems. Now, can I continue uninterrupted please?'

Knowing he was beaten, Tobias McMillan briefly nodded his head.

'Good. Firstly, those two young ladies you paid to give Marcus Weavell an alibi will now conveniently realise that they made a mistake and you will use your contacts to ensure a retrial is ordered. Do you agree?'

Nothing.

'Tobias, do you agree?' Cornelius lifted the camera out of his pocket to reinforce the point.

The nod was almost imperceptible.

'Okay, now, you know the name of the person who has been leaking information out of Gloucester Road Police Station. I am going to read you a list of names and you will nod when you hear the name of the mole.'

One by one, Cornelius read out the names of his colleagues at the station. It was the seventh name that elicited a nod of the head. He read it out again to be sure, his heart sinking in the process.

'Okay Tobias, I'm leaving you in peace now, but before I go, you need to know that these photos will be stored on a secure cloud based server, and in the event of anything happening to me, they will all be released to the papers.'

Without saying another word, he turned and walked away, leaving the barrister wondering how the hell he was going to get himself free.

***

Cornelius spent nearly thirty minutes walking around Victoria Park; the bright sunny Sunday morning was a stark contrast to his mood. The park teemed with family life. Couples cooed at their babies as they pushed them around in expensive buggies, dog walkers ambled along the footpaths and children laughed and yelled as they clumsily kicked an old football on the grass. They all looked happy, not that Cornelius was envious; he was on the lookout for one particular person.

Eventually, Cornelius saw him strolling along a wide pathway flanked by common lime trees, distracted by the boisterous behaviour of his lurcher. He was within five metres of Cornelius before he recognised him.

'Lucas! I'm surprised to see you here.' His tone was relaxed and casual.

'Well, I'm here for a reason – I'm looking for you.'

Malcolm Williams's expression changed as tension crept up his spine.

'I know, Malcolm. All I need to find out now, is why.'

'Know? Know what?'

Cornelius didn't reply. He stared at the sergeant and waited.

'What are you on about?' His quivering voice was giving away his emotions.

Cornelius broke his silence.

'Leaving the phone in John Brawley's desk was a bit risky, but you had to dump it somewhere when you received a call from Elliot Chorley who thought that the phone had been compromised. It was a smart move as well; Brawley was my number one suspect for leaking the information about me. But Brawley was a healthy bugger who never ate cakes or sweets, and that phone had a sugary residue all over it. In any case, he had already set off to

Donald Parfield's by the time the last call to the phone was answered.'

'Lucas, I don't know what you are talking about, I don't have time to listen to this crap.'

Malcolm started to walk away, but Cornelius grabbed his arm.

'Tobias McMillan has confirmed it was you Malcolm.'

'That's bollocks.' Despite his verbal defiance, Cornelius saw the fear in his eyes.

'It's just you and me Malcolm, I'm not wired, nothing you tell me is admissible. I only want to know why.'

Malcolm Williams stared off into the bright morning, trying to work out how to get out of his predicament. He reached into his wallet and pulled out a photograph that was folded in half and passed it to Cornelius. It was a picture of a young red-headed girl skipping out of school, a bright beaming smile on her face as she saw someone waiting for her in the near distance. It looked as if it had been taken with a long lens, her cheerful cherub-like face unaware of the camera.

'That's my granddaughter, Molly, she was six last month. I found an envelope waiting for me at the station with that photo inside. The envelope also contained a razor blade. One week later, I received some instructions. I was to steal the heroin from the evidence room and leave it at a prearranged spot. It wasn't easy, but I managed to take it, and I hoped that would be the end of it. I guessed it had something to do with Palmer, but then I was instructed to give information to that shit McMillan, which confused me. I reckoned that maybe Palmer didn't want the risk of Weasel being locked up in a different nick to him and wanted him kept on the outside for when he was released. The phone was supplied to me, and I received another set of photos of Lucy playing in the park close to her home. This time there was a hypodermic needle with the pictures and instructions to ring Elliot Chorley with regular updates on the progress of the investigation.'

'You never knew who it was?'

'No, the instructions were always printed out and left for me at the station ...'

He still couldn't bring himself to look at Cornelius, but a tear rolled down his cheek.

'I'm sorry Lucas, you mean a lot to me, but I'd sell the whole sodding lot of you down the river to protect my family and keep them safe. You might not understand, but that's me and I'll happily take the consequences.'

Cornelius could understand. He'd beaten up a reporter, lied about how he'd apprehended a killer and given heroin back to a gangster so he could blackmail a barrister. He was no better than Malcolm and certainly in no position to judge.

Cornelius turned on his heels and walked away.

About the author

By Which We Are Judged is the first novel by Les Finlayson.

Les spent more years than he cares to admit working for Somerset County Council in a variety of roles. Before that the dairy, automotive and confectionary businesses also acted as paymasters. Although he held the desire to write a novel for a number of years, it was not until he successfully completed his master's degree that he found the confidence to write *By Which We Are Judged*.

A lifelong fan of crime novels, he was inspired to write *By Which We Are Judged* whilst pruning the leylandii trees that border his house. For those people who have not yet read the novel, that may seem just a little odd!

Les lives in Taunton, Somerset, with his wife Debbie and two badly behaved dogs.

First published in Great Britain in 2018 by Les Finlayson

Copyright © Les Finlayson 2018

Cover design used under licence.

Les Finlayson has asserted his right under the Copyright, Designs and Patents Act 1988 to be identified as the author of this work.

This book is a work of fiction, any resemblance to actual persons, living or dead, is purely coincidental.

Version 1.0 ISBN 9781999595623

This book is copyright material and must not be copied, reproduced, transferred, distributed, leased, licensed or publicly performed or used in any way except as specifically permitted in writing by Les Finlayson, as allowed under the terms and conditions under which it was purchased or as strictly permitted by applicable copyright law. Any authorised distribution or use of this text may be a direct infringement of the author's rights and those responsible may be liable in law accordingly.